Francis Plug
How To Be A Public Author

Paul Ewen

GALLEY BEGGAR BRITAIN

By the same author:
London Pub Reviews

First published in 2014 by Galley Beggar Press Limited
37 Dover Street, Norwich, NR2 3LG

Typeset by Ben Cracknell Studios Ltd
Printed in the UK by Clays, St Ives plc

Sections of this novel have previously appeared, in modified
form, in *Five Dials* (Issue 7) and *Sport* (Issue 41)

A CIP record for this book
is available from the British Library

ISBN 978-1910296-43-1

Francis Plug
How To Be A Public Author

PRAISE FOR *FRANCIS PLUG*

"*Francis Plug* is a brilliant, deranged new comic creation... It's the funniest book I've read in years, and I hope the hugely talented Ewen sells half a million copies." (*The Sunday Times*)

"So funny you find yourself giggling long after you've passed the joke... Pure – and purely pleasurable – silliness." (*The Times Literary Supplement*)

"Plug's eye for detail and ear for scathing one-liners are memorably poetic... In this hilarious account of the lonely lives of authors, Ewen has created a modern comic masterpiece." (*New Statesman*)

"Wickedly comic... One of the funniest books of the year." (*Front Row*, BBC Radio 4)

"Francis Plug rampages across the literary scene like an alcoholic Mr Pooter... it's one of the funniest books I've ever read." (*The Times*)

"I howled with laughter." (*Town & Country*)

"Francis Plug, fictional author of this wonderful book, can be instantly elevated to the pantheon of infuriating, inspired nuisances, alongside Henry Root and, God forbid, Dennis Pennis. ... It's surely a parable for our times." (*The Guardian*)

"For those with a taste for dark, unpredictable, and sometimes surreal comedy, this is a book of invigorating originality. The character of Francis Plug himself is a creation of twisted genius." (*The Sunday Express*)

"Paul Ewen's *How To Be A Public Author by Francis Plug* has been the best kind of find; a real word-of-mouth hit. Think New Grub Street mixed with Chris Morris." (*The Big Issue*)

"*Francis Plug* brilliantly sends up the whole literary circus." (*Open Book*, BBC Radio 4)

For Linda

INTRODUCTION

Bookish folk aren't what they used to be. Introverted, reserved, studious. There was a time when bookish folk would steer clear of trendy bars, dinner occasions and gatherings. Any social or public encounters would be avoided at all costs because these activities were very un-bookish. Bookish folk preferred to stay in, or to sit alone in a quiet pub, reading a good book, or getting some writing done. Writers, in fact, perhaps epitomized these bookish traits most strongly. At least, they used to.

These days, bookish people, such as writers, are commonly found on stage, headlining festivals, or being interviewed on TV. Author events and performances have proliferated, becoming established parts of a writer's role. It's not that authors have suddenly become more extroverted – it's more a case that their job description has changed.

Of course, not all writers are bookish. Not in the traditional sense of the word anyway. Some are well suited for public life, particularly those from certain academic backgrounds where public speaking is encouraged and confidence in social situations is shaped and formed. These writers may even be termed 'gregarious', and are thus happy being offered up for speaking engagements, stage discussions and signings. Good for them. But the others – the timid, shy and mousy authors – they're being thrust into the limelight too. That's my lot. The social wipeouts. Unprepared and ill-equipped to face our reader audience. What's most concerning is that no one is offering us any guidance or tips.

We're expected to hit the ground running, confident and ready, loaded with banter, quips and answers. It's a disaster waiting to happen.

That's why I've decided to study the ways of the literary event. The know-how necessary for survival as a public author. This book is a culmination of that. It follows in the fine tradition of *The Paris Review*'s 'Writers At Work' series, teasing out methods and tips from the biggest literary names. Unlike their interview format however, this collection is based on first-hand experiences and observations at real author events. By attending in person and documenting the smallest details in true author style, I've managed to collate a rich mine of information pertaining to the public skills of our most noted writers. Stage etiquette, audience questions, book signings, wardrobe, performance. Invaluable knowledge for those of us forced to become public authors too.

The authors I have chosen to focus on specifically are Booker Prize-winners. Writers at the coalface of public interaction, under the most intensive public scrutiny and spotlight glare. If role models are to be found in the world of public authors, surely this is the group in which to find them. Hopefully we can all benefit from their valuable expertise and knowledge.

Francis Plug

Midnight's Children

Salman Rushdie

To Francis Plug

[signature]

JONATHAN CAPE
THIRTY BEDFORD SQUARE LONDON

The water in Salman Rushdie's glass is rippling. The glass itself is perfectly still, sitting flat on the even table surface, but the water inside is rippling. It's *Still* water, but it's rippling. I know it's *Still* water because I can read the label on the bottle. *Still Spring Water.* I'm sitting in the front row. I can see it with my own eyes.

Salman Rushdie has barely touched his water, unsurprisingly. The water was placed on the table shortly before 18:30, and he didn't sit down until 19:07. So it's been sitting there, warming, for nearly forty minutes. Imagine what it must taste like now, especially under all those bright lights. Like a heated swimming pool, or a glass of hot-water bottle water. Sometimes I drink the warm water in the shower when I'm washing my face, but I don't swallow it because the taste is like something from an ornamental frog in a garden pond on a very hot day. So instead, I spit the water out down my tummy. And then I give my tummy a good soap down.

Bacteria thrives in warm water. It's rampant in waterbeds. I heard of a couple who never cleaned their waterbed, not once. You're supposed to add chemicals to keep the heated water free from bugs. But this couple didn't. Perhaps they didn't know they needed to, or maybe they just forgot. Anyway, one day they were preparing to move house, and they emptied the contents of the waterbed bladder into their bath. The water that began to sludge out of the valve was filled with dozens of little scaly

5

things with legs and no eyes. Little hairy mites, kicking about in their clean white tub. The couple were horrified. But there was more to come. A squelching noise was heard, and out slid a huge slimy worm, two metres in length, maybe more, thicker than your thumb. They'd been sleeping on that. Sleeping on a bed of worm.

So don't drink the complimentary water at your author events, because you might get worms.

There are other dangers too. Perhaps your unattended water bottle in the empty auditorium has been tampered with. We only have to look at the lessons learned from Agatha Christie. People in her books are forever being poisoned. She even spells out what the poison is and how it's administered. In their drinks. The organisers of this event must be only too aware of Agatha Christie's back catalogue, and of the brugmansia flower, formerly known as the datura, a South American pendant-shaped plant belonging to the *Solanaceae* family, also famed for its spicy night scent, which is used by Amazonian tribes as distilled poison to tip their arrows. It doesn't take an idiot to work this out.

Tonight's event was scheduled to begin at 19:00, but Professor John Mullan, who's asking all the questions, and his guest, novelist Salman Rushdie, didn't sit behind the light pinewood table until some seven minutes after. Authors, I've noticed, are always running late. That's why, unlike other celebrities, they aren't paid loads of money to advertise expensive watches. In contrast, I entered the Shaw Theatre this evening at 18:20, which is why I've secured this top-notch seat in the middle of the front row. If Salman Rushdie were on TV, I would need to move further back because the light would be bad for my eyes.

Earlier, after saving my seat with my coat, I ran through the empty theatre playing Cops and Robbers. Assigning myself the role of robber, I darted down a row, between the folded up chairs, with my right hand tucked under my sleeve holding a gun. When I reached the wall and realised there was no escape, I spun around, drew my gun and begun firing randomly, shouting AAARRGHH!! A policeman shot me in the face, and I fell backwards over the row of seats below, my legs sprawling in the air. It was all quite real to life, with mild concussion and everything, so I ended the game early and slowly crept amongst the rows, loudly flipping all the seats. Another thing you can do before your author event is stock up on complimentary wine.

Drinks Table Woman: Back again?

FP: Yes, that was very tasty, thank you.

Drinks Table Woman: And you want another glass?

FP: Yes please.

Drinks Table Woman: [*Holding up bottle.*] White?

FP: Um, yes white and red, thanks.

Drinks Table Woman: White *and* red?

FP: Why not! [*Laughing nervously.*]

Drinks Table Woman: One of each?

FP: OK! [*Laughing nervously.*]

Drinks Table Woman: You're quite early aren't you? Still half an hour yet…

FP: Yes. Do you have any Kasmiri brandy?

Drinks Table Woman: Kasmiri brandy? No…

FP: Any Mercurochrome?

Drinks Table Woman: No, just the wine.

FP: Right. Does any of the wine contain pickled water snakes? For virility?

Drinks Table Woman: No, it's just ordinary wine. With grapes.

FP: OK. Maybe I could take a bottle. Save me… save you pouring all the time… [*Laughing nervously.*]

Drinks Table Woman: You want to take a bottle?

FP: Ha, ha. Yes.

Drinks Table Woman: Hmm. I'm only supposed to give out one glass per person. And you've had three glasses already. Three glasses, plus an entire bottle would be like… seven large glasses…

FP: I'm like a lawn, aren't I? A lawn.

The empty bottle now stands beside my shoe as Salman Rushdie discusses his Booker Prize-winning novel, *Midnight's Children*. Right now he's talking about the use of topical issues.

Salman Rushdie: … anyone who tries to incorporate, particularly contemporary history or contemporary political material into a contemporary novel, it's a very frightening thing to do because, you know, the subject always changes, whether it's next week or next year or in five years time…

The Sauvignon Blanc kept its chill far better than Salman Rushdie's water. Why didn't the Shaw Theatre offer him a jug of iced water? Maybe they thought he'd be impressed by the fancy bottle and the fact that the water came from a spring. Oh dear. If a half-wit like me can see through that silly guise, I'm afraid Salman Rushdie is very likely appalled. Other stage performers have people running on from the wings with fresh drinks, but Salman Rushdie is lumped with water that probably smells like a wet mitten drying on the radiator. What if he takes a large swig and has to spit it out? Where will he spit it? In his hand? What will he do with it then? Tip it into his pocket? And what if there's too much water to fit in the cup of his hand? Will he keep it in his mouth instead and gargle it? Or will he allow it to run out of his mouth and down his bearded chin? No, he will do no such thing. This is a literary event, and Salman Rushdie has a reputation to uphold as a distinguished man of words. He will be forced, against his best wishes, to swallow the warm water, resigning himself to the fact that he mustn't drink any more, even though his throat is dry from all this talking, something he's obviously not used to because he's a writer, and writers don't talk, they sit quietly.

Just to reiterate, DON'T drink the complimentary water at your author event.

The ripples on Salman Rushdie's water, I believe, are being caused by a series of deep sighs. Sighs that are escaping through his nose. I'll describe Salman Rushdie's nose, just as others may, in turn, describe yours. It is not a monumental organ, but it appears to have a lot to say for itself. From bridge to bow, it is about the length of a modern mobile phone, and it resembles a bunch of small, upside down flowers that have been pinned to his face without a message. The nostrils are shaped like melting clocks, and their generous girth offers flume-like passages for volumes of air to travel both down and up. A pair of stylish glasses are affixed to his nose – I'm not sure of the exact optician or designer, but perhaps closer scrutiny on internet images will confirm this. It's important to note that his goatee beard and moustache, which are succumbing to grey, are neatly trimmed.

The event is taking place in front of a live theatre audience, but it's also being recorded for future public use. On the surface of the desk, alongside the warm *Spring Water*, is a recorder device and some microphones. A young man plugged these in shortly before 19:00, and he now sits behind a side desk, wearing headphones and facing the audience like a courtroom typist, recording the facts. The purpose of this electronic gadgetry is to save the author's voice as an audio 'Podcast', which will be accessible for free on the worldwide web. It must put even more pressure on the author because every word he says is being kept alive for the entire world to hear. Not only words but other noises too, like laughs, snorts and sneezes. My smoker's cough will probably make today's file. I once dropped a bottle of scotch at a similar event, and it made a loud thud on the floor, and I cursed a bit. I suspect you could also hear me laughing by myself, and, on that occasion, weeping.

These recordings don't describe the authors themselves, however. Their gestures, their body language, their trousers. Hopefully the book you are now reading will assist in these respects, as will any such events you attend as an audience participant yourself (recommended).

Salman Rushdie and the professor are sharing a microphone on the table. But if your voice is soft and projects poorly, you might require your own, attached to your lapel. However, this may need to be removed if you're drinking wine instead of water because you may well start talking much louder. You might even begin shouting.

FP: [*Aloud.*] Why did I only get one bottle? I should have got two.

I met Salman Rushdie earlier, as it happens, because I was lighting up a Gold Flake cigarette outside the theatre just as he arrived. He was, and is, smartly dressed in a dark suit with shiny black shoes, a white shirt, and a gold tie with strawberry splotches. I assume his publishing company are fitting the bill for his expensive attire, because no writer worth his salt is going to own a suit of their own. No way. When I dress to go out, I dress to go outside, into someone's garden. But it's worth having a parent/grandparent on stand-by if your publishing company is not forthcoming in this respect, or if you happen to be a successful self-published author.

Salman Rushdie is a short man, which is a consolation, because so am I. Writers don't have to be pin-ups. An athletic build is not a prerequisite, and in fact, many writers are beginning their careers just as professional footballers are finishing theirs. This may be why you don't see big-name male authors advertising the latest hi-tech razors. Because their faces are just too wrinkly.

As Salman Rushdie approached the Shaw Theatre, I nervously waved him in, as if he were a taxiing aircraft.

Salman Rushdie: Hello. Would you like me to sign your book?

FP: Yes please. To Francis Plug. Francis with an 'i', Plug with one 'g'.

Salman Rushdie: *Francis Plug.* Is that you?

FP: Yes.

Salman Rushdie: What an interesting name. *Francis Plug.* It sounds like the name of a fictional character...

FP: Yes, but I'm real.

Salman Rushdie: Of course.

FP: I'm not a talking mule, for example. In a haunted house.

Salman Rushdie: No. [*Slight pause.*] But as Saleem Sinai says, 'What's real and what's true aren't necessarily the same'.

FP: Sure. But he also calls his penis a 'soo-soo'. [*Laughs.*]

Salman Rushdie: OK, thanks.

FP: [*Still laughing.*]

Saleem Sinai is the name of the central character in *Midnight's Children*. Francis Plug is my name. As names go, I suppose it's quite memorable. People forget my face, but they don't forget my name. This has helped me stay invisible and blend in (apart from a particular 'Butt Plug' period). Of course, as an author, anonymity goes out the window. You become a name *and* a face. That's why it makes sense to prepare. It makes all the sense in the world.

Salman Rushdie's book is set in India and contains many challenging narrative conventions. This makes the professor very excited. He would clap his hands if he could. John Mullan, a pink-faced gentleman, is a professor of English literature, and tonight he's wearing a tight black top. It looks like the same top he wore at a previous event. Maybe it's his good luck top. It reminds me of those tight tops that are difficult to take off. If you try to pull them over your head, they often get stuck there and you can't see. And you panic slightly, afraid that you're going to suffocate, or that someone will walk up to you and punch you in the stomach. The professor has a lean frame, so his tight black top suits him well, but I imagine he'll struggle later tonight when he tries to take it off before bed.

Audience questions are a popular part of most author events, and I want to ask Salman Rushdie about his socks, because I can see them there, poking out. But then I notice my hands and think otherwise. They look like a worm's hands, all muddy and slimy, with little gardens beneath the nails. No one is going to pick a hand like that, even if I'm right here in the front row, frantically waving it about like a big mucky moth. No, I'll have to go and give them a thorough wash and scrub, just as soon as I relieve myself. In fact, they'll need a good going over before my piddle because I'm not about to touch my modesty with those filthy monsters.

Salman Rushdie: … So for instance the spittoon, I mean it's just a spittoon, that's all it is: it has in itself, intrinsically, no metaphorical meaning…

Salman Rushdie is in the middle of a serious point, so I creep past the stage on tip-toes with my dirty hands held up to my chest like a quiet mouse's paws.

Once my wee is wee-ed and my hands are stringently cleansed, I duck outside for a quick State Express 555 cigarette. My £8 ticket is equivalent to two and a half well-filled glasses of wine.

So far I've had seven glasses, so I'm up. Still, you can see a half-decent band for £8. And bands have fancy stage lights. In 2044, it will probably cost £1,111 to attend an author event, and us authors will be talking within enclosed, bullet-proof boxes. Perhaps we're currently experiencing the golden age of author/reader interaction, but I suspect, for most contemporary authors, it's nothing but a friggin' nightmare.

There doesn't appear to be anything outside the theatre to draw the crowds in for tonight's event. No inflatable Salman Rushdie figure with long, billowing limbs, for instance. Not even a banner that reads: NEXT ATTRACTION! SALMAN RUSHDIE! TALKING! LIVE ON STAGE!

It's just a matter of time, I suppose.

The wine table is unattended, so I help myself to another bottle before heading back into the theatre. Salman Rushdie looks over to me as I scuttle towards my seat, and the professor's eyes are diverted by my re-entry also. It must be distracting to have someone moving about like a frilled lizard while you're trying to talk. But at least I didn't walk out on them. I came back. And my sparkling hands smell of lovely flowing bathroom soap.

FP: [*Aloud.*] Mmm… Milk & Honey.

The condensation from the wine bottle leaves damp stains on my trousers. I'm also starting to feel very drunk. There are two Salman Rushdies now, so I try looking at them through my wine glass, holding it up to my eyes.

FP: [*Aloud.*] He's quadrupled! There are four of him, three of him! FOUR! THREE! FOUR! TWO! NINE!
Woman Sitting Beside Me: Ssshhhh!!

13

The wine in my tummy is sloshing. Salman Rushdie is attempting to answer an audience question about characters that have gone beyond his control. But the calm of his gentle voice is broken by my hiccups. I stick my hand up.

Professor Mullan: Yes, the young man there, in front.
FP: SORRY. [*Hic.*]
Professor Mullan: Um…
FP: I'M REALLY [*Hic.*] DRUNK.
Professor Mullan: I see.

The professor quickly picks out someone else, and Salman Rushdie engages them with a thoughtful response. I slump back, feeling like a bit of a dick.

Later, weighed down by a leather satchel, I stumble out of the auditorium, possibly gripping a wine bottle.

THE
FAMISHED
ROAD

Ben Okri

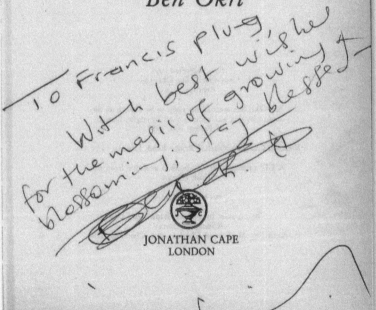

JONATHAN CAPE
LONDON

In Ben Okri's Booker Prize-winning novel, *The Famished Road*, the road swallows people up and feeds them into its stomach. It reminds me of the speed humps I have to navigate in my work van. Unlike the more popular white vans, my van is grey, a tone conducive to its age.

To avoid the police I steer my van down London's back streets where I'm forced to encounter roads blighted with these friggin' speed humps. Driving over them is like trying to shave a face covered in warts. It's like driving some hundred years ago, especially in my van, which is nothing short of an old shit-heap.

Of course, you can't use words like 'shit-heap' when you're an author, on stage at the Hay Festival, for instance. D.H. Lawrence was using the 'C' word way back in the 1920's, but I think the world's grown up a lot since then. Booker Prize-winners don't tend to blaspheme in their events, because they probably assume, quite rightly, that their audience really wouldn't care for that.

Of course, that doesn't stop said authors using swear words in their books. James Kelman's Booker book is loaded with expletives, including 'stupid fucking fuckpig bastards'. And Hilary Mantel refers to 'a four-penny fuck' and a 'leek-eating cunt' in just one of her winners. I don't remember any such coarseness in Ben Okri's novel, although I do recall the trees having very odd names, like iroko, baobab and obecke.

This evening I've come to hear Ben Okri talk politely at an Oxfam shop. It's near the British Museum, in Bloomsbury, not far from where D.H. Lawrence used to live. There are no chairs left, so I'm standing at the back, which is actually the front, facing the windows onto Bloomsbury Street. After scrimping up a suggested donation of £6 and placing it into an empty fishbowl, I take a glass of red wine in receipt. Although I finish the wine very quickly, I only return for one further glass because Oxfam is a charity, and it wouldn't be very charitable to drink all their wine, or to try and recoup my donation, after donating it, in the form of said wine. Instead, by reaching beneath the chair legs of those sitting in front, I manage to take quick swigs from their floor-bound glasses, as a sort of seating tax.

It was Ben Okri himself, in *The Famished Road*, who wrote:

Learn to drink, my son. A man must be able to hold his drink because drunkenness is sometimes necessary in this difficult life.

That's why I always carry a hip flask of whisky with me. We'll hopefully explore the area of 'author confidence' later, in more detail.

Ben Okri has just arrived through the main door of the shop wearing a black suit and a cream shirt without a tie. It's all a bit awkward, because we were expecting him to appear from the wings somewhere. Instead, as I say, he just walked through the main door. So an Oxfam representative has quickly whipped him off out the back somewhere, in case people started talking to him, before his event. He's really dressed up for the occasion, in his suit. But unfortunately he's forgotten his reading glasses, because the Oxfam representative has just asked if anyone has a pair he can borrow. Patting all my pockets, desperate to assist, I end up waving a pen around.

Oxfam Woman: Yes?

FP: I have this.

Oxfam Woman: A pen?

FP: Yes.

Oxfam Woman: It was some reading glasses we were after…

FP: Thank you.

On a previous occasion, Ben Okri had been browsing the bookshelves here in Oxfam's Bloomsbury shop when a staff member recognised him and invited him back to give a talk. He had been picked out in public, identified purely because of his appearance. His face was now familiar, like the Honey Monster, for instance. As a public author, this is a very real consequence that you must be prepared for.

Until his death, American author J.D. Salinger kept well away from prying eyes, spending a great deal of energy in safeguarding his famous work, *The Catcher in the Rye*. Thomas Pynchon, another American, has also adopted a reclusive, hermit lifestyle, with only one or two photographs of him known to exist. These are examples of authors who have successfully avoided the public glare. To combat meddling reporters yourself, try and refrain from splaying out on pavements, or slumping in the doorways of neighbourhood pubs. Doing these things may build up a reputation for yourself that you could really do without.

Ben Okri is actually unwell this evening, but he has turned up regardless, soldiering on. Instead of being curled up in bed with Vicks on his pillow, he is out in Bloomsbury, all flashed up in a fancy suit and a stranger's pair of glasses. There are many lessons to be learned from this, but most clearly is the sense of self-sacrifice that Ben Okri has displayed this evening, and from which we the audience have most certainly benefited. Oxfam is a charitable entity, so Ben Okri is giving his time tonight for free. The Oxfam representative mentioned that they'd done a scour of many local branches, sourcing all of Ben Okri's titles that had been donated and handed in. Therefore, Ben Okri won't secure any new book sales tonight, because the books have all been bought already.

He's also sick, so he is effectively sacrificing his personal health this evening also. When you're sick you can't write, in which case you try and get well as quickly as possible. Rather than do that, Ben Okri has chosen not to let down his hosts and the large crowd who have turned up to hear him read and speak. And unlike other big authors who beat a hasty retreat as soon as their stage time is up, Ben Okri has agreed to stick around to meet his readers and sign their second-hand books.

He's sweating profusely, leading me to think he is actually close to death.

FP: Are you OK?

Ben Okri: I'll survive, I'm sure. Thank you.

FP: You are a credit to the pioneering spirit of the public author.

Ben Okri: Well, you're too kind. [*Pause.*] *Francis Plug*? Is that you?

FP: Yes. Have you heard of me?

Ben Okri: No.

FP: Oh. Because I've actually made a bit of a name for myself in residential gardening.

Ben Okri: Ah, you're a gardener.

FP: Yes… but I'm an author too.

Ben Okri: Are you? What books have you written?

FP: I haven't written any yet.

Ben Okri: Oh.

FP: But… I'm writing one at the moment. Right now. And you're in it.

Ben Okri: Me? I'm in your book?

FP: Yes. It's going to be brilliant.

Ben Okri: What's it about?

FP: Um, well, I can't tell you. I'd have to kill you. If you don't die first. Of your illness.

Ben Okri: OK. I guess I'll just have to wait and read it when it's finished.

FP: Yes. [*Pause.*] Thanks for not swearing tonight.

Ben Okri: Did you think I might?

FP: No, I didn't think you'd stoop to that. [*Pause.*] I liked that bit in *The Famished Road* where Madame Koto is moving a table in her bar and she farts.

Ben Okri: You liked that did you?

FP: Yip. [*Laughs.*] It was funny.

Ben Okri: Hmm.

FP: I'm glad you didn't cark it before you signed my book.

Ben Okri: Yes, most fortunate...

Tending gardens is an OK job because I get to work alone, and this very much suits my inward and lonely author credentials. I used to think that a writing career would be quiet and peaceful too, but of course that's all changed. Now you have to work a crowd. Ben Okri this evening is a case in point. And on top of their events, authors are also expected to be more interactive with their readers online. They're now encouraged to 'connect' with their audience and 'make friends' on social networking websites and the like. Maybe some authors are comfortable making 'cyber friends'. But I'd rather spend my spare time writing a book than writing about what I had for lunch. Writers don't make friends, they lose them. Especially drunk writers.

I transgress...

BARRY UNSWORTH

SACRED HUNGER

To Francis Plug –
with best wishes!

Barry Unsworth

HAMISH HAMILTON · LONDON

While reading Barry Unsworth's Booker Prize-winning novel, *Sacred Hunger*, I found myself perched in the dizzying heights of a ship, like the Liverpool Merchant featured in the book. It wasn't actually a ship, of course – it was an old oak tree, and I was high amongst the foliage, having just escaped from my client, Mr Stapleton, who owned the tree and the surrounding garden and property. He had arrived home unexpectedly, finding me lying on my back on the lawn, attempting to pedal a 'sky bicycle'. A short distance from my resting, sodden head was a freshly laid pile of vomit.

FP: It wasn't me, Mr Stapleton. It must have been someone else.

Mr Stapleton: OH, SOMEONE ELSE, WAS IT? SOMEONE ELSE CLIMBED OVER MY NINE-FOOT FENCE AND PUKED THEIR GUTS OUT, RIGHT NEXT TO YOU, FANCY THAT!

FP: Maybe… it was a badger…

He was very angry, Mr Stapleton, he was pulling at the collar of his shirt and stretching his neck out, trying to find extra room for his bigger, redder neck. Very noisy, shouting at me, scaring the birds away from London, the little sparrows, scaring them away into the countryside. And the tits.

23

I stopped pedalling and stood up, turning into a gorilla.

FP: OO, OO! AH, AH! OO, OO! AH, AH!!

My hands curled into fists and I fiercely beat my chest, roaring. Mr Stapleton was quiet and stood quite still. His whole face tightened, resembling a face drawn with felt-tip pen on a taut balloon. Picking myself off the ground like a gorilla, I ambled quickly across to the oak tree in the corner of the garden, rolling my arms before me in their rolled up overall sleeves. Climbing the trunk with strong nimble fingers, I continued my ascent until high amongst the foliage, hidden from view. Once safely clear of immediate danger, I began to shake the upper branches like a mad, mad monkey. This was designed to confuse, to ward off an attack by a group of outsider monkeys in order to protect my own inner group of monkeys.

After the roaring and the beating and the shaking of the branches, I fished inside my pocket and produced a pack of Cutter's Choice, some papers and a box of matches. Far below, a lot of yellow leaves were gathered on the lawn. I'd have to rake those up later.

Mr Stapleton is a banker, but he doesn't look like one. He's part of the new 'rock star' breed. Unlike his predecessors, he's not geeky and awkward. In fact, he looks more Baywatch than MoneyWatch. He's a tall fellow, broad and white, with tanned skin, most likely achieved via ultra-violet bulbs. A 'home counties' background, in his late 30's perhaps, with pale eyes, light brown hair (darkened with gel or 'fudge'), and a thin unfurling nose, scarred at the bridge, as if broken and swiftly fixed. Handsome yes, but in a dastardly, villainous way.

It's not surprising we have our run-ins. Ultimately, we're wired very differently. He's a hard-edged investment type, a mover and a shaker. Whereas me, I'm more of a meek, bleeding heart, lacking any of that ruthless drive stuff, or capitalist fervor. We may as well be from different planets. It amazes me that I've lasted this long as his groundsman. But I came recommended by the Hargreaves, an elderly couple whose garden I tend in Highgate. According to them, Mr Stapleton was taken by the fact that I was a writer. That has to be some sort of sick joke.

I sat like Hughes, in the crow's nest. Hughes is a minor character in *Sacred Hunger*, but he's the person I remember the most. Barry Unsworth's historical epic follows the journey of a slave ship from Liverpool to the Caribbean and onwards to Africa and the Americas. Hughes is part of the English crew making the journey. The ship is packed with human life, unbearably so, but for one tiny place, high up in the rigging. It is there, in the crow's nest, that Hughes resides, shut off from the others in his own swaying, elevated world.

I ended up sitting in the rafters of Mr Stapleton's oak tree for two and a half hours. Being up a tree wasn't the worst way to pass the time. I had my smokes, and also a cheeky little bottle of scotch. Also, the wind through the leaves sounded like stones being washed and shaken in a sieve, and I enjoyed watching the clouds being kneaded into various contortions of dough, as if by unseen jointed knuckles on a floured chopping board of sky. Still, there were more important things I could have been getting on with. And there lies the problem for the author of today; too many other concerns prevent you from actually writing. Things like money, working to earn the money, angry people, turning into a gorilla, hiding like a gorilla in a tree to escape the angry people. When you could be writing.

One thousand oak trees were needed to make a slave ship, according to Barry Unsworth's research. (His book is a thick tome, possibly using many oak trees in its production too.) Firs were also employed in the process, forming the construct of the mast, and elms were intricately carved for their role in the figurehead decorations. When I met Barry Unsworth, I hadn't yet read his novel, so I couldn't ask if Hughes was based on him. But as a writer used to solitude, Hughes rang a bell with me, so perhaps he rung Barry Unsworth's bell too.

Barry Unsworth's talk was at the University of London in Holloway Road. But the tickets were quite expensive, so instead of buying one, I awaited him in the foyer.

One of the ladies on the desk was very nice, and knowing I couldn't afford to attend she offered to help me meet Barry Unsworth when he arrived.

Nice Woman: Are you studying at the university?
FP: The 'University of Life'.

The more serious audience members began turning up, so I sat patiently in the foyer, squeezing my hands until all the blood disappeared, perhaps shooting up my arms.

As timed ticked on, it seemed that Barry Unsworth was cutting it rather fine for his own event. It's worth considering how one should time the arrival of one's own public appearances. It would be terrible, for instance, to arrive too early and to be waiting around with everyone staring at you. They might even ask questions before you have a chance to get some drinks in. At the larger venues, it's likely there will be a rear artist's entrance where a doorman will shake your hand with a white glove and tell you by name that you have been expected. Perhaps another member of staff will lead you to your dressing room where a rack of clothes awaits, a stocked fridge hums, and some mirror lights buzz. As the auditorium fills with anticipation, you can sit out back, doing the 'turkey head' to some 'bopping tunes' before bursting on stage to a rapturous welcome. But you can't do that at the smaller places. At the University of London Holloway Road Theatre, it's probably best to arrive just as the train's whistle is blowing, so to speak.

Barry Unsworth knew exactly what he was doing. He arrived just in the nick of time, and was accompanied, I think, by his wife, and also another couple, as if they'd all just enjoyed a lovely pub meal, perhaps at the Lord Nelson nearby. I'd stopped in there earlier myself, but I hadn't thought to look out for Barry Unsworth. Which was silly. Of course that's where he'd be, prior to a gig. At the pub. It made all the sense in the world.

The nice lady on the desk had to reach up to put her hand on Barry Unsworth's shoulder, due to him being a noticeably tall man, and with her other hand she pointed towards me, cowering near the entrance doors, as if someone had just punched me hard in my testis. Barry Unsworth's height, coupled with his Booker Prize literary status, made him an imposing figure indeed, especially to someone who was denying him a cut of his ticket price profits. But in fact he was a quiet and gentle man, and my initial concerns about being seized by his large hands and upended on the foyer floor proved unfounded. While all the paid-up ticket holders were somewhere inside, waiting, Barry Unsworth sat next to me, having a chat.

Barry Unsworth: You'd like a book signed?
FP: Yes, please. This one.
Barry Unsworth: Ah, you've got it all prepared.

Owing to previous misunderstandings with authors who could not understand my confused lamb-like bleatings, I had written my name on a slip of paper, providing a clear guide to my full title and its correct spelling. As a public author, signing books, it's crucial that you listen carefully to people, even the muttering ones.

Watching Barry Unsworth intently, I noticed that he continued talking as he wrote, his left forearm keeping the title pages spread so his pen was unimpeded.

FP: Are you worried about tonight?

Barry Unsworth: In what way?

FP: Getting up in front of all those people, talking to them...

Barry Unsworth: Well, a little. It's been a while since I've done this sort of thing. I'm looking forward to the discussion, though. It should be interesting.

FP: But you've had a few drinks, right?

Barry Unsworth: Have I?

FP: For the nerves. At the Lord Nelson.

Barry Unsworth: The Lord Nelson?

FP: With your delicious pub meal, granted.

Barry Unsworth: Um... no. We ate at a restaurant. And I just allowed myself the one modest glass of wine...

FP: I think you should ask for some more wine inside. If I were you, I'd ask for two bottles.

Barry Unsworth: Two bottles of wine?

FP: Ask the university people. That lady, maybe? And whatever happens, you mustn't drink the water, because it's full of long squiggly worms.

Barry Unsworth: Really?

FP: Yip. This long. [*Stretching arms out, with hands on either end of the arms.*]

Barry Unsworth held my pen out so I took it, together with my copy of his book, and smiling warmly he stood up. He was dressed smartly too, while I was in my gardening gear with cheap brandy breath.

Barry Unsworth: Thanks for the advice, Francis. Nice to meet you.

FP: Thank you, Barry Unsworth. Good luck.

I remained sitting in the foyer, studying Barry Unsworth's signature. The 'r' in Francis, combined with the 'F', looked a little like a fire extinguisher. This was uncanny because I have a real fondness for fire extinguishers, and long to one day discharge one. They're like guns, but guns for good. In fact, if William Burroughs, the American writer, had aimed a fire extinguisher at the glass on his wife's head, perhaps she would still be alive today.

He was a very nice chap, Barry Unsworth, and I was slightly sad to see him walk off towards the throngs. I hoped they would look after him and I hoped he'd get plenty of free wine. As for me, I decided to go and spend the price of the ticket and more on whisky and Scotch, and maybe some vodka also. Not everyone has to go and get very drunk all the time, but some of us do.

Sadly, Barry Unsworth passed away not long after this was written. Of all the Booker Prize-winners I have encountered, he was without a doubt one of the most humble, considerate and nice. This may be in part because he lived the last years of his life in the Italian countryside, well away from the crowds and the stresses of British literary life.

HILARY MANTEL

WOLF HALL

*Francis Pryg
with good wishes*

Hilary Mantel.

FOURTH ESTATE • London

HILARY MANTEL

BRING UP
THE BODIES

*To Francis Pryg
all good wishes*

Hilary Mantel.

FOURTH ESTATE • London

When I turned up to the Hilary Mantel event, I was aching all over, and perhaps a bit smelly. I'd spent the day engaged in the removal of a tree stump, the remains of an eighty-year-old sycamore.

In this day and age, very few gardeners will contemplate stump removal without the aid of winches, or motorised stump grinders, or mini excavators. Personally, I find such advancements alien and confusing. Tending the land is a simple process, without need for modern gadgetry, and since such contraptions should not be operated when under the influence of alcohol, I usually resort to the good old-fashioned spade. A chainsaw is the exception to this rule, used when there isn't enough garden space to go around the stump and you're forced to go through it. Taking a dangerous chainsaw into my own hands can prove hairy however, especially in the afternoons, after a lunchtime visit to the pub.

It always saddens me to see a tree toppled, but removing stumps is traumatising too. Perhaps it's the roots, so resistant to exposure that they seem to cling onto the deepest reaches of the earth with desperate fingers. It's a feeling you may share too, when you think of your own life to come, as a public author.

I started with a spade, digging a hole around the base of the stump. A rented chainsaw awaited quietly on a paved step nearby. My own chainsaw was pawned off some months before, to cover financial difficulties at that time. The more I dug, the more frequently the roots appeared, all needing to be painstakingly chopped with secateurs. Occasionally I'd stop and dry retch like a yawning spider monkey. Once beneath the stump itself, the spade became useless, and I reverted to a trowel and my blistered and mud-stained hands. Eventually, thanks to ceaseless toil, the stump began to wiggle like a loose tooth, no longer harnessed to the mother ship. A final struggle then ensued, involving a desperate, shouting heave. And there it was, unearthed, laying sprawled on the lawn like an escape pod from a NASA rocket. I lay alongside it for a time, breathing heavily, physically shaking with exhaustion. Sweat leaked down my head and neck. Why do I do this, I thought. I should be sat behind a mahogany writing desk! With an ink quill! After a reviving swig of scotch, I removed the small spindly roots still attached to the stump and fired up the chainsaw, jitterly slicing the remaining trunk into circular segments, which I planned to sell later, on the Internet.

WHEELS FOR FLINTSTONES CAR
SET OF FOUR (PLUS SPARE)
STARTING BID: £0.99
POST & PACKAGING: £725.00

Dead on my feet, I walked slowly to Draper's Hall, like a huge, furry Snuffleupacus. All around were the high-rise buildings of the City of London, home to the financial district. Like novelists, investment bankers spend all day dealing with imaginary, fantasy things that don't actually exist. Unlike writing, it pays very well, even in our current dire economy, which they caused. Nobody's bothered to turn the lights off in their buildings tonight, to save money.

Despite the earlier sunshine, it's now very cold out in the City of London, something you tend to notice when you're standing

32

in a queue in the middle of the road. After slowly creeping forwards onto the pavement, we edge into a plush corridor lined with imposing portraits from a century long past. At the other end of the queue, deep in the warm bowels of the Drapers' Hall, two women sit behind a table checking surnames. One has been allocated A–M, the other the N–Zs. I find myself inexplicably drawn towards Woman II.

FP: 'Plug'.
Woman II: *'Plug'*?

A suited man with a moustache directs me towards a ludicrously fancy staircase, which I ascend with some difficulty, given my aching body. Upstairs, a clean-shaven younger man, also suited, ushers me into the palatial 'Court Room', towards the free wine. There is loads and loads of free wine. Other drinks are free too, like juices, and perhaps water, but the wine glimmers all the brighter. The man behind the drinks table has his hands behind his back like a policeman. He isn't pouring drinks because they've been poured already, into lots and lots of glasses. Instead, he simply stares at me. Perhaps he smells me also. I take two glasses and wander over to a most impressive woven tapestry, mounted on a side wall. There are two such tapestries in the Court Room, and I discuss these aloud with the intended recipient of the second glass of wine.

As author events go, this is, without a doubt, the glitziest I have ever attended. In fact, it's possibly the flashest building I've ever been in, full stop. For an emerging author, it's almost too much. Too excessive, too unobtainable. After all, to reach these sort of heights, you have to be properly special. As the first English novelist to win the Booker Prize twice, Hilary Mantel has no doubt earned her stripes. But for the rest of us, it's probably worth preparing for a back-of-the-shop affair, with zero drinks and an audience of zilch.

We're invited to make our way into the Livery Hall, the venue for the talk. Unfortunately, unlike other Guardian Book Club events, drinks must be left outside. Having to leave a table still laden with full wine glasses is something that weighs heavily on my heart. So I don't. I choose to remain in the Court Room, drinking the free wine.

Drinks Policeman: Please make your way through to the Livery Hall, sir.
FP: I can't let all this lot go to waste, can I? [*Raising two new glasses.*] To Hilary! To Hilary!! Edmund Hilary! To Edmund Hilary!! To Sherpa Kensington!!

I'm escorted in person to the Livery Hall. As I enter, John Mullan, the interviewer, is declaring that Hilary Mantel has 'finally made it'. By which he means her success, rather than her late arrival. But this success, it turns out, is not the only reason for the opulent surroundings. The rather stunning Livery Hall is also the site of Thomas Cromwell's former townhouse, and therefore intrinsic to the two Booker Prize-winning books Hilary Mantel has penned. The Hall itself is almost circular in shape, adding to the grandness, and the chocolate-brown marble pillars and narrow balcony above lend a sort of theatrical dimension. Ceiling paintings depict narrative scenes, possibly Shakespearian, and a further collection of large austere portraits adorn the walls. Queen Victoria takes pride of place behind the raised stage, upon which the author, Hilary Mantel, plays her part, on a chair.

I sit drink-less on my own chair, which is solid and wooden, with a leather base. There are no cheap, flip-up seats in the Livery Hall. Even the red carpet is richly threaded, its ram motifs also appearing in gold upon the marble pillars. Normally a setting such as this would guarantee a more refined type of patron, but tonight's event is open to the public, so any old scruffbag can waltz in. I scour the crowd, looking for scruffbags.

Hilary Mantel's event is full of old people, which is nice. Old timers are great. Many of my favourite pubs are propped up by elderly folk, and there's something reassuring about this. Perhaps it's because old people are too frail to be threatening, or just wise to all that tough-guy stuff. Old people don't try too hard to be cool, and being cool is something that us drinkers aren't very good at either. When you're drunk, it takes a bit longer to process things and to put your trousers on, for instance. Same for the oldies.

Hilary Mantel's microphone isn't working. She can still be heard, but only faintly, through John Mullan's mic. He makes no attempt to swap, so he's either unaware of the issue or he's a mic hog. Given the chill outside, there's understandably a lot of coughing. Instead of curling up in front of the fire with a good book, the public have come out in the freezing cold to hear an author talk instead. To combat their hacks and wheezing, Hilary Mantel must project her voice even more, without a mic. A woman hobbles up the side aisle towards my end-of-the-row seat. She is attempting to stifle a bad coughing fit, and is thoughtfully exiting the talk in order to save the rest of us her germs and bloody great racket. I clap politely at her gesture as she passes, and she stares at me with bulbous, stricken eyes.

Hilary Mantel has a tall bottle of water to herself, so as not to catch anything from John Mullan. When she answers his questions, she faces her audience, looking around us all, often with a broad smile. Unlike most authors, she genuinely seems to be enjoying herself. Of course, when you've secured a gig in a place like this, knowing that you've 'made it', who wouldn't?

Her outfit tonight appears suitably glamorous. She wears a striking red top, loosely fitting, which is heightened by a thick black necklace. Hopefully I'll see this necklace in closer detail at the signing, allowing for a more detailed report in my 'attire' notes. With all those marble pillars and royal portraits behind her, Hilary Mantel could easily pass as a Head of State. In fact, she looks a bit like Hilary Clinton. OK, her red top clashes somewhat with the red carpet design, but it's not as if she's sitting on the floor. She's sitting way up there, on a stage.

A man with a trimmed beard and glasses suddenly mounts the stage too, but he's not a streaker, or a Father For Justice. He's one of the tech people, and in a swift, no-nonsense manner, he deftly switches the two microphones. Hilary Mantel, the feature act, is finally given a proper voice.

Hilary Mantel: I can really feel like I'm on the microphone now.

We're not out of the woods yet, however. As question time is announced, the public address speakers emit a truly deafening screech. It's enough to make me cower, literally raising my arm in protection. For all the historical opulence of tonight's setting, they're really struggling with the tools of the modern ways. As a featured author in such a case, your hands are tied. When the technology melts down, dear reader, all you can do is shrug and persevere. Tonight, Hilary Mantel epitomizes this defiance with her high spirits and cheery smile.

The distractions aren't just technical. While the author valiantly answers questions from the audience, John Mullan waves his arms about like a mad man. He is gesturing to a young woman with a roving microphone, before pointing wildly to anyone with their hand up. The microphone woman has a very nasty cough herself, and all this running around isn't helping her one iota. As an author, you must be wary therefore of not only catching your readers' filthy germs, but also those of the event subordinates too. It may come to pass that your voice projection needs to be sacrificed in favour of a white surgical mask, as worn by the likes of Japanese tourists and Michael Jackson.

A man asks about the phrase 'the tail of her eye', which he's noticed has been used in both the Cromwell books to date. But Hilary Mantel is unaware of this repetition, and there is an awkward moment as the man, having inadvertently highlighted a 'slip', stammers somewhat sheepishly. Hilary Mantel makes light of this, but then another raised hand queries the number of lovers that one of her real-life characters is purported to have. Again, Hilary Mantel is put on the spot and must defend her work. But she does, and the matter is quickly resolved. None of the questions are too critical. The large audience is here to fawn in her presence. They're on her side. Any real critics remain silent. Still, some of the questions are extremely tedious. They're more concerned with historical facts and less with the fictional construct for which Hilary Mantel has no doubt spent years of her life creating. She must be thinking: *Hello? Can we actually talk about my friggin' book please?* Having studied her body language closely however, I've noticed no sign of rolling eyeballs or foul curses discreetly mouthed. This restraint is something we can all learn from. One person asks why less of Thomas Cromwell's private life is aired in *Bring Out The Bodies*, the second book, and Hilary Mantel explains that his life became increasingly consumed by public affairs. Perhaps Hilary Mantel's own life is now going the same way.

Hilary Mantel is said to live in 'Budleigh Salterton', but I don't buy that. According to an article in a national newspaper, she supposedly entertained a journalist in her beachfront home, before they both wandered into town together and dined at a local restaurant. It was even claimed that Hilary Mantel's husband Gerald had picked the journalist up from Exmouth Station. But Exmouth is in Devon. It just doesn't add up. If a writer moved to Devon, to get away from it all, the last thing they'd do is invite a journalist (and a photographer) to come traipsing through their house. Hilary Mantel may be most amenable to her interviewer and large audience tonight, but as for inviting a journalist into her home, in 'Budleigh Salterton'... hello?

Her signing session is in the Drawing Room, another resplendent affair, furnished with huge mirrors, chandeliers, and sculpture busts of the Queen and HRH the Prince of Wales. A table is set up at the back, and I'm lucky to secure a good queue position, to help me escape quicker for a smoke. I'm keen to ask Hilary Mantel about the fictional construct of her books. But instead, I find myself discussing the conspiracy.

Hilary Mantel: I'm not quite sure what you're getting at…

FP: I think we both know it's a cover-up, don't we Hilary Mantel.

Hilary Mantel: A cover-up? Is that so? What's your theory, then?

FP: Well, I think *you* wrote that article yourself, to put people off the scent. So they couldn't track you down and pester you.

Hilary Mantel: Do you now?

FP: Yes ma'am, I do. 'Budleigh Salterton'? [*Shallow laugh.*] As if! That's not a real place. It's clearly some coastal town of fantasy, dreamed up by your extraordinary imagination.

Hilary Mantel: Hmm…

FP: Don't get me wrong, I think it's brilliant, I really do. It's such an ingenious ploy, for getting all those leeches off your tail.

Hilary Mantel: In fact…

FP: Seriously… [*Holding out fist.*] … respect.

Hillary Mantel: Next please.

All that wine has been shamefully cleared away, so I skirt about the City streets, in need of a wee. Down a narrow alleyway, I happen across the Jamaica Wine House, which is actually just an old pub. It's full of bankers in identical suits, but I find a spare table, so decide to stop in and collate my notes. The cost of my ale is quite reasonable, which seems a bit unfair, given the silly money earned by its customers.

Upon leaving, I encounter a group of bankers outside, swearing loudly. It really isn't in keeping with the cultured night I've had.

FP: King Henry didn't appreciate coarse language.
Banker: What?
FP: Henry the eighth. He didn't appreciate coarse language.
Banker: You got a problem or something?
FP: People have gone to the Tower for saying less.
Banker: For saying what?
FP: Leek-eating cunt.
Banker: You calling me a leek-eating cunt?
FP: The people don't give a four-penny fuck.

They're a bit aggressive, some of these bankers. Not like the ones that work in actual banks, like J.K. Rowling used to. These chaps give me a talking to and a dressing down, even though I was only quoting from a Booker Prize-winning book, from one of England's pre-eminent writers. Bristling, I stagger off, a dark cartoon cloud hovering over my head. I suppose most people wouldn't recognise a reputable author, or their work, from Adam, so when in public, my advice is simply to keep your head down.

POSSESSION

A ROMANCE

—❖◈❖—

A. S. BYATT

For Francis Plug

from

A S Byatt

Chatto & Windus
LONDON

FP: Mr. Bevill? It's Francis Plug, the gardener.

Mr. Bevill: Oh yes.

FP: I can't come over today, I'm afraid. 'Cos I'm sick. I'm curled up in bed.

Mr. Bevill: Oh dear. Well I hope...

FP: Look, I'm about to go into a tunnel so I might cut out...
[*Beep, beep, beep.*]

I can't really afford to skive off work at the moment, but A.S. Byatt is doing a midday event at Foyles bookshop. And before that I want to visit the London Library's Reading Room.

The London Library is situated in the northwest corner of St James Square, not far from Piccadilly Circus. It's a favourite haunt of Roland Michell, one of the central characters in A.S. Byatt's Booker Prize-winning novel, *Possession*. While there, I might rub shoulders with other writers of my day and age too. On the way I pass Hatchard's, London's oldest bookshop, which is also mentioned in *Possession*. I look eagerly in the windows, hoping to see my own book on display, before remembering that I haven't finished writing it yet, let alone getting it published.

FP: Der!

I'm prevented from entering the Reading Room of the London Library due to a series of turnstiles, which can only be activated by electronic cards. To have a card you must be a member. The bespectacled woman behind the reception desk gives me a pamphlet, which outlines the fees. Life Membership makes sense financially, in the long run. Young people are required to pay the most, because they have the most life left in them. For those aged 18-25, a Life Membership costs £16,800. I ask the woman if I can sit down on the seating provided in the reception area, to mull things over.

FP: [*Aloud.*] £16,800? Ha, ha, ha! £16,800! £16,800! Ha, ha, ha!! Ha, ha, ha!!!

Seriously, how can Roland Michell afford that? He's only a young lad, and in *Possession*, he's a lowly academic. His girlfriend, Val, carries him financially, like a sack of spuds. Being a writer, A.S. Byatt must struggle with her membership fees too, although she at least has benefited from the £50,000 Booker Prize cheque. Yet she was writing about the Reading Room *before* she'd won the Booker Prize. And she also said she would spend the Prize money on building a swimming pool for her house in France...

I decide to make the most of my time in the London Library reception area by writing a poem. I entitle it: *Poos and Wees in the London Library*.

When I get to Foyles, there's time to spare before the A.S. Byatt event starts, so I stand in the window display, facing out to Charing Cross Road. I'm next to the recommended books, with my hands on my hips. A passing woman slows to look inside, so my hands and arms dart out like directional arrows towards the display. I smile warmly with my head tilted, my mouth open, but she hurriedly moves on. No sale!

Most of the people passing the window don't bother looking in at all, even though the books are arranged in quite a striking way.

If my book was in the window, I would try to make sure it had some kind of protruding rod attached to it. The book itself would be cradled in a battery-powered pendulum stand, causing the rod to swing forth and repeatedly tap on the window, thus attracting passers-by. Maybe the rod would be a drumstick, securely fixed with masking tape to my book. The tilting pendulum stand would be a sort of metronome instrument that worked like an outward windscreen wiper, its momentum projecting my book like a child on a playground swing, thus allowing the rod, drumstick or otherwise, to strike the glass with a tapping noise, thus drawing attention from passers-by. Swinging back, and forth, back, and forth, repeating the persistent tapping on the glass.

I use my pen to tap on the window, and yes, sure enough...

Security Guard: Excuse me, sir. Can you come out of there please?

FP: It works, do you see? When I tap my pen on the glass, the people turn and look into the window. Where the books are. You might want to...

Security Guard: This way please, sir.

Even bookshops now have big burly chaps protecting them. It's difficult to understand this, because as the London Riots proved, bookshops are the last place marauding gangs want to trespass.

Security Guard: *Now* please, sir.

FP: Look! [*Vigorously thumping on window, gesturing to passers-by.*] Look in here please! Lovely books! Look at the lovely books!

The Gallery is an enclosed room in Foyles, away from all the bookshelves. I'm sitting in the back row on a chair that is clown-nose-red. On the floor near my chair is an A4 paper sign that reads: *RESERVED*.

I retrieve this for later use, because when you drink by yourself in pubs and you go out for a smoke, or to the toilet, your seat is often stolen in your absence.

A film camera is mounted on a tripod just inside the door, and a second tripod firmly grips an extended microphone. Seated behind a desk, Antonia S. Byatt wears a thick black woollen jumper with an exceptionally large roll-neck collar. If she unravelled this collar, it would envelope her face and continue up her head like a kind of funnel. She has a roundish face, greying hair, and a CBE.

There are 25 different spotlights in the room, and eight central lights shaped like thin watermelons, or blowfish. These all work to highlight A.S. Byatt's best side, and any other sides as well. The closer I stare at her, the more she reminds me of an illustrated personification of the wind. I imagine her, perhaps in ponse to a heated question, forcibly blowing us all backwards, every time she leans forward to make a point, I firmly grip ide of my chair.

.S. Byatt: I think it's very dangerous to put real people, who you know, into books. People who are unable to respond.

In *Possession*, Roland Michell and his friend Maud attempt to get into the minds of the poets they are thoroughly studying. Watching A.S. Byatt being questioned in public, firstly by the interviewer, and now by members of the audience, it seems as if we are trying to pry into hers too. I wonder if, despite this crowded event, she's thinking about her writing room and her piece of chalk cliff from Flamborough Head in Yorkshire. Or the magpies and green parakeets in the tops of the nearby ash trees.

I know what A.S. Byatt's writing room looks like, because there was a photo of it in the newspaper. It was part of a weekly series in one of the Saturday review sections showing the desks and computers of well-known authors, and the environments where they write and create. Alongside each photo was a written description from the author themselves, talking about their room and where they got this chair from, and what that painting was of, and who gave them that knick-knack. Unfortunately, opening up your personal life like this is a common path for the modern public author, which you need to be prepared for. On the plus side, I suppose it's the closest you'll ever get to being on MTV 'Cribs'.

Although the mystery and wonderment of A.S. Byatt's writing room is gone, I am still left to imagine what the rest of her house might be like. In my mind, the hallway is shaped like an underground tube station. Large posters fill the blackened walls, pasted over wads of other large, browning posters, and each poster is filled with tiny words in 8-point type. The hallway floor is made from sliding tiles, like in that Jamiroquai video, except much faster. The walls of the huge lounge are covered with hundreds and hundreds of stuffed animal heads, and each head is talking, reading a different audio book aloud. *Beowulf*, for instance, is read by an anteater, while Balzac's *La Peau de Chagrin* is being voiced by a little lizard head. The bathroom is arranged like a service station forecourt with a petrol pump shower nozzle, petrol pump taps, and a cash machine. And the kitchen is compromised of a huge set of teeth, each molar housing a different appliance, cupboard or drawer. At mealtimes, the top set of teeth raise up and a retractable tongue sticks out, which is the kitchen table.

A.S. Byatt is signing books at a table that is wooden and plain. She seems like a friendly and warm person. Like a lovely warm wind. My hands are sweaty because of all the lights.

FP: Hello, A.S. Byatt.

A.S. Byatt: Hello.

FP: Um… do you mind if I mention you, the *real you*, in a book?

A.S. Byatt: What sort of book?

FP: Um, it's a book about author events, about authors in public, interacting with the public.

A.S. Byatt: So it's non-fiction?

FP: Kind of. I mean… if I used this conversation, for instance, it wouldn't be *word-for-word*, because I have a terrible memory. So I'd have to improvise.

A.S. Byatt: Hmm. What is the point of it, exactly? The book?

FP: Oh, it's… it's like a kind of guidebook. A self-help guide.

A.S. Byatt: A self-help guide?

FP: Yes.

A.S. Byatt: ?

FP: Um… so… what about the London Library?

A.S. Byatt: What about the London Library?

FP: I mean, how expensive is *that* place?

A.S. Byatt: Is it?

FP: Um… it might be. [*Awkward pause.*] Did you happen to notice those clown-nose-red chairs?

A.S. Byatt: Where?

FP: Just there.

I step down to the front row and drag out one of the chairs. Picking it up with my perspiring hands, I clumsily place it over my head and face.

FP: See, A.S. Byatt? I look like a clown…

The Pillars of Hercules is approximately 20 seconds walk from Foyles bookshop, via an alley that smells of musty piss. It is the former pub of choice for Martin Amis, Ian McEwan and Julian Barnes. Martin Amis' writer's room was in the paper too. It was 'a detached building at the end of a small concrete garden', with a glass ceiling 'covered in leaves and squirrels.' He hasn't won the Booker Prize, although his Dad did.

Julian Barnes famously referred to the Booker Prize as 'posh bingo'. When he went on to win it, he said: 'The Booker Prize has a tendency to drive people a bit mad.' One of his earlier books, *Flaubert's Parrot*, is a fictional account of an actual writer, Gustave Flaubert, the author of *Madame Bovary*. In it, Julian Barnes makes some interesting points about the reader's desire to pursue the author:

Why does the writing make us chase the writer? Why can't we leave well enough alone? Why aren't books enough?

Ian McEwan has won the Booker Prize too. Now he and Julian probably pick up the drinks tab, while Martin bemoans his lack of major prize money.

Martin Amis: You shits!

The three friends must worry that the old ways are going out the window, especially with the Booker Prize opening up to the Americans. Another big debate currently is whether digital books will replace physical books. Personally, I don't think so. Wearing a digital watch was cool when I was a kid, and where are they now? My own theory is that digital books were actually designed by NASA for astronauts, to reduce bulk. The galaxy is also very dark, and digital books light up. But they've stopped the space shuttle missions now because they're too expensive and they keep blowing up. This has left the digital book suppliers

47

with a warehouse full of the things that they can't shift, so now they're trying to flog them to everyday earthlings.

A couple stand near me at the bar, so I bring them into my debate.

FP: It's a total scam. You don't need space ware. You madam [*pointing finger into woman's tummy*] are not Lieutenant Uhura, and you sir [*pointing finger into man's tummy*] are not Captain James T. Kirk.

I stand outside the Pillars of Hercules like a small smoking stump, still smoldering after an earlier bush fire has been contained. My head is filled with troublesome thoughts. Whatever the future holds, it's likely that I will remain poor and will continue to be hounded for my Self-Assessment Tax returns. The tax people who post the computer-generated letters with the highlighted words could do well to be a bit more sympathetic. Like my bank, they clearly have no understanding about the all-encompassing nature of writing. I also worry about how clever A.S. Byatt is, and whether, as a fellow author, I'm a thicky.

But fear not, fellow authors. We're only five chapters in! Great success awaits us!

to Francis Plug

JULIAN BARNES

THE SENSE
OF AN ENDING

for

Julian Barnes

JONATHAN CAPE
LONDON

Like A.S. Byatt, Julian Barnes seems pretty smart too. Some authors do book signings at Asda, but Julian Barnes took to the stage in the Sheldonian Theatre, Oxford.

The Upper Gallery in the Sheldonian Theatre is home to the 'cheap' seats. This may be because the 'seats' are basically just wooden floorboards tiered on different levels. The backrest, therefore, is the legs of the person sitting behind. Prior to the event beginning, I enjoyed a few drinks across the road in the White Horse, a pub which has welcomed the likes of Winston Churchill, Bill Clinton and Inspector Morse. But I've come to regret those drinks after being crammed like a sardine into my £15 seat. The more spacious Lower Gallery seats are £25, while the Ground Floor seats are a whopping £50. In aeroplane terms, that would be likened to first class, with Julian Barnes as captain and his interviewer, Hermione Lee, as co-pilot. Apart from extra legroom however, and a non-reclining backrest, the first class ticket holders aren't particularly well serviced. They have a decent view of the captain, but like the rest of us, it turns out they'll have no opportunity to ask him questions in today's event, or even to get their books personally signed afterwards. They must be nervously hoping for some kind of laser-show accompaniment to justify the price of their tickets. The ceiling of the theatre might feature a magnificent fresco, depicting an allegory involving cherubs and burning clouds, but there is no net bulging with balloons, awaiting release.

The performance does begin with a ceremony, however. Julian Barnes is presented with the Sunday Times Award for Literature, which takes the form of a ceramic black and white pot with dual handles. Given I missed seeing him receive his Booker Prize, it's a good opportunity to witness the protocol for such an occasion. In his dark grey suit and pale blue buttoned shirt without tie, Julian Barnes is most gracious. His brief speech is modest, articulate, and also light-hearted. He mentions Hilary Mantel's dominance of the year's literary awards, saying he expects her to fling open the doors at any moment, demanding his prize too. Once this interlude is over, he sits down and sips water from a short, stubby drinking glass. Hermione Lee gets the interview underway, keen to explore a link between all of Julian Barnes' many books. He, on the other hand, is very reluctant to do so. His elbow is on the table alongside, his closed forearm facing Hermione Lee in a decidedly defensive pose.

Julian Barnes: I don't normally look back over my oeuvre, apart from at occasions like this, when I'm forced to. I don't find it very helpful.

Oh dear. This isn't very entertaining. It's all a bit serious and grim. The ale from the White Horse is pressing, but I'm absolutely penned in. There is no question of a quiet exit for a wee, let alone a cheeky cig. Down below, on their free-standing chairs with mauve fabric, the £50 crowd are clasping their heads. It's as if they're sat before a telly in a William Hill, watching their £50 greyhound biting the bums of the other dogs, at the back of the pack. But then Julian Barnes begins recounting a story about his grandfather killing chickens and we all perk up. His memory of this involves a neck-wringing device, whereas his

52

brother remembers a decapitation instrument, with the chicken's head falling into a basket, its neck spurting blood.

This is a great pointer, emerging author. The event is going badly and everyone is anxiously biting their teeth, particularly those paying special money. It's all building towards a disaster. But the author introduces a piece about decapitating chickens and the event is saved. If we follow this example, and have a story up our sleeve about ironing a fish, say, it just might save the day.

With all parties now happy, Julian Barnes stands up and seizes his ceramic trophy. He then ascends, dramatically, into the air, propelled by tiny wires, previously unseen. Both of his hands grasp the handles of the pot, while his elbows piston, like chicken wings. Up in the rafters, in the cheap seats, we are finally given a close vantage point of the author as he flits before us. He has a hands-free microphone attached to his head, and he begins singing, repeating the chicken death tale in verse. Suddenly his head tips forward, falling off entirely, into the black and white pot with a clunk. From out of his neck protrudes a fountain of confetti, and the crowd erupts in applause.

In retrospect, it all sounds difficult to believe. Perhaps Julian Barnes was onto something when he wrote in his Booker Prize-winning book:

The last isn't something I actually saw, but what you end up remembering isn't always the same as what you have witnessed.

Afterwards, I bolt down the spiral staircase, descending further to the basement loos. Julian Barnes is beneath the theatre too, huddled some way from the toilets with a small entourage. His head intact, he now wears a long, army-green trench coat.

Postponing my urgent wee further, I approach with my book and its dedication slip.

FP: That was quite something, that flapping about in the air. And your decapitating head...
Julian Barnes: I beg your pardon?

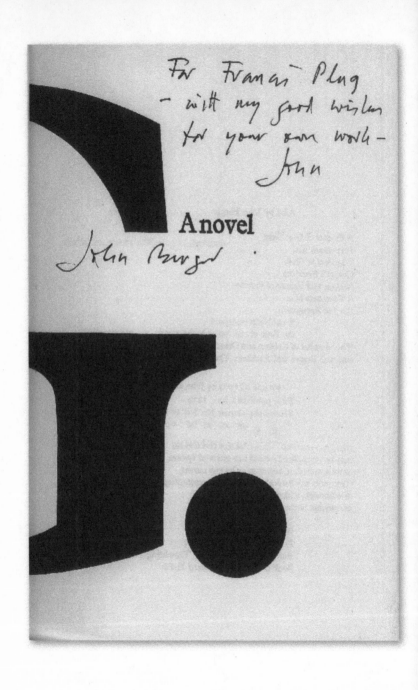

For Francis Plug
— with my good wishes
for your own work—
John

A novel

John Berger

The role of an author is not what it used to be. But gardening's not the job it was either. Today for instance, once these bulbs are planted and this jasmine and ivy are chopped back, I have loads of leafs to rake up, loads. That's because autumn is getting later, due to the exhaust fumes from all the SUV vehicles. The fumes are raising the greenhouse gas levels, so heat is being retained in the atmosphere, mucking up the weather systems. It's not my job to fix it, it's the government's, but they haven't. Instead, they drive around in Jaguars and fly about in jets.

These environmental changes are set to become the gardener's equivalent of the computer era. Temperatures are going to get even more topsy-turvy, and if us gardeners don't evolve we'll be left behind. Still, the edges of the lawns will always need trimming I suppose, and the jasmine won't stop growing. People with computers still use staplers.

Buckingham Palace is a very useful place for manure. It's horse-poo heaven, especially around the cobblestone periphery and on the large stretch of reddish road known as The Mall that leads towards the gates. By collecting a few pats, scooping them into plastic bags, I'm helping to beautify the surrounds for the overseas visitor, sparing their clumsy sightseeing feet the plops. Otherwise, it'll wedge between the rubber patterns of their shoe soles and they'll only go and traipse it through Harrods later, or The Ritz.

Horses are mentioned quite often in John Berger's Booker Prize- winning novel, G. They're depicted as honourable creatures, as weapons, and as lasting smells on one's hands. At one point, a galloping horse's head is even compared to a penis. Today, John Berger is appearing at the Institute of Contemporary Art (ICA), situated further along The Mall, towards Trafalgar Square. I can't really afford the price of a ticket, which doesn't matter, because it's sold out.

John Berger is perhaps the most notorious of all the Booker Prize-winners. When awarded the prize at the official ceremony in 1972, his subsequent speech provoked a wrath of controversy. He accused the Prize sponsors, Booker McConnell, of contributing to the modern poverty of the Caribbean, suggesting they had amassed their wealth via exploitative means. He subsequently announced that he would give half his prize to the Black Panthers, whose socialist and revolutionary thinking he could align with his own Marxist beliefs. Much criticism of his outburst would follow, and he would be sidelined from the other writers of the day, branded a rebel. Now living far from the literary scene, on a remote farm high in the French Alps, it is fair to assume he can escape from the encroachments of the media and the public, and meddlesome people like me.

The best time to collect free horse manure from The Mall is after a big procession, such as a royal wedding, or the demise of a Queen Mum. That's when all the horses come out, and they tend to get kind of jumpy because of the crowds and the motorbikes and the TV cameras, and they poo more. Fresh horse poo usually hits the ground in large balls. The texture is not too dissimilar from that of a hot cross bun; the dark brown exterior looks as if sugar has been baked into the crusty coating, while the insides have a light yeasty quality, which is often exposed after the steep drop to the hard road. The more intact the balls, the easier they are to scoop into my plastic bags, but even the splattered yeasty bits can be herded and corralled by scraping my dustpan across the rough, tarmacked surface. My clients would be most impressed if they knew that the Queen's horses were making their flowers grow, not the common plop-plops of some bog-standard sheep or cows. Special delivery poo, thanks to Her Majesty and Francis Plug.

My copy of G is secured within a plastic bag also, to keep it protected from the poo. It's a first edition, and it's not actually mine, so it's important that I keep G from the poo of the gee-gees.

A hardened poo is rolling down my tilted dustpan when two police officers approach.

Policeman: What do you think you're doing there, sir?
FP: Ahm... I'm just taking some of the horse poos away.
Policeman: And why would you be doing that, sir?
FP: Ahm... to put in the garden...
Policeman: To put in the garden. What's your name, sir?
FP: Francis Plug.
Policeman: Francis *what?*
FP: Plug.
Policeman: Plug? As in bath plug?
FP: Mm.
Policeman: That's your real name?
FP: Yes.
Policeman: Can we see some ID, Francis *Plug?*

I fish my card out of my wallet.

Policeman: *Francis Plug.* Unbelievable. Let's have a look in your bag then, Francis *Plug.*

I open the flap of my satchel.

Policeman: Hmm. That'll be the horse poo, then.
Policeman II: [*Sniggers.*]
Policeman: What's in that plastic bag there?
FP: A book, called *G*.
Policeman: *G?* Pass it here, please. Why's it in a plastic bag?
FP: Because of the poos.

I look at my gardening boots.

Policeman: Well, Francis *Plug...*
Policeman II: [*Sniggers.*]
Policeman: I'm going to ask you to move on now and
to refrain from removing any more HORSE POO,
understood? Because that's the home of the QUEEN just
there and we don't like people crouching on the road near
the QUEEN'S HOUSE. It's a bit SUSPICIOUS. Are we
clear?
FP: Yes.
Policeman: Right, well on your way then. And no more of
your horse poo collecting, Francis PLUG!

They're laughing, the two police officers, they're laughing
at me. My hands are shaking, putting the dustpan back into
the white plastic bag. The dustpan is light blue and it's smeared
with traces of browny green poo. It smells of horse poo, which
is a nice smell, a country smell, a good smell. My hands
continue trembling as I zip up the bag, but I'm not acting
suspiciously. I am not. I'm not even looking at the Queen's
house, just collecting poos off the road, cleaning the surrounds,
helping the tourists. My face and neck are burning as I walk
away from the Queen's house.

FP: [*Muttering aloud.*] YOU BLOODY IDIOTS. I WAS NOT BEHAVING IN A SUSPICIOUS… CAN YOU EVEN READ? MAYBE YOU SHOULD LEARN TO READ BECAUSE YOU'RE NOT VERY CLEVER YOU KNOW.

When I get to the ICA, I go straight to the bar to fill up.

FP: A drink please, a lovely drink.

Some people sitting near me in the bar are discussing a smell. This reminds me of a passage in *G* where John Berger describes the smell of the earth during a heavy storm, just as the rain first hits and begins to soak in. It smells, he writes, of meat.

Man: It's shit. It definitely smells of shit. That guy there.
Woman: Say something! It's disgusting!

A chair scrapes.

Man: Excuse me mate. There's a really bad smell coming from over here. It stinks of shit, frankly.
FP: It's not coming from me.
Man: Well, it's coming from your direction. And it only started when you arrived. It's definitely coming from you, somewhere.
FP: No, it's from the horses. From their bottoms.

I fiddle about in my satchel, producing some horse poo, waving it around.

Man: Yurk!
FP: The police tried to arrest me for this, two of them. But it was on the road, outside the Queen's house. It wasn't actually in a horse's bottom at the time.

Man: Yurk!

The man begins talking to the barman who looks across at me, following the direction of the man's pointed finger.

Barman: Sorry, sir. You're going to have to leave.

FP: But I need to have some drinks, I really do. I'm going through a bit of a rough patch.

Barman: [*Shaking head.*] I'm afraid you can't stay in here. That smell is very bad. The other customers are complaining.

FP: It's a fresh country smell. Like . . . like *Black Beauty.*

Barman: No, people are trying to eat in here. OK? You're putting people off their food.

FP: But why are they eating in here? This is a bar!

Barman: Come on, sir.

FP: But... but what about those elephant poo paintings? Remember? In that art gallery. Where was it? People paid good money to see those.

Barman: [*Shaking head.*]

FP: Can I at least finish my drink?

Barman: [*Shaking head.*] I need you to leave now, sir.

FP: [*Loudly humming* Black Beauty *theme tune.*]

John Berger is inside Cinema 1, so I sit on the red leather bench seat outside, waiting for him to emerge. It's a pointless exercise, really. If I want to offer you guidance on how to be a public author, I need to be inside the cinema, with the public author. At best I can wait and pick up some tips on how to sign books, and maybe some insights on author fashion. What else can I hope for? That simply by standing close to a real-life famous author, that some of his precious aura and talent may somehow be distributed to me? Transferred like pollen, blown across the air currents and sprinkled about my person?

RIDICULOUS!

I'm not the only one waiting. A man sitting further along the bench seat has a black bag with three or four John Berger books in tow. I've seen him at signings before. His motivation, I reckon, is a monetary one. His nose is a nose for investment.

Having unwrapped my book, I lay it on my lap, just in case some gland secretions from my sweaty hands should seep into the jacket design and spoil the red colour pigments. To keep the book steady, I hold my knees together, imagining I am a woman from the 1950's who is wearing a pretty dress, waiting to be asked for a dance. Looking up, I am surprised to find the book investor standing over me.

Book Investor: Do you know where that smell is coming from?

FP: Which smell?

Book Investor: Can't you smell it? It's like manure. Animal poo...

FP: Maybe it's these leather seats...

Book Investor: Are you waiting for John Berger?

FP: Yes.

Book Investor: [*Nodding towards my book.*] You don't see many hardback copies of G. [*He produces an almost identical hardback copy from his bag.*] Of course, I've got one...

He looks at the copy in his hand, turning it over, comparing it with mine.

FP: You know, John Berger once said: 'Imagination is not, as is sometimes thought, the ability to invent; it is the ability to disclose that which exists'.

Book Investor: [*Shakes his head.*] Did he?

FP: Do you believe in goblins?

Book Investor: No. Do you?

FP: Yes.

He walks quickly across the large black tiles embedded with craggy stone chips. When he sits down he pulls his jumper up over his nose.

John Berger's event is running over and now people are congregating for the screening that follows. A few people sniff the air, others whisper. They are screwing up their noses as if they've never smelled a farmyard before. It's starting to get to me. The police interrogation. The lack of drinks. And now this. Courting unwanted attention via crumbly balls of poo. I can feel myself losing it.

FP: What am I doing here? Learning to be a public author? But I'm in the foyer. Stinking of shit. Little craggy stone chips, stinking of shit...

The doors to Cinema 1 are suddenly thrown back and a crowd of people begin to blow out like air from a balloon. The book investor slips in with the crowd for the next event, fighting against the stream of those exiting. Is John Berger signing books *inside the theatre?* Should I be forcing my way in too? No, there he blows, he's breaking through the counter-flow. His arm is held firmly by a younger woman who directs him straight to the automatic doors and out towards The Mall. I scramble up to follow, bumping my way behind, as if gripping the tail of John Berger's imaginary cloak.

Outside, he stands with his head bent forward, lighting a cigarette. Despite the wind's bitter bite, he is covered in little more than a buttoned shirt with the sleeves rolled up. He's not a tall man, John Berger, but he seems quite a fit and sturdy fellow, such as one who might chop his own firewood. It seems difficult to believe that he's beyond his eightieth year, and as such, one of the oldest winners of the Prize. Only three Bookers were awarded before his, and only one of their recipients is still above ground.

John Berger is quickly ringed by admirers, seeking first-hand contact with the object of their regard. It's hard enough avoiding 'social' smokers who want to chat outside pubs or other public buildings, but when you're a recognised author, you're even more of a target. My advice, in such a case, would be to have your car parked nearby so you can smoke inside with the doors locked, the tinted windows up, and the car alarm activated.

Lighting a cigarette with trembling hands, I attempt to hold the filter end steady and inhale the smoke, just like John Berger is doing.

Standing on the edge of the group, I feel as if I am attending an awkward social gathering that I've only been invited to out of politeness. With no formal queue in place, our presence around John Berger seems smothering. Putting myself in his position, simply wanting a quiet smoke, I feel smothered too. My nerves, already frayed, are beginning to snap.

Before long, a couple of brazen hangers-on, including the book investor, thrust their books forward without subtlety. I hang back, hoping to get some of the smaller crumbs from the more feisty ducks. However, the young female aid, aggrieved by the leeching crowd, attempts to get John Berger towards the road to flag down a taxi. As he moves off with her, I catch his eye from my awkward background foothold, holding up my book hopefully. He stops and I apologise.

FP: I'm really sorry about the smell.
John Berger: Hmm... what *is* that smell?
FP: It's my poo. My *horse* poo. The Queen's horses...
John Berger: [*Laughs.*] Fair enough! Just a signature?
FP: No, no, to Francis Plug. Please.
John Berger: Francis with an 'i'?
FP: Yes, please.
John Berger: And Plug...
FP: P.L.U.G. I'm... I'm a writer too.

John Berger: Are you? Well, keep hard at it, won't you?
FP: I will!
John Berger: Um… are you OK there, Francis?
FP: [*Nodding, reaching for handkerchief.*]
John Berger: You're sure?
FP: Yes. Thank you very much. Thank you.

I feel like I'm walking through a waterfall as I re-enter the ICA, searching out the toilets. I'm leaning on the basin when the door behind me shudders open, so pushing the push-down taps, cupping the water, I manically splash my face and hair.

FP: [*Shouting.*] I'VE GOT WATER IN MY EYES! TAP WATER!

ff

KAZUO ISHIGURO

The Remains of the Day

To Francis Plug,

[signature]

faber and faber
LONDON BOSTON

The Christmas season is a busy one for booksellers. Some shops hold special events, with multiple authors all signing books at once. Waterstones' Hampstead store is a case in point. And this year they have a Booker Prize-winner to boot.

The air is thick with murderous fog, but I'm not concerned. After all, this is safe-as-houses Hampstead. The last unrest or disorder here probably dates back to that scamp, Dick Turpin.

After a lengthy spell in a local historic pub (a pub so old, they even played a Portishead album in its entirety), I venture to the high street, seeking out the village Waterstones. The Christmas authors have yet to show, so I wander out back. In the children's area a well-dressed mother is crouching with her young boy, reading him a story on a mat. The mat is a fluorescent purple colour, and the cushions look very soft and inviting. I lie there for a while, eyes closed, wafting up clouds of sour whisky. But needing to keep alert, I start arranging the mats into a wrestling ring.

The mother and her little boy are by no means intended as opponents, but perhaps, by virtue of their position on the mats, they become unwillingly embroiled in my 'Slam Down' title. I can only guess at this, because my head is inside a cushion cover, and I am flexing my biceps, shouting.

FP: AAAHH… OOOMMFA!!

A short time later, feeling a little sick, I sit up, removing my mask. The woman and the boy are nowhere to be seen. Dozens of books lie strewn over the mats, and one of the bookcases has fallen over. I wipe up the sweat patches from the mats, and tidy the books and shelving. Then I stride back to the front of the shop with my chest out, like wrestlers do when they've won.

A number of authors have arrived in my absence, including Kazuo Ishiguro. He is signing books already, and a small queue forms before him, like a Pinocchio nose. Rather than purchasing his new book as a seasonal gift for loved ones however, the people awaiting signatures are holding the books they arrived with. These unashamed attendees are specialist bookshop types, queuing to raise the value of their first editions. Like them, clutching a first edition also, I will not be making the cash registers ring.

The other authors are standing around with their arms folded, like the back-up members of a literary band who no one recognises because they aren't the lead singer. I recognise Howard Jacobson [yet to be a Booker winner himself], and also political spin-doctor Alastair Campbell who, presumably, is used to lurking in the shadows. Both men stand behind their respective desks, talking to each other, and I begin listening into snippets while I wait for the Ishiguro queue to die down a bit.

Alastair Campbell: So, do you live around here?

Howard Jacobson: No, I live in Soho. But this is my old stomping ground.

Alastair Campbell: *Soho.* You weren't one of those placard-waving shits in the Iraq demonstrations, were you?

Howard Jacobson: I'm sorry?

Alastair Campbell: You know, those drippy 'Not In Our Name' types. That's not your crowd, is it?
Howard Jacobson: Um…

One of the visiting booksellers interrupts them, approaching Howard Jacobson with an old hardback copy of his first book *Coming From Behind*.

Howard Jacobson: [*Lamenting.*] They're only interested in my old stuff. No one wants to buy my new books. Over twenty-five years ago I wrote that.

Alastair Campbell catches me giving him a hard stare and folds his arms tighter, leaning back on his shoes. I don't register the name of his book, but I think it's called *Alastiar*. He's a good fiction writer by all accounts.

A woman stands near another desk, and at her feet is a cute little dog, a spaniel. I crouch to pat the spaniel and it becomes all excited, putting its paws on my shoes and licking my nose.

FP: Hey, hey! What a nice little dog you are!
Woman: Yes, I've written a book about her.
FP: Excuse me?
Woman: I've written a book about her.
FP: What? You've written a book… about this dog?
Woman: Yes.

There is no queue for the woman, or the dog. Not a sausage. I feel bad about walking away, shaking my head, but I do.

Kazuo Ishiguro is a shortish chap who, perhaps in deference to the other authors, has chosen to remain standing despite having a dedicated table and chair to sit at. After signing my book, he surprises me by extending his hand, the tool of his trade. Although a seasoned pro of the public author circuit, it's a rather amateur mistake. Because anyone who's seen a televised 'Slam Down' title would know all too well of the naïve opponent handshake. My first instinct therefore is to pull the unsuspecting challenger around in a wide arc and slam him into the ropes, from which he would spring back into my stiff-arm clothesline. But I let him off with a warning, having already gripped his hand for far, far longer than is deemed appropriate.

Christmas is a very quiet time for gardeners. Work virtually grinds to a halt over the winter months, and we become little squirrels, calling on saved reserves over the lean times. Unfortunately, I never stock up. Any such forethought is overridden by immediate demands and spiraling debts. Thus I find myself, sitting at home on Christmas Eve, nervously sharpening my tools.

The other residents of my building have, I think, left, returning to their family homes for some traditional cheer. There hasn't been the usual tell-tale signs of their habituation, generally highlighted by the thumping on the walls or ceiling as I perform my late-night improvised dances. Things came to a head one night when I came back from the pub and decided to blow the dust and hairs from my carpet into the stairwell with my leaf blower. I happened to look up and noticed half a dozen people, all screaming at me, just a few steps away. The blast from the nozzle was directed towards the woman from Flat 2, pressing her thin nighty firmly around her bosoms, and when I pointed and laughed, her boyfriend kind of attacked me. I woke up in the landing with whisky breath because I hadn't brushed my teeth before bed.

I do regret my drunken noise. As a writer, of all people, I should understand the desire for peace and quiet in one's home.

Like they say in that TV advert with Ian McEwan: *Everyone needs a place to think.*

My mother includes a letter inside her Christmas card:

Dearest Francis,

Sorry to hear that you are being followed by spies dressed as street cleaners. We can understand that they would be very keen to get their hands on the book you are writing, particularly if, as you say, it exposes certain fairy tales as works of fact.

All the same, it's good to know that the imminent death you predicted for yourself in the previous letter has not been realised.

How is your very good friend Salman Rushdie? It sounds like you have acquired a greater sense of confidence since we last saw you. Fancy kissing Hilary Mantel! On the mouth! Hope your dinner together in 'Budleigh Salterton' was a success. Are you eating well generally and taking care of your health? Your handwriting is getting more and more illegible – we hope this is because, as you imply, you keep forgetting to remove your gloves after operating heavy machinery.

Thank you for the offer of the new twenty-bedroom house with the unending treasures and riches once your book is published.

Love Mum & Dad.

We won't be having a family gathering this year. I spent last Christmas with my sister Claire and her family. Although she started speaking to me again in July, Claire is adamant that I will never share Christmas with them again. It's fair to say that her husband Rick and I don't see eye to eye, but we're family, so I've always tried to make an effort. Despite his regular criticisms of my drinking, amongst other things, he still tries to out-drink me.

Shortly before Christmas lunch last year, in front of his elderly mother, I pulled down his trousers and pants and gave his diddle a sharp flick. Fending off his rage by running behind the table, I proceeded to pelt him with some funny little sausages, and a volley of mince pies.

There's a family gathering in Anne Enright's *The Gathering*, but it's a gathering for a funeral.

To Francis Plug

The Gathering

—

Anne Enright

JONATHAN CAPE
LONDON

When I arrive at Anne Enright's event in Bloomsbury, I'm very, very late. I'm also a bit worse for wear, and the cover of her book is smeared and streaked with blood.

The door of the London Review Bookshop doesn't squeak, and there is no bell. But my shoe manages to give it a shuddering thump because, although my body has stopped outside, my feet have decided to stroll on in. At the back of the shop, beyond the mass of heads, some of which briefly turn, Anne Enright is being thanked. There is a burst of thunderous applause, which helps rouse me, peeling back my sleepy, frog-like eyes.

The crowd begin rising to their feet, signalling the end of the talk, and I stumble forward, blending into the stately queue that is forming between the chairs. The movement of the queue is haphazard, and lacking the means to focus, I find myself stationary and vacant, with large gaps opening up before me. At other times, I ram into the bottom of the man in front.

FP: Sorry. Again.

Having drunk my overflowing cup of top-shelf spirits, I now pump this back into the air as a foul, pissy mist. Despite purposefully choosing Irish whiskey to celebrate the evening with Anne Enright, I worry I'll melt her face as she signs my bloody book. So I squeeze out three capsules of minty gum, placing them onto my palm like pills, before administering them into my open mouth. What I really need is an Irish coffee because I'm dreadfully tired.

Anne Enright is wearing blue, or so I imagine it. She also wears a necklace made from chain links, like that from which a bath plug might hang. Not the little ball chains, but the rectangular, brick-shaped links with the missing middles. The end of her necklace is concealed beneath her top, so perhaps a rubber plug lies hidden there too.

FP: Sorry about the blood.

Anne Enright: Is that blood?

FP: Yes.

Anne Enright: *Your* blood?

FP: Yes. It's a long story.

Anne Enright: Is it a good story? I like a good story.

FP: It's OK, I suppose.

Anne Enright: So…?

FP: Well, basically, I stopped by the Plough pub, near here, before your event. But it was packed, so I went upstairs, to the upstairs bar, which was empty. But the actual bar itself, upstairs, was closed. So I climbed over the shutters and fell head-first onto a sink, and then onto the floor.

Anne Enright: Ouch!

FP: Then I took your book out of my satchel, to make sure it wasn't creased or dented, and some blood fell on it, from my head, via the sink.

Anne Enright: Oo dear. Are you alright then?

FP: There's more. I then realised I was behind a bar. A *bar*. With loads of drinks. Like Irish whiskey. *Irish* whiskey. It was all free, effectively. Which is why I missed your talk, I'm afraid. End of story.

78

Anne Enright: Well, that's quite…

FP: Oh, and when I climbed back over…

Anne Enright: Yes?

FP: … there were people sitting at some of the tables. And I fell very near some of them.

Anne Enright: They must have got quite a shock.

FP: I have no idea.

Anne Enright: Well. I don't think I've ever signed a blood-splattered book be…

FP: Aaaarrrgghh!

Anne Enright: What?

FP: I just bit my tongue!

Anne Enright: Oh.

FP: Instead of my… chewing gum!

Anne Enright: You're really in the wars, aren't you?

FP: [*Nodding, wincing.*]

Anne Enright: 'To Francis Plug'. Is that you?

FP: Yes.

Anne Enright: What an interesting name. I'm always on the lookout for interesting names. But I can't say I've come across a 'Plug' before.

FP: J.G. Ballard asked me if it was French.

Anne Enright: Did he? Yes, it could almost be French, couldn't it?

FP: But it's not *Ploog*. It's *Plug*. As in bath plug. Like your… your…

Anne Enright: … ?

FP: Thank you. I'm just going to the toilet now.

Anne Enright: OK. Very nice to meet you.

FP: There's a sign over there, for the toilet. A toilet in a bookshop? Whatever next? Hairdryers?

Anne Enright: Who knows? Bye, Francis Plug.

FP: When I sit on the toilet, I sit backwards, facing the cistern. Because you can use the ceramic lid as a reading desk.

Anne Enright: Well, that's…

FP: Yes. But sometimes, when I stand up, I lose my balance and fall backwards, onto my wiped bottom.

Anne Enright: Bye then…

It's a handy tip that, fellow authors. The toilet cistern writing desk. Particularly when you need to balance your precious writing time with other occupations, like myself.

The toilet in the London Review Bookshop is at the bottom of a very steep staircase. It's a bit precarious, but once you reach the small basement room, you can be comforted in the knowledge that you're cushioned from sudden air-strike by thousands of books. When I clamber back up to the shop, I loudly click my fingers in time with every new step I ascend.

THE BONE PEOPLE

KERI HULME

SPIRAL
in association with
HODDER AND STOUGHTON
AUCKLAND LONDON SYDNEY TORONTO

Keri Hulme is probably having a BBQ-style Christmas. A bit of grilled grouper perhaps, maybe some squid, a bit of cod. Smoke in her eyes, sunlight too, on the beach. Because it's summer down there in New Zealand. No one said you had to have snow. Bethlehem wasn't layered in the stuff on the holy day. They were all wearing sandals, so the New Zealand model is, in fact, more accurate.

In the preface to her 1985 Booker-winning novel, *The Bone People*, Keri Hulme describes living five hundred miles from her publisher, not having a telephone, and receiving 'only intermittent mail delivery'. Her life appears to mirror that of her book's central character, Kerewin Holmes. Like Kerewin Holmes, Keri Hulme lives in an isolated coastal community in a house she built herself. To my knowledge, she has never surfaced in the UK for an author event, not even appearing at the coveted Booker Prize ceremony at London's Guildhall. This may be due to the fact that she resides on the opposite side of the world, cut off, even from her own compatriots. Booker-winners from Australia, South Africa, India and Canada have all taken the stage in London, along with numerous Irish writers, and expatriated British authors, such as Barry Unsworth and John Berger. But I suspect Keri Hulme will always keep her distance, happier to be hidden away, maintaining a low profile like Kerewin Holmes in *The Bone People*.

In terms of Booker Prize-winners, she is not alone in her desire for privacy. Anita Brookner too, avoids public events, despite the continuing appearance of her numerous, well-reviewed books. Ruth Prawer Jhabvala, who sadly passed away recently, had been living in America as a retired screenwriter, well out of the literary 'scene'. David Storey and Stanley Middleton have also died during the writing of this book, both steering clear of the limelight in their later years at least. Of the living winners, most seem to emerge solely to promote new books, being otherwise content to get on with their real jobs. Perhaps they're on Twitter and Facebook too, but I wouldn't know.

For those of us anxiously preparing for an authorial life in the spotlight, the Keri Hulme model is incredibly enticing. But I imagine many prospective publishers will be uncomfortable swallowing such a proposition. Even though the larger houses have their own marketing and PR people on board, they still expect their authors to fulfill that role too. One solution, it seems to me, is to skip the country. It's much harder to show up for that theatre event/signing when you've absconded to a remote beach near Franz Josef Glacier. The flipside to this, dear reader, is that you could end up off the publisher radar, and may even be forgotten. [*Laughing.*] Like that's a bad thing!

After spending much of Christmas Day in bed, I finally venture out. There is no indication of anything special in the air. No rainbows, no falling glitter, no unicorns. The traffic lights change from green to orange to red, but not fast enough to be decorative or pretty. The grey sky seems to exist at street level, overpowering the exhaust fumes and the gas from the rotting fridges.

There are a few familiar faces in the Boston Arms, and I offer a tip of my tight-knit woollen hat as I approach the bar. It's the human interaction that's so important at Christmas, the shared camaraderie, the revelling in the cheer. It isn't a day to be an author, sitting at home, wallowing in self-interest. Christmas is a time for togetherness, celebrating, and dancing in the style of one pumping up an inflatable floating device.

Old Man: Look, here comes your mate.
Old Man II: Oh, Jesus. It's the original jingle bells.
Old Man: Yep. Jingle-bloody-jangle, all the way to the friggin' nuthouse.

From the outside, the Boston Arms looks like a rocket. It's the kind of pub where Flash Gordon might drink. In my opinion, it's the most impressive looking pub in the world. I've seen pictures of the Atomium in Brussels, and the Boston Arms in Tufnell Park is very like this. The only real difference being that the Boston Arms is a pub, with Venetian blinds. On a previous visit I operated the blinds cord, synchronising their opening and shutting with the blinking of my own eyes.

FP: Open. Shut. Open. Shut.

The Chinese woman turns up, selling her DVDs on Christmas Day. When she pings off the rubber bands, the films spill out from their flimsy stack like fish from a net. After a quick sift, one of the young lads buys three of her catch, and she beats a hasty retreat. If the publishing firms all sink into oblivion following the digitisation of books, I might have to sell CDs of my stuff in the Boston Arms too.

An older couple sit at an adjacent table, and seeing me peer through the blinds, they attempt to strike up a conversation.

Old Woman: Waiting for someone?

FP: No, thank you.

Old Woman: Are you here by yourself, then?

FP: Have you seen the traffic? It's like a herd of wild animals out there. The buses are big red elephants, the black cabs are black lions, the cars are gazelles, the trucks are buffaloes, the vans are zebras, the mini-cabs are monkeys, the bicycles are rabbits. No, the trucks are *rhinos*, the *vans* are buffaloes. The motorbikes are ostriches…

The older couple look at the selection of drinks on my table and slowly stiffen. The woman turns towards the man.

Old Woman: Little Julie will be starting school next year…

On my other side, to my left, a group of people are having a great time. They are laughing and taking photographs of each other, because it's Christmas Day. When they catch me watching, they ask me to bunch in for one of their photos. Afterwards, the photographer looks at the image on the screen and he's somewhat puzzled.

Photographer: Your face has gone all weird. Look, you can see the veins in your forehead. It's like you're trying to squeeze one out.

FP: That's my happy face.

There's still 45 minutes of Christmas Day left, but despite having no work to rise for on Boxing Day, I head home, slip into bed and am soon huddled up, eyes shut, beneath the sheets.

Until I hear a queer bubbling sound. It's coming from the bottom of my bed. Bubbles float up past my kicking feet, perhaps emerging out of a treasure chest, in a sunken ship. Twisting around, I descend quickly, diving with flappy cheeks, past the angelfish, the gobies and the snapper, down to the bottom of the bed.

To Francis Plug,

The White Tiger

ARAVIND ADIGA

Best wishes,

Atlantic Books
LONDON

The New Year isn't so new anymore, but despite this I haven't made much progress with my writing. With every passing week there seems to be more reports pertaining to the end of the book, but clearly not my one. In search of guidance and inspiration, I decide to visit the London Book Fair.

From the outside, the Earls Court Convention Centre looks like a cartoon duck's head. Uniformed police patrol the wide, cigarette-littered steps, while fancy cars pull up, driven by professional drivers. Perhaps Balram Halwai, the chauffeur and central protagonist in *The White Tiger*, is one of these. Maybe his boss Ashok is in town to pick up a few novels. All the male attendees appear to be attired in suits, while the ladies are mostly wearing trousers. It seems very formal for a bunch of books.

In the foyer area, sniffer dogs snuffle about my legs, looking for terrorists. One of the dogs is a Labrador and the other is a spaniel, and their noses are quite different, despite their unified talent. Why the London Book Fair would be a security target I really can't say. Maybe they think that authors are going to go mental because their advances have been slashed. The terrorists who rammed their car into Glasgow airport were supposedly doctors, so who's to say that authors aren't capable of blowing something up too?

Rather than just buying a ticket, I'm told I have to register. To register will cost £45. Wait a minute. £45? Just to see some old trestle tables piled up with messy books?

FP: Is this some sort of sick joke?

The cashier is quite adamant that they *do not* give discounts to poor people. I could try and bolt through, but I suppose the dogs would get me. Departing quietly, I sit out on the steps with the cigarette butts, before adding my own. Then I walk around the side of the building, flanking it, until I find an open fire door to the rear. For the smokers, like me.

It's not what I was expecting, the Fair. I thought it would be filled with books, like the weekend market on the Southbank. But there are no trestle tables. Instead, it's more like a department store at sale time. Flimsy, roofless stalls resembling perfume counters house publishers and their brand new books. The independents are in small, cosy boxes, while the big corporates are set up in large stage set-type zones, their latest wares displayed amidst publicity banners and signs. The Fair is supposed to last for three days, but I wonder how I'm going to fill the next ten minutes.

Fortunately, it takes a good hour to circumnavigate the entire ground floor. Each aisle is referenced alphabetically, such as Aisle A, or Aisle F, and each exhibit has a numerical code that is preceded by the aisle letter, such as A405, or D515. These are displayed on signs that protrude out from the stalls like tags on jean pockets. Buddha's Light Publishing burns incense on their table front. Another stall offers free biscuits. These are the interesting exhibits. The other 100 or so are really rather dull, to be honest. There are no shackled grizzly bears, no conjoined twins, no 'lobster boys'. I follow a food trolley for a time because it makes an entrancing rattly noise.

The highlight of the Fair is probably the building itself. Huge square posts support an Olympic-scale structure that divides into Earls Court One and Earls Court Two. In the upper reaches of Earls Court One are white canopy strips and massive ribbed air conditioner tubes. Earls Court Two, in contrast, has a bare curved ceiling, making it resemble a hangar, where aircraft might be stored. In each, electrical wires and cords drape down from the rafters like underwater oxygen tubes, pumping life to the ground far below. But both could use a gardener's green fingers, to brighten them up. Some token plants have been placed along the main thoroughfare, but for the most part the place is a horror of blandness. Personally, I would take a literary approach to the foliage, starting with a beanstalk that reached all the way up to the ceiling. A pigeon flutters around inside Earls Court One, before settling on one of the overhead rafters. I watch it for about 20 minutes. Somehow, like me, it's found a way in.

A particularly large exhibition space announces the international focus of the Fair, which is India.

FP: Is Aravind Adiga here?
Indian Exhibition Representative: Aravind Adiga? No, I'm afraid not.
FP: OK, fine. No skin off my nose. I've met him before, you see. Oh yes.

Aravind Adiga is signing copies of his Booker Prize-winning book, *The White Tiger*, at Waterstones' Gower Street branch, just off Tottenham Court Road. Tall vertical banners in the windows feature his photo, and large bold headings read:

MEET ARAVIND ADIGA.

About twenty-five to thirty people have queued in an orderly fashion, their positions contained by stretchy canvas strips, like those to be found in banks or post offices. The signing desk is covered by a large black cloth with a Waterstones logo. It drapes all the way to the floor, so I'm unable to see what sort of shoes Aravind Adiga is wearing, in order to replicate the style myself. Behind him is a large sheet of Waterstones wallpaper mounted on backing board, like the sponsorship logos behind talking football players. As a backdrop for author photos, it's rather drab. At my signing event, I'd like an image of a huge shark, so when people took photos of me it would look as though I was inside the shark's mouth, being eaten. In Aravind Adiga's case, he could have used a hungry white tiger. It's an opportunity missed.

Aravind Adiga is bald through the middle of his head, and the remaining arid sections are closely shaved. When he bends down to sign each book, his scalp is bared, and I find myself imagining him soundly asleep in bed, while I stand alongside, looking down, fully dressed. His novel is displayed on the desk, in book and audio-book format, and half a dozen plastic cups are piled on top of each other beside a jug of un-iced water, just in case he needs a new cup for each gulp. If I was Aravind Adiga, I would request a row of cocktail shots, one for each book signed.

With the desk close by now, I stand out to the side in order to see around the cloth and glimpse his shoes. They are black formal shoes, but above these are a pair of informal blue jeans, hiding behind the desk like a casual television newsreader's beach trunks.

I wonder if Aravind Adiga has cultivated a photographic 'look' for the many shots he is asked to pose for. My look, that I've been practicing in front of the mirror, is based on Macaulay Culkin in the film *Home Alone*. I practice it again as I stand in the signing queue.

Aravind Adiga: Are you alright?
FP: Yes, thank you. [*Pause.*] Do you mind if I take a photo?
Aravind Adiga: No, go right ahead.
FP: I don't know how to work the camera in my phone, so I'm going to take a photo with my mind.
Aravind Adiga: OK...
FP: [*Laughing.*]
Aravind Adiga: ?
FP: In my photograph you've got spaghetti coming out of your mouth. It's all down your jacket.
Aravind Adiga: Spaghetti?
FP: [*Laughing.*] Yes. Spaghetti!

The Indian stand have missed a trick by not having Aravind Adiga as a meeter and greeter. But it seems he, and other published writers, have been spared today. The success of their works has instead been left in the hands of the well-dressed folk with the laminated passes.

Unlike the other delegates, I don't have a pass on show. Some are affixed to hips, but most are clipped to lapels. The green passes and the orange passes seem to be the most VIP. These allow elevator access up to the 'International Rights Centre'. Here, the 'chosen ones' look down on us from the lofty heights of an exclusive balcony area. When I join the queue for ascension, a bouncer-like gatekeeper rebuffs me.

Gatekeeper: Where's your pass?
FP: Actually, I'm an *author*.
Gatekeeper: No. You need an orange or green pass.

FP: I must have left it at the biscuit place. Did you know you can get free biscuits around there, at the biscuit place?

Gatekeeper: No.

FP: Why don't you pop around there, for some free biscuits? I'll look after this...

Gatekeeper: No thanks.

The Harper Collins exhibit is one of the largest in the London Book Fair, and it backs right onto the main boulevard, or 'high street', of Earls Court One. The carpet they have chosen is black and business-like, and the majority of the space is taken up by the 40-50 tables and accompanying chairs where people sit talking, not reading. Their conversations seem rather earnest. Two people stand up from one of the tables, so I rush in and nab it.

Harper Collins Representative: Excuse me.

FP: Sorry, this table's taken.

Harper Collins Representative: Um... there's actually a queue for this table. Do you have an appointment?

FP: I'm an author.

Harper Collins Representative: A Harper Collins' author?

FP: No.

Harper Collins Representative: Right. Well, I'm afraid this table is booked. There are people waiting to sit here.

FP: My book is for sale. To the highest bidder.

Harper Collins Representative: [*Rubbing his hands over his eyes.*] OK, we're actually trying to *sell* books in here. Rather than buy them.

FP: It's a very good book. Seriously. You better snap it up 'cos everyone's hot on its heels.

Harper Collins Representative: Look, why don't you try upstairs? [*Pointing to the top of the escalator.*] That's where the book buying is going on. Not down here, I'm afraid.

FP: Sure. I'm also up for public events. I can really work a crowd.

The rep holds my chair for me.

I try a second time to ride the central escalator.

Security Guard: Excuse me, sir… SIR! You must have an
    orange or green pass to go up the escalator.
FP: To ascend it, you mean.
Security Guard: Can I see your pass please?
FP: The thing is, I'm actually an *author.* May I pass?
Security Guard: Not without an orange or green pass, sir.
FP: I cannot pass without a pass?
Security Guard: No, sir.
FP: What about pasta? Can I pass with some pasta?
Security Guard: No, sir.
FP: Lovely pasta? Lovely bit of pasta?

I head back out the fire doors for a cigarette. I have a drink
too, which I brought with me. Another smoker, a woman, eyes
me with suspicion. On her hips is a prized green pass for the
upper level. I give her a big smile, hoping to rein in my forehead
veins. She looks away, so I produce some scrap paper and begin
writing notes for my book at the London Book Fair.

Green Pass Woman: Wow, look at your tiny writing! That's
    amazing. So small and neat.

She is suddenly right next to me, bending down from her
tottering heels.

Green Pass Woman: What are you writing?
FP: It's a book. I'm an author. A wordsmith.
Green Pass Woman: An author, really? Wow. We don't get
    many of those here. What's your name?

FP: Francis Plug.
Green Pass Woman: Francis Plug? Who are you with?
FP: Um… no one.
Green Pass Woman: Oh.

She flicks her cigarette, inclining her head to blow smoke in the air like an ornamental frog spouting an arc of water across a manicured garden pond.

Green Pass Woman: Well, don't go blind, Francis Plug.

She begins walking away.

FP: Um, can I come up…

She finishes walking away.

While walking around the perimeter edge of the stalls in Earls Court One, looking for pigeons or rattling trolleys, I pass a sign that reads: STAIRS TO ALL LEVELS.

Passing through a side door, I proceed up some wide cascading stairs, as if wearing a very, very long flowing gown. On the first floor appears to be a separate theatre venue, but I continue to the second level, which opens out into a vast concreted area, resembling a multi-storey car park. Far across to the left are some temporary divider walls, and from here comes the sound of clinking plates and rattling cutlery.

Service staff are busying around outside, but they barely raise an eye at me as I pass far through a narrow gap in the walls, emerging at the back of a restaurant dining area. Walking casually through the restaurant, I make my low-key entrance into the buzz and hype of the VIP International Rights Centre.

Unlike the ground floor, there are no exhibits or stalls. Instead, tall locker units dominate the space, each allocated to different literary agencies. Beside these are numerous tables where brief conversations are taking place. When one person gets up and leaves, they are quickly replaced by another, like a speed-dating event. It's all very regimented and serious.

A stocky, tattooed man passes by with a full water cooler bottle under each arm. An older man and woman wait impatiently for him at the dispenser with their plastic cups. After replacing the new water barrel on top, the serviceman is not thanked. He's barely finished his task when the old woman leaps in with her cup, as if she's just survived a plane crash in a remote wood and is intent on consuming the other passengers, despite a recent airplane meal.

Because it's so close to the ceiling and the billowing waves of white tarpaulin, it feels like I'm in the clouds in the exclusive International Rights Centre. The surroundings themselves are rather dreary, lacking any sort of colour or interest, but the view from the balcony is really quite something. The roof-less exhibits below, with their spouting exposed wires, take on a strangely enticing form, like a town after a hurricane. Feeling safe from harm's way, up here in the nest, I'm suddenly brought back to ground by a shouty voice.

Green Pass Woman: Francis Plug! How did you get up here, you rascal!

FP: Um…

Green Pass Woman: [*To another woman.*] He's an author! I met him downstairs. He has this tiny, creepy handwriting…

Other Woman: An author? What are you doing up here?

FP: It's got a lovely view, I think. And you?

Other Woman: We're literary agents. You probably shouldn't be up here.

FP: Literary agents! Ha, ha!

Other Woman: [*Looking at watch.*] And I've got a meeting now, so...

FP: Oh...

Green Pass Woman: Me too. Bye, Francis Plug. Don't let them catch you up here, you naughty boy!

The two of them wander off towards the tables. Literary agents. What a stroke of luck. I need to get myself a spot at one of those tables.

I turn to find a security guard standing right beside me.

Security Guard: Can I see your pass please, sir?

The balcony is just there. The Fair delegates are scuttling about below like very large ants.

FP: Don't come any closer... or I'll jump!

My arm is held very firmly as I descend the escalator, and after passing the spaniel and the Labrador, I'm flicked down the entrance steps like a spent cig.

Just down the road from the Earls Court Exhibition Centre is the Lillie Langtry pub. A sign juts out on Lillie Road, so I walk towards this, pointing at it.

A chatty old timer gets started on me as soon as I sit down.

Old Timer: Tough morning?

FP: Yeah. I've just come from the London Book Fair.

Old Timer: What, down at Earls Court?

FP: Yes.

Old Timer: You ever hear of a writer called William Burroughs? American fella?

FP: Yes, of course.

Old Timer: He used to drink in here.

FP: Really? I didn't know...

Old Timer: Yeah. He was holed up at the old Empress Hotel. It used to be right next door there. But they pulled it down and stuck up that Hotel Lily thing.

FP: Wow. Did he ever shoot anyone in here?

Old Timer: Bill? I don't think so. No, he was pretty quiet. He sat over there [*pointing*], and he was always dressed smartly, in a suit...

FP: A suit?

Old Timer: Yeah, always. [*Pause.*] Have you ever shot anyone?

FP: No. But I was thinking of blowing up the London Book Fair. Imagine that. It'd be raining books. And the books would be on fire.

Old Timer: Well, you take care now...

No other Book Fair delegates have followed the steps of William Burroughs to the Lillie Langtry, although one of the cleaning staff turns up wearing a pass, which is blue.

As well as shooting his wife dead, William Burroughs took lots of heroin and engaged in homosexual acts before those sort of things really became acceptable. Yet he is regarded as one of the great twentieth century authors. A lot has changed since his time, of course. You have to keep your nose clean now. I think he would have struggled to sit on stage for long periods with nothing but warm water, for instance. Still, he wore a suit, so maybe he would have got along just fine.

Schindler's Ark

Thomas Keneally

To Francis Plug

Shalom

Thomas Keneally

HODDER AND STOUGHTON
London Sydney Auckland Toronto

On the day of the Thomas Keneally event, I am blessed with the prospect of paid work. The Hargreaves are a pleasant and kind elderly couple, and their Highgate grounds require some general maintenance and tidying. Like their neighbours, they live on a huge tract of land that necessitates much tending.

Mr Hargreaves: Here he is, here's our Francis Plug.

FP: How are you, Mr Hargreaves?

Mr Hargreaves: Very well there, my boy. No forced entries.

FP: No forced entries?

Mr Hargreaves: No. No forced entries, no revenge killings, no beheadings. I haven't been slain since you saw me last.

FP: Well, the day is still young...

Mr Hargreaves: Yes, I suppose you're right. Still time for me to be dragged along the streets tied behind a motorbike, or some such.

FP: I'll try and keep an eye out for you, Mr Hargreaves.

Mr Hargreaves: You're a good lad, Francis. And how's that book of yours coming along?

FP: Slowly, but surely...

Mr Hargreaves: Very good, very good. Tell you what, someone should write a book about *you*, with a name like yours.

FP: I don't think anyone would read that... unless it had a twist.

Mr Hargreaves: Well, maybe the twist is that you work in the nude. Like you did on your birthday.

FP: Oh yes, I'd forgotten about that. [*Pause.*] Hmm, this jasmine needs cutting back…

Tending to wall-climbing plants offers a rich opportunity to stare into the windows of other people's houses, like in *Confessions of a Window Cleaner*. But I've never seen anything rude at the Hargreaves'. Mrs Hargreaves is too old to be a MILF. As far as I'm aware, no pizza deliverers have ever turned up with penises protruding through the bottom of the pizza boxes.

They have a separate category for Mrs Hargreaves' lot, just like the bookshops have 'Crime' and 'Science Fiction' categories. She fits into the 'Grannies'. You have to take your hat off to those porn people because they're very well organised.

Of course, like the authors, the musicians, the screenwriters and the gaming people, the porn people too are suffering. No one wants to pay for their efforts any more. All that rooty-tooty for nothing because it's available for free, on the web. The public are the new porn stars, apparently. Hopefully they don't know that at the Boston Arms, because some of that lot aren't half ropey.

Mrs Hargreaves: [*Hands on hips.*] Good morning, young Francis.

FP: Hello, Mrs Hargreaves.

Mrs Hargreaves: You could use a bit of fattening up, couldn't you? When are you going to shave? You're starting to look like one of those paedophiles. I'll bring out some fresh baking later, shall I?

Mrs Hargreaves leaves newspaper pages on the floor inside, so I don't stomp mud through the house when I use the loo. I also have my own hand towel, to prevent smears and streaks on the linen. Sometimes I shake the hands of esteemed authors, like Kazuo Ishiguro, no doubt passing on worm and manure elements. I still use one of those old-fashioned unhygienic handkerchiefs too. It's a wonder I haven't wiped out the entire writing community and their followers. As a public author therefore, it's worth considering the use of elbow-length dishwashing gloves at book signings, and a large, easy-wipe kitchen apron. Personally, I'm on the look-out for an apron that reads: MR GOOD LOOKIN' IS COOKIN'.

My bank balance is in a bad way. To keep some aside for my Thomas Keneally evening, I spend my lunch hour on Parliament Hill, rather than the pub. Occasionally a tired or infirm stroller angles their way towards my bench, but when they see my mucky clothes and whisky bottle, they sigh and press on.

I try and think of other ways to save money. Perhaps if I baked a huge cake I could live off that for a week or so. There wouldn't be any fancy decorations, but if I had any icing mix left I could make a figurine and lie them on their stomach in their undergarments sunbathing on top of the cake.

Something hairy rubs against my dangling arm, causing me to freak out. It's only a dog however, a friendly, medium-sized brown dog. It seems pretty excited about something because its tongue is out. I lean down and scratch behind its ears and it laughs.

FP: You like that, don't you?

As I tickle its hairy neck, I feel something round and metallic. It's an engraved plaque, attached to a leather collar. On the plaque is written 'ROX', and there's a mobile phone number.

FP: Rox. Is that your name?

Rox continues to laugh silently as I add her mobile number to the 'Contacts' section of my phone. A shrill whistle sounds, causing Rox to dart away, ears pinned back. I rub my fingers together, watching brown dog hairs fall gently towards the grass of Parliament Hill.

Later, as I'm packing my gear up for the day, Mrs Hargreaves gives me an envelope and old Mr Stapleton winks.

Mrs Hargreaves: Here's a little extra for you, Francis. To help with your book. Get some food into you. And some toothpaste wouldn't go amiss either...

Fifty quid. They gave me fifty quid at Christmas too. I'm a bit overcome. Thanking them most kindly, I shuffle off, wiping my eyes.

Before heading into town, I pick up a small tube of travel toothpaste and a nectarine.

Thomas Keneally is an Australian author with big Hollywood connections. In 1982, he won the Booker Prize for *Schindler's Ark*. Steven Spielberg brought this to the big screen using the amended title, *Schindler's List*. This evening's event is at Waterstones' mega Piccadilly store, and I settle into the 'Studio Lounge', the in-house bar on the fifth floor. Australians are renowned for drinking quickly and manically, like a bunch of yobbos. But I sit quietly and drink slowly, hopefully setting an example for any of Thomas Keneally's compatriots. Nick Cave, the rock star/author, is also Australian, and according to a flyer on the table, he too has an impending Waterstones event. I pocket the flyer, interested to learn publicity tips from an author who gets showered with knickers.

'Studio Lounge' is a terrible, terrible name for a bar, and the surroundings are void of character and charm. Despite this, I'm impressed that a bookshop is serving top-shelf drinks. This is Waterstones' flagship store, and as well as five separate levels, there's an event calendar constantly filled with impending author visits. In truth, many of the 'authors' are actually just celebrities who happen to have books out, with little input towards the actual penmanship, I'd imagine. It is these celebrities, for the most part, whose photos are displayed on the walls of the shop's stairwell, rather than actual authors who write actual books. Still, the celebrity titles are popular sellers, and their sales offer publishers a pot of money to spend on 'real' writers. And as long as the stairwell walls of Waterstones Piccadilly are filled with chefs and singers and politicians, they hopefully won't need awkward photos of our silly mugs, right authors?

From what I've read, Thomas Keneally is a very nice chap, and I pay special attention to his talk, hoping to learn how I can interest Steven Spielberg in this book too. The prerequisite smoking break is suppressed, as is the scotch in my pocket, and the pressing need to wee. Apart from some discreet note taking, my crucial form of remembrance, I sit quite still, clenching my entire body tight, as if undertaking a coach journey around treacherous mountainside verges.

Thomas Keneally has a laughing face, so perhaps he doesn't take life too seriously, except when penning atrocities, such as the real-life story of concentration camp victims during the holocaust. Despite being well into his seventies, he also retains a very fresh-faced, cheeky look about him, like a balding, bearded boy. His white beard is restricted to his chin, so it looks like his head is emerging through the top of a cloud.

In his author's note at the start of *Schindler's Ark*, Thomas Keneally writes:

I have attempted to avoid all fiction... since fiction would debase the record, and to distinguish between reality and the myths which are likely to attach themselves to a man of Oskar's stature.

Despite its subsequent links to the superficial glamour of Hollywood, it is a novel firmly rooted in the real world. And despite being a character in a novel, Oskar Schindler was a real person. Thomas Keneally is a real person too, and even though the Booker Prize is only awarded to works of fiction, maybe my book will be up for a shout as well.

At one point in *Schindler's Ark*, Oskar Schindler becomes immensely aggravated and attempts to lift the top of a table as if it were a desk lid. After the talk, as Thomas Keneally adds a signature to my book, I position my thumbs beneath the underside of the signing table and heave with all my might.

FP: Nggghhhaaahhh!!
Thomas Keneally: What the heck!
FP: It's not a desk lid, is it? It's a secured, inflexible table top!
Thomas Keneally: Yeah, no shit!

The Hargreaves' advance is all gone, so when I pick up a bottle of cheap whisky, I also pick up the ingredients for a very large cake.

Sifting flour and breaking eggs is fun, and I start throwing kitchen utensils over my shoulders, like the Swedish chef on *The Muppets*.

Soon after, however, I start to cry. Instead of adding two *tsps* of baking powder to my cake mixture, I've added two *tbls*. The cake has ballooned up inside the oven, cascading onto the racks beneath, and now the whole gloopy mixture has caught on fire. There's smoke everywhere. It's a friggin' disaster. With no one around to sympathise, I decide to text Rox.

SET CAKE ON FIRE. CRYING NOW. HAVE TO EAT RAW POTATOES.

A short time later, I receive a reply.

SORRY, WHO IS THIS?

She got my text. What a clever dog.

WE MET ON THE HILL. AT THE BENCH? I SCRATCHED U AND U RAN AWAY…

I wait nearly eleven minutes for a reply, but there isn't one. Rox is probably busy carrying a stick, or some slippers. I decide to send her another text.

HAVE U GOT A STICK IN YR MOUTH? I CAN SCRATCH U AGAIN U KNOW…

There is still no reply from Rox, so I start to clean the oven because the sticky cake residue is beginning to cool and solidify.

JOHN
BANVILLE

THE SEA

To Francis Phy

J. Banville

PICADOR

Every week, countless new author events are listed throughout Britain. My focus on Booker Prize-winners has helped narrow my participation at these, but occasionally, cost permitting, I have widened my net for other tasty fish. Booker bridesmaid Beryl Bainbridge was such a case, as was J.G. Ballard, and Nobel Prize winner, Doris Lessing. I've also seen a number of visiting American authors, such as Bret Easton Ellis, Joyce Carol Oates, Douglas Coupland, and various Pulitzer Prize-winners. Most of these authors appeared comfortable with their public personas, although Dave Eggers reputedly finds author events, 'aggressively boring'.

Irish writer John Banville seems unenthused also. Soon after winning the Booker Prize for his novel *The Sea*, he was quoted as saying:

We writers are shy, nocturnal creatures. Push us into the light and the light blinds us.

His quote seems to echo the sentiments of Max Morden, the central character in *The Sea*:

To be concealed, protected, guarded, that is all I have ever truly wanted, to burrow down into a place of womby warmth and cower there, hidden from the sky's indifferent gaze and the harsh air's damagings.

When I read that John Banville would be speaking to a crowded London Review Bookshop, I immediately decided to attend, imagining a shrieking man, melting and writhing on the floor.

In *The Sea*, Max Morden recalls a summer when, as a boy, he was befriended by a well-respected family, enabling him to scale the social steps and join the chosen elite. When I find myself amongst the attendees of author events, I have a sense of what he means. In my experience, it is often the intelligent, well-read, well-to-do classes that frequent such literary gatherings, and the John Banville event proves no exception. Having secured access, I feel like the pigeon in the Earls Court Convention Centre, not quite sure how I actually got in.

It's difficult to know the exact dress code for these bookish occasions. Authors, as we've seen, tend to make a big effort, perhaps borrowing suits and formal dresses from their well-heeled publishers. As an audience participant, part of me acknowledges a certain reverence that comes with the presence of the Booker Prize-winner themselves, and also my fellow audience who are, more often than not, exceptionally groomed. At the same time however, the seats in the London Review Bookshop are plastic fold-out chairs; we're in a bookshop, not Grosvenor House, and books themselves are read on toilets by people with bare bums. The woman seated to my left is all fancied up in a brown sequined dress, and her leg is positioned across her knee, causing her suspended leather-strap shoe to breach my space, the area in front of my chair. When I give her foot a polite little pat with my hand, beckoning it back into its rightful zone, she takes exception. Her voice sounds like a photo enlargement being slowly printed out at a photo processing shop.

Fancy Woman: I-BEG-YOUR-PAR-DON?

Her foot still bobbles in my region, so I push it again and give her shoulder a little nudge.

FP: Get out.

Her face flushes with colour and her pincer hand squeezes my fleshy side hard.

FP: Ow!

Swivelling on my bottom, I raise my feet to the side of her chair and begin shunting her out into the aisle. Incensed, she leaps up, pulling her chair from beneath me, and stepping forward, she kicks my shins.

FP: Ow!

We are pawing at each other, as if with flippers, when a red-fingernailed woman in front turns and hisses:

Red-Fingernailed Woman: Stop it you two!

John Banville must be waiting in some side room, drinking wine for the nerves, or brandy perhaps, like Max Morden favours in *The Sea*. I too am drinking, having helped myself to a bottle of Sauvignon Blanc from the complimentary drinks table. This bottle now sits on the 'Current Affairs' shelving, to the right of my seat, and while waiting for John Banville to appear I begin to browse the titles, keen for a diversion from the unnecessary sighs and huffing that continue to blow out of the woman alongside, like volcanic smoke from Iceland's Eyjafjallajökull. None of the books have been pre-signed, and I attribute this to the fact they've been written by journalists, academics, and other unsexy people.

111

It is interesting to think however, that someone will purchase the very book I happen to be holding, and they will take it back to their house in some borough or village and read it. Having digested a small passage of text myself, for free, I decide to add a passage of my own. Tearing a page from my notebook, before tearing this again, in two, I write, upon the first sheet: SEE PAGE 241.

Inserting this between page numbers five and six, I proceed to write on the second sheet: BEWARE THE DWARF INSIDE YOUR BODY. BEWARE THE LITTLE STARING DWARF THAT PEERS OUT THROUGH YOUR BODY. YOU HAVE A LITTLE DWARF INSIDE YOU. IT'S LOOKING OUT OF YOUR EYES, MAKING THEM TWITCH ABOUT. IT'S STARING OUT OF YOUR EYES. A LITTLE DWARF!

Glancing around at the lightly chattering audience with their single helpings of wine, I discreetly insert this second note between the crisp pages numbered 240 and 241, before replacing the book into its shelf slot.

What motivates the author event participant? What makes them seek out the quivering human flesh, blood and bone marrow of the author? The fiction author in particular? Surely they, the audience, have the prerequisite imaginative skills necessary to follow the author's invented work in the first place, and yet they seek to crush their flight of fancy by exposing themselves to the factory machinery as it were. They have to follow Mickey Mouse and Minnie Mouse back to the changing rooms and smell the sweat from the red-faced puppeteers. Maybe, if novels were less fictional, the reader could get their reality hit from the book instead of the writer. My book, at least, is based on fact, so hopefully all my public events will be cancelled due to lack of interest.

The downside to writing a factual book is that when it is sold here, in the London Review Bookshop, it won't be pressed closely between Sylvia Plath and Edgar Allan Poe, in the fiction aisle. Maybe I should add a bit about a man who turns into a turnip. Or introduce a singing squid. I am, after all, heavily influenced by the works of Dr Seuss.

The complimentary wine is tasty, and I'm drinking it rather fast, but I'm certainly not cut when I hear a voice introduce the evening's author as Benjamin Black.

After the audience applause, a man sits at the table, absorbing the glare. Unlike most author events, there is no accompanying interviewer, so he faces the crowd alone, as if representing himself in the dock. He begins reading from a book, but it isn't *The Sea*. It isn't even a John Banville title. It's a book by Benjamin Black. I paid good money to see John Banville. Enough for a couple, three brandies. But having come to hear Max Morden through the voice of John Banville, I am dished up Benjamin Black instead.

Benjamin Black has a rich Irish voice, and his physical features match the photos of John Banville I have previously studied. John Banville's writer's room appeared, like A.S. Byatt's, in a weekend newspaper supplement. His Dublin study has bright red carpet, postcards affixed to the white walls, and a thin rug beneath a table, which may well conceal an escape hatch. According to the text he wrote to accompany the photo, he puts the chain on the door, thinking himself unassailable. But he isn't, because we are inside it. Myself and thousands, perhaps hundreds of thousands of others. Because his Dublin study is on the worldwide web now.

John Banville, it emerges, also writes books under a secondary name, and tonight at the London Review Bookshop he has come as the other. Thinking about it, he isn't the only author with a pseudonym or an alter ego. Ian Rankin is Jack Harvey, Ruth Rendell is Barbara Vine, and Iain Banks also wrote as Iain M. Banks. However, I thought these were names to be hidden behind, to protect the identity, to safeguard the truth. But John Banville isn't even wearing a disguise. He could have donned a false moustache, or an Ace Frehley painted face. But he must have forgotten.

Does Benjamin Black have his own writer's room? Maybe it's inside one of those mysterious doors on the Underground that read: DANGER RISK OF ELECTROCUTION.

Or perhaps he writes in a secret chamber in the side of a hill, accessible only by driving ones car into a cave. Could it be that John Banville is the Bruce Wayne character and Benjamin Black is the caped crusader? I nod vigorously in the London Review Bookshop, tapping the side of my nose.

When Benjamin Black reads from the passage in his novel, he doesn't hold the book right up to his face, obscuring his head. But it's something for you to consider, authors. And perhaps you could read from a special tailor-made edition, A0-sized, so if you squatted down, you could also block out your torso and legs, existing purely as a timid, mousey voice with shoes. Benjamin Black meanwhile, holds his book out like a red cape, as if daring the assembled crowd to stampede. It is surely just a matter of time before those pre-drinks of his wear off and he begins to clutch his cheeks and wail.

The free bottle of wine I claimed earlier is empty, so I decide to head back for another. The drinks are positioned to the right of Benjamin Black/John Banville himself, who, having finished the passage from his book, is now addressing the gathered literati with anecdotes and amusing tales.

Before selecting a drink, I set about scrutinising the author's performance from the wings. He is a big strapping fellow,

Benjamin Black, with the right sort of physique for lifting cars. But he doesn't appear grizzly or dangerous, like Ernest Hemingway. He clearly feels no need to live up to some big-guy image, so there are no tales about tree felling or monster trout punching. His hands actually look rather soft and prissy, although I'm very sure they could rip that book of his in half.

He's desperately under-disguised however, and so, after some time has passed, I set about capturing his attention with a series of arm flaps, as if engaged in a chimp dance. His speech falters slightly, like a car that continues to move after its engine has fallen onto the road. I ring my hands around my eyes.

FP: [*Mouthing the words.*] Your mask! Your mask!

After enquiring of my gestures with a pensive stare, Benjamin Black returns his attention to his audience. So I discreetly slip him a scrawled note that I have folded inside my knotted handkerchief. The note reads: TIE THE HANKIE ACROSS YOUR FACE!

A staff member attempts to direct me back to my chair, positioning himself between me and the free wine. Over his shoulder is a Fire Exit door, and a green plastic sign above features a graphic character running urgently and pointing to his bottom, as if it were aflame. The doorframe is painted a sullen road surface grey, and in its centre is a single large glass pane. Running quickly towards the glass door with a protruding arm and shoulder, I smash right through, falling amidst the shards like a brick with a note tied to it that reads: YOU'RE FINISHED.

The swift, sharp sound of broken glass is replaced by an unpleasant, whining alarm. After picking myself up, brushing off the fine shards, I beckon to Benjamin Black/John Banville, holding my arms forward and upwards in a gesture of flight. It is time to deliver him back to the quiet solitude of his cave, an action given greater resonance by the droning alarm, and by the noisy kerfuffle now erupting within the boisterous confines of the London Review Bookshop.

To Francis Mop —

THE FINKLER QUESTION

Howard Jacobson

Best Wishes

Howard Jac...

BLOOMSBURY

LONDON · BERLIN · NEW YORK

The night before Howard Jacobson's event, around 1 o'clock in the morning, I have a craving for some stinky cheese. The 24hr grocers in Tufnell Park doesn't sell stinky cheese, so I have to go to a supermarket. Tufnell Park doesn't have a supermarket, so I have to drive to Camden.

Thinking I might get some cheap wine too, I release a shopping trolley from its shackled row, having to put down a deposit, by way of a £1 coin. As long as my £1 remains in its slot, I suppose, technically, it's my trolley.

I never usually shop in supermarkets because I eat very little and supermarkets are very big. But there's something appealing about a massive public place, in the middle of the night, with very little public in it. I stop first at the fresh fruit aisle. When I've peeled off about sixty or seventy stickers from the apples, bananas and kiwis, lining them up along the bars of my trolley, I push forth in search of stinky cheese and cheap cask wine. On the way I pass the books. Supermarkets never used to sell books. In the old days they just sold groceries, and if they were a particularly well-stocked branch, maybe some Blu-Tack. But then they became these giant super stores, offering everything from TVs to car insurance. Most of the books are bestseller paperbacks. It's difficult to tell one author from the next, or even what the titles are, because the covers are plastered with large discount stickers. The discounts make them very cheap indeed.

Cheaper, in fact, than a block of cheese. Cheese that's produced in a single day by a cow eating grass. Writing a book is a little more difficult. But while the cow is rewarded with pastures of grass upon which to graze, I'm forced to take a second job, mowing lawns.

The discount stickers on the books are much larger than the apple and banana stickers, so they take up more room on the bars of my trolley. Prying them off the books is a fairly straightforward procedure, like removing a snail from a lettuce leaf. When there's no more room on the trolley, I put the little oval fruit stickers on the books instead. They're a far more tasteful addition to the covers, and they're not so shouty. You can actually read the titles and the author names, and you get a fair indication of value because the books are being sold at about the same price as the bananas.

I decide to keep my £1 trolley, bundling it into the back of the van. But on the way home, I stop next to Camden Lock and release it over the bridge, as if it's a dolphin that's been forced to perform hoop tricks for sardines.

Nick Cave's event is on the same day as Howard Jacobson's. The people in his signing queue are younger and more 'alternative' than those at most author events, because Nick Cave is a rock star. However, he's also the well-respected author of a poetry collection, and today he's promoting his lauded second novel. Perhaps, with his literary credentials, together with his wild rock 'n' roll ways, Nick Cave is the perfect blueprint for the novelist of the future; quiet, solitary and disciplined, yet loud, crowd-pleasing and mental.

As well as writing books and performing music, Nick Cave is also an actor, revered for roles in feature films. His creative talents seem endless. Of course, all of these creative industries are now threatened by people who want their talents for nothing. So what will happen to the next Nick Cave? Will there be a place for him, or her?

When he arrives at Waterstones Piccadilly, Nick Cave has a small entourage, and he walks upright, holding the hand of a beautiful woman. He's ushered past the queue towards the back of the shop, like an official in a fast lane to the Olympic stadium. He wears a black, pin-striped suit, but it's not a suit that we could hope to get away with, authors. It's a shiny, shimmery suit. And his white shirt has a pink trim near the buttons, which is completely unorthodox. And unlike all those male writers with goatee beards, Nick Cave is clean shaven. It seems clear that modern authors have a heck of a lot to learn.

The fact that he's an author too however, restricts Nick Cave to certain rules. For instance, if the water on his table is warm and tepid, he mustn't dash the bottle to the floor or smash up his chair. That isn't the way authors behave. On the other hand, because he's a rock star, he can choose to overlook certain pleasantries. For instance, today Nick Cave is only signing his *new* book, and just one copy at that. Individual photos with the author are not allowed, due, it's claimed, to 'timing restrictions'. I'm not sure about hand shaking, but personally, I'd be too scared. After all, he might jerk me across the signing table and press his mouth against my ear and whisper:

Nick Cave: Don't give me that 'Francis Plug' shit. Do you
    think I was born yesterday? You get a signature and that's it,
    motherfucker.

Before signing commences however, Nick Cave is handed a copy of his book and positioned before a temporary wall of Waterstones logos. A barrage of photo flashes engulf him, and though he remains standing upright, it looks like he's being gunned down.

Clapham Junction is famed as Europe's busiest train station, but tonight the trains are drowned out by loud, bass-heavy music from the Book Slam venue over the road. The Grand is an old theatre that's been transformed into a rather happening bar and club. Bouncers patrol the entrance, and security guards wear suits and earpieces that seem to be made of 1950's telephone cords. My name's on a list at the door, and fortunately it's arranged in order of first names, so I don't have to blurt out 'PLUG' in a very uncool way.

There's a proper stage inside, although it isn't ludicrously big, like the ones on the Southbank, or those used by Nick Cave. It's characterful, as befitting an old theatre, and yet imposing enough to fill me with fear. An author is going to mount that stage later, by himself. I don't even know Howard Jacobson, but still, I harbour butterflies for the man. These are exacerbated by the presence, on stage, of a full drum kit and a Yamaha keyboard. Has my 'rock star author' prophesy been realised already? Has the lectern been replaced by a full backing band? It's worth knowing how to drink, dear reader, because God help the shy sober writer on stage with a Yamaha keyboard.

In front of the stage is a pit area with fifteen large round tables, each covered in black tablecloths and red glass candle lights. My very early arrival has been rewarded with a choice of tables in the front row, including one directly in front of the microphone stand. Two places on this central table have been pre-reserved, so I place my collection of drinks next to these, patting them.

The surrounding tables fill quickly as other Book Slammers arrive, and subsequent arrivals sit or stand at curved benches on either side, or at the back, near the bar. There are also people seated above, in the middle level tier of the theatre, as if expecting to see *Swan Lake,* or *The Lion King*. Some of them are in special private booths, where royalty would sit, or the two old gents from *The Muppets*. And then Howard Jacobson and his wife/partner turn up, sitting at my table, right next to me.

FP: Ha, ha!

Howard Jacobson collected £50,000 for his Booker Prize win, so he can afford the drink prices at the Grand, which, while not extortionate, are substantial enough to cover the security guards and the regular dry-cleaning of their suits. I've had a few of these drinks myself, so I boldly make the first show of conversation with the evening's drawcard.

FP: Hello.
Howard Jacobson: Hello.
Howard Jacobson's Wife/Partner: Hello.

I'm trying to think of other words I know when a waiter appears with a black bucket and collects my empty whisky glasses. Howard Jacobson is drinking wine and his glass isn't empty. He has, I notice, big frizzy hair, as if his head were a cushion and the stuffing had been pulled out of a tear in his scalp. His eyes are droopy, like a sad dog's, and his nose has the shape and form of a vegetarian sausage. He wears a navy blue suit jacket, no tie, and the light shirt beneath has two, maybe three buttons unbuttoned.

A man from the organisation committee introduces the evening, and as he stands directly above, it strikes me how high the stage is. It isn't very wide or deep, but from our immediate proximity, it seems death-defying. The author Jackie Kay, who's up first, admits that the Book Slam experience is a world away from her previous talks at Milton Keynes Central Library.

When Howard Jacobson leaves to take the stage himself, I realise he's wearing grey flared suit trousers, tightly pressed into place by a black belt. His shoes are black too, and some reading glasses, also black, are produced when he's towering over us, on stage. He holds his book, *The Finkler Question*, in his right hand, while his left hand is hidden from sight inside his pocket.

Howard Jacobson: I thought I'd read something clean for my first 'set' and something not so clean for my second 'set'.

After his first 'set', a man comes on stage and adjusts the height of his microphone, like a roadie. I disappear away to the toilet. When I return, a band is performing on stage. The female singer's top is gold and very sparkly, and she has red streaks through her hair. She is far more dazzling than Howard Jacobson, but it's not a competition. The drinks have loosened me up, so I make a show of producing my copy of *The Finkler Question*. As its esteemed author signs it, I broach the subject of the stage height.

FP: It must make you shudder, peering over that. It's like Beachy Head.
Howard Jacobson: Beachy Head? Hmm, not quite…

I slowly push one of my whiskies across the table towards him, as if sharpening its base on an adze.

FP: Here. You'll need some nerve to do that.

I'm really quite drunk when Howard Jacobson is called away to address his public for a second time. Which is why I follow him, joining him on stage, just to see what it's like. This is where my real undoing starts. It starts with my legs slung either side of the Yamaha.

FP: Jump on, Howard Jacobson. Come on, forget all this. I'll drive you back to London.
Howard Jacobson: *Back* to London? You go, Francis. Go back to wherever you came from.
FP: C'mon, let's go. Let's go. Let's go, Howard Jacobson. [*Patting Yamaha.*] Jump on.

Howard Jacobson: It's the humiliation that makes us human, ladies and gentleman.

Notoriety can be a way to sell books, my reader friends, but it's not a path that Booker Prize-winners tend to tread. I'd also strongly advise that you actually have a book to sell before even thinking about that most slippery of slopes.

PAT BARKER

The Ghost Road

To Francis Phin

Best wishes,

Pat Barker

VIKING

Today I'm back working at Mr Stapleton's. He lives in a very pretty Primrose Hill street, full of willows, lavender and well-manicured Moroccan broom. My van resembles a wedge of spinach in his well-polished street. His car, an executive German saloon, would equate to a Saloon Bar in pub terms, while my van would be more of an unrefined Public Bar. Some of his neighbours own large and imposing 4WD vehicles, and this, I think, is because their gardens are so big, they think they're in the countryside.

Mr Stapleton lives by himself in a huge four-bedroom house. His girlfriend sometimes stays over, but she presumably beds with Mr Stapleton, which still leaves three disused rooms. Perhaps these rooms are reserved for imaginary people, connected to Mr Stapleton's work with financial investments. The doorbell chime seems to resonate throughout the chambers of a cavernous castle. It's the same chime as Big Ben, but Mr Stapleton's name is Leonard.

Mr Stapleton: I've been going through your invoices and a few things don't add up.

FP: Oh.

Mr Stapleton: On the second of February you charged me for the rental of two wheelbarrows.

FP: Oh yes.

Mr Stapleton: *Two* wheelbarrows.

FP: Mmm.

Mr Stapleton: That's a mistake, isn't it? What would you need *two* wheelbarrows for?

FP: I think… there were lots of leaves.

Mr Stapleton: What?

FP: And snails. Loads of those big snails.

Mr Stapleton: No, that's ridiculous. You put all the leaves in the large plastic sacks, that I *also* get billed for, and then you carry them out to your van yourself. I've seen you. You don't even use *one* wheelbarrow.

FP: Umm… [*Pause.*] … Maybe the wheelbarrows, that were carrying the leaves, were *inside* the plastic sacks…

Mr Stapleton has loads of money, gazillions, but he's at pains to share as little of it with me as possible. My hard-earned taxes are bailing out his lot and paying for their fancy haircuts. But instead of supporting me in turn with a little sympathy, he's badgering me about wheelbarrows. This is not conducive to great literature. I'll have to escape down the pub at lunch.

Like J.K. Rowling, I write a good deal in my lunch break. She started the Harry Potter series while working in a bank, and she must have picked up plenty of tips about money because now she's got more than the Queen. Still, I'm surprised she managed to get beyond the first chapter, given how unreliable those bank pens are.

When I write in a pub, by hand, people look at me strangely, as if I'm up to something. The customers seem to think I'm an eavesdropping undercover cop, while the staff probably take me for a pub reviewer, exposing their dirty curtains and stinky Gents. People who type on electronic devices are ignored, but because I write with a pen I am somehow more of a threat. Maybe it doesn't help that I sometimes yabber aloud, and repeatedly jab my pen at invisible people's eyes.

Cigarette breaks upset my flow of writing, causing me to stop and go outside. When I first began writing, I could smoke undisturbed at my table, never needing to surface for air. But since the ban, I have been forced to emerge and make use of my blowhole, as it were.

I'm desperate for a fag on the train ride to Pat Barker's gig. Wanstead is way out east, near Grange Hill. I'd always assumed Grange Hill was totally made up, but it's not. The tube train emerges into daylight at Stratford, before submerging again like a porpoise after Leytonstone. Counterbalancing my hands, I weigh up whether Wanstead will be an island or an underwater cave.

When I arrive at Wanstead Library, I'm a bit late and the audience is already seated. There's still plenty of wine left on a rear table, so I take a few glasses, even though the drinks-table man watches as I sit on a back row chair by myself. The event has been organised by Newham Bookshop. They must be hoping the audience don't notice all the free library books, especially the Pat Barker ones. I'm guessing they're just a little shop, Newham Bookshop, and therefore too small to host the likes of a Booker Prize-winner and all of her many followers. Having Pat Barker in your tiny shop would be like hosting a Nick Cave gig, by which I mean one of his proper stadium gigs, as opposed to him in a chair, behind a table.

Tonight's event is in a large room, adjacent to the main library, which boasts white painted brick walls, and a slatted wooden ceiling in the style of a Scandinavian beehive. The sizeable crowd is comprised mainly of older women who, like me, sit on fold-out chairs with padded green cushions. If we were in Newham Bookshop, there would probably be standing room only, and with all this free wine knocking about, the poor old books might get soiled, particularly if you get any of those mad crowd surfers with their wayward legs and feet.

A woman from Newham Bookshop does a quick introduction, and Pat Barker begins reading behind a simple, chapel-like lectern, possibly from the Reformation period. Because we're in a library, it's like being read a story at story time, were it not for all the wine, and the story about a man's horrible facial disfigurement. I had expected Pat Barker to sound northern, because that's where she lives, in Durham, but instead she almost sounds local. Maybe this is a new publishing directive in regards to author events – doing regional accents. Pat Barker is very convincing, although she might do better to adopt more of an Essex twang next time. I wonder how she gets on in Hay-On-Wye? Or Galway, Heaven forbid!

Her new book is part of *The Ghost Road* trilogy. However, she doesn't like the word 'trilogy' because she thinks it places unwanted pressure on the expectations of her next work. She only found out she was writing a 'trilogy' when she read about it in a newspaper.

Pat Barker: It was news to me!

Now seated, her presence exists purely in terms of her local voice, due to my short stature, in the back row. She may as well be hidden behind a mask, like the disfigured character in her new book. The interviewer, also now unseen, is a bearded man from Newham Bookshop, and he chats with Pat Barker on a modest stage. Tonight was billed as Pat Barker's only London event for her new book, so Newham Bookshop are like giant killers, scoring a massive coup for Wanstead. This may explain all the plentiful wine, which might explain the many audience questions.

Q: Do you consider yourself a historical writer?
Pat Barker: My settings may be historical, but I very much write about modern issues, such as prejudice.

Q: How do you distinguish between biography and fiction?

Pat Barker: Biography tends to focus on 'great' people, while fiction focuses on everyone else.

Q: Are you a political writer?

Pat Barker: Certain injustices get me boiling with rage, and I write about these, so I guess that makes me a political writer.

In the row in front I spy the book investor chap from the John Berger event. He's come all the way out to Wanstead too. We probably should catch up afterwards, discuss our shared author event interests, chew the fat. But I think such a politeness would end badly. I'll end up confessing about the horse poo in my bag at the ICA, and he'll recall a time when he was privy to me shouting obscenities, or parading wee-stained trousers. So when he catches my eye, I simply raise my chin slightly, while he turns away quickly, appearing to blow into a small invisible whistle.

As 8 pm approaches, the introductory woman from Newham Books begins creeping up the side of the aisles with a mixed bouquet of flowers. The cellophane wrapping is terribly noisy, so any sense of surprise or delight is lost. But it's a very nice gesture, although the chance of getting such a gift all the way back to Durham, alive, is miniscule at best.

The signing takes place on stage, and Pat Barker sits behind a square, wobbly table. Upon this is placed a half-pint glass of red wine, courtesy of the bearded interviewer. Again, it's a very nice gesture. But I fear for the public's books, worried that the force of Pat Barker's wrist and signing hand may put said books at great risk, via the wobbling table, and the contents of her glass with its page-destroying crimson dye.

FP: Shall I hold that for you?

Pat Barker: There's no need, thank you.

FP: Steady...

Pat Barker: What?

FP: No, you're right. Sorry.

Pat Barker: *Francis Plug*? Is…

FP: Did you know Grange Hill was real?

Pat Barker: Grange Hill?

FP: Yes, it's a real place. Not far from here.

Pat Barker: Is that right?

FP: I'm going to go there. Right now, in fact.

Pat Barker: Good for you.

The train connections to Grange Hill are few and far between, and it's quite late by the time I pull up to the station. I almost invited Pat Barker along too, but at the last minute I bottled it. I didn't have any sort of plan in place, and spontaneity isn't one of my strong points, particularly when it involves the fast-pace, mad-cap world of Grange Hill.

Upon exiting the station, I find myself in the middle of nowhere. Some taxis are parked outside, which I take as a bad sign. I ask one of the drivers where the nearest pub is.

Taxi Driver: That would be the King William IV, in Chigwell. About a mile away.

FP: A mile away?

Taxi Driver: [*Indicating left.*] Up this hill here…

FP: Is that Grange Hill?

Taxi Driver: I suppose so.

FP: Is that where the school is?

Taxi Driver: No.

FP: Oh. Where is it?

Taxi Driver: What?

FP: The school.

Taxi Driver: What school?

FP: Grange Hill.

Taxi Driver: There is no school in Grange Hill.

FP: Ha, ha!

Whatever you do, don't agree to an author event in Grange Hill. There are no pubs, none at all, and apparently they don't even have a school. In Grange Hill!

Paddy Clarke
Ha Ha Ha

Roddy Doyle

Secker & Warburg
London

It's the first time I've been to the Guardian's flash building in York Way. The Scott Room on the first floor has no tiered seating. This means my second-to-back row seat again denies me a clear view of the author, despite his modest raised platform. Further along my row sits the literary editor of the Guardian. She glances at the bottle of red wine I have obtained without a glass, from the drinks table outside.

The stark white walls of the Scott Room support strange brass handles, as if concealing huge vertical drawers filled with dead humans, or butterflies as large as tablecloths. At the front of the room, two ceiling-mounted 'bubbles' safeguard security cameras, perhaps secretly filming the authors as they talk, picking up on peculiar ticks, such as the squeezing of an ear between thumb and forefinger, or the prodding of a pen into a clothing-shrouded bellybutton.

Because Roddy Doyle's elevation is not sufficient, he appears to me only as a bald scalp, like a first quarter moon phase. I'm put in the position of a little ten year-old boy, unable to peer over the adults. When Professor Mullan voices the title of Roddy Doyle's book, I laugh openly. *Paddy Clarke Ha Ha Ha*. It's the first time I've actually heard it spoken aloud. It's funny, the *Ha Ha Ha* part. And, according to the professor, it's also the best-selling Booker-winning book of all time.

Roddy Doyle: I suppose I should be pleased about that.

Roddy Doyle talks quickly, in a soft voice, with an Irish accent. It isn't enough that I can't see him; I have to keep my ears pricked too. A professional photographer is clicking noisily away with her camera. She has a very large lens protruding from the front, like a pile of stacked pint glasses. At one point I see her creeping along beside the aisles, as if she were some red-cheeked colonial hunter with a blunderbuss and a hard, sand-toned safari hat. I'm also distracted by the literary editor of the Guardian, who I catch whispering to someone in the row behind. But I make no attempt to scold her because maybe she'll criticise my future work and bury my hopes and ruin my life.

At question time, a rather posh older woman asks Roddy Doyle if he can explain what a Chinese Burn is, and also a Dead Leg. I stare towards this woman with cross-eyed, ping-pong ball eyes. Some of these literary people aren't quite as sharp as you might think. Roddy Doyle explains very patiently what the two things are, but inside he must be pulling a total spazzer face.

A thick white cloth covers the signing table, draping down to floor level. It would make a great fort, under there. In *Paddy Clarke Ha Ha Ha*, Daniel Boone signs his name on a tree, and Paddy, or someone else, signs their name in wet cement with a stick. This makes me think that signings are on Roddy Doyle's mind a lot.

Roddy Doyle's shaven bald head means he has less hair to comb, but also more face to wash. Around his head he wears glasses, and in his left ear is an earring stud. He wears a striped, navy blue suit jacket, a dark shirt, blue jeans and hiker-type trainers. Around his wrist is a watch with a black strap. He drinks water out of a clear glass, putting his fingerprints on it, like an autograph.

Roddy Doyle: *Francis Plug*?

FP: Yes. Not 'Sinbad'.

Roddy Doyle: ... Right.

FP: Actually, I'm going for a drink just now, and I'd be most honoured if you would join me. To help with a book I'm writing.

Roddy Doyle: Ah. Well, actually...

FP: The pub is called the Flying Scotsman. It's very near here, in King's Cross. Caledonian Road. I'll get the first round in.

Roddy Doyle: Look, thanks Francis, but I'm afraid...

FP: I'm afraid too. The Flying Scotsman. Caledonian Road.

Roddy Doyle's signature was written with a biro pen, so it's harder to read, especially here in the Flying Scotsman. I may as well read with my eyes closed. Dark and skanky, that's the general vibe. A bit of a murky den. From the outside it looked closed down and boarded up. I began to panic until I saw the message on the blackboard sign: WE ARE OPEN. PUSH THE DOOR.

I hope Roddy Doyle finds his way OK. He might think I've given him the run-around. In retrospect, I probably should have dropped by first, before inviting the likes of him, a Booker Prize-winning novelist, to some random pub. A sign behind the bar reads: PLEASE BE PATIENT WITH THE BAR STAFF. EVEN A TOILET CAN ONLY DEAL WITH ONE ARSEHOLE AT A TIME.

I wander round to the back of the bar. Here it's very dark indeed. The handful of chairs and stools are all taken, so I lean against a side wall. A ledge on the wall leads towards the only lit area, which is a stage shaped like a half-sandwich. The ledge is narrow and raised, just enough to be uncomfortably high for the resting of elbows. Roddy Doyle isn't very tall, so fingers crossed he can reach the ledge and that the comfort proves sufficient. I hope he doesn't want to eat.

FP: 'Do they do food?' [*Laughing.*]

Pinned to the wall above the ledge is a handwritten note on a sheet of A4 paper. The note reads:

MOBILES
ARE NOT TO BE USED IN THIS BAR AREA!!
INCLUDING TEXTING. IF CAUGHT TAKING
PICTURES OR VIDEOS, YOUR PHONE WILL
BE CHECKED AND ERASED.

The entrance door is hidden away from sight, as if it were a cave opening, far from where I now stand, deep inside a mountain. The distinct lack of light has, I notice, resulted in damp patches. A pair of pointy heels walks across the stage, belonging to a woman who's removing her negligee.

The woman mock-shivers to her small audience before dropping her negligee onto stage left. Her knickers land near the back, to the right. She has tattoos in many places, such as her arms, her bum, her shin, and on the lower nape of her neck. Some of these stretch taut across her skin as she showboats her flexible calves. Now she's writhing like a snail or a slug when it moves its mollusc body forward in slow slithery ripples. Her backing track is *Maria Mariana* by Carlos Santana. I hope Roddy Doyle likes Latin American music. Maybe she'll do an Irish number.

FP: [*Laughing.*] She's slapping her own bottom!

Another woman approaches, walking from person to person with a plastic cup that contains £1 coins. I make a bit of small talk.

FP: Roddy Doyle's on his way here now. The Booker Prize-winner.

Coin Lady: Who?

FP: Roddy Doyle.

Coin Lady: What did he win?

FP: The Booker Prize. 1992.

Coin Lady: ?

FP: I've met loads of Booker Prize-winner.

Coin Lady: Have you?

FP: Yep. Tonight Roddy Doyle agreed that there were comparisons between *Paddy Clarke Ha Ha Ha* and *Lord of the Flies*. He thought both shared elements of childhood cruelty, although he pointed out that the third person narrative in *Lord of the Flies* was quite different from his own, which deliberately 'strolls and meanders'.

Coin Lady: Wow. [*Rattle, rattle.*]

The first performance ends and there's a bit of clapping. There are no stagehands to pick up the woman's clothes, and the sexy dancing fantasy vanishes when she shunts her knickers up her legs.

The toilets are a bit grim, and I worry what Roddy Doyle will think. He's yet to show, but his signing queue was a long one, and there are the official hands to shake and the pleasantries to dispense with. Despite the dim lighting in here, it's not a large pub and I'm confident he'll find me once he's worked out the code of the entrance. And I'll wave out to him, like a madman.

My favourite dancer is the one who pulls back the elastic on the bra she's removed and pretends to fire it like an arrow from a crossbow. I give her a note to pass on to Roddy.

Dear Roddy,

Decided to press on – spent £8 on lady dances, the same amount as your ticket! Anyway, I hope you'll join me for a drink at Filthy McNasty's pub. It's on Amwell Street, off Pentonville Road, towards Islington. If you pass me in your chauffeur-driven car, please pick me up. I'm a bit drunk but I'm better company like that. See you soon.

Francis Plug.

It's a tough old climb up the hill from King's Cross. The Flying Scotsman wasn't really conducive to uninterrupted literary chat. It wasn't a pub for Booker Prize-winners, like Roddy. It could tarnish his reputation. I'm relieved therefore to have directed him elsewhere. To a pub called Filthy McNasty's.

I wait and wait, like a small boy alone at the school gates. It'll be alright, Dad's going to pick me up any minute. Except he doesn't.

When I leave, I'm drunk as a skunk. The street outside appears in slow motion because my eyes take longer to open, like a pair of mucky rubbish bin lids. When prised ajar, the sparkles off the street lamps are dazzling, almost overpowering the vista before I'm ready to take it all in.

I head north, towards home. I should be tucked up tight in bed.

MOON TIGER

by

Penelope Lively

ANDRE DEUTSCH

I'm getting a bit old for these 'big nights'. It's hard enough getting up early to garden, let alone focusing my head to write. Most Booker Prize-winners are a bit long in the tooth, and perhaps that's why they're successful. They've put aside their hard drinking ways and the trivial distractions of youth to get down to some serious work. That's why you rarely read about them in the tabloids. They're far too grown-up for unruly behaviour. DBC Pierre is perhaps the most rock-'n'-roll of the list, but his wild years were held, for the most part, before his literary acclaim. V.S. Naipaul is quite a controversial chap, although the headlines he makes are for scandals of a Prince Philip nature. And Salman Rushdie has made the front pages across the globe, but ultimately for writing a book, not for eating the head off a bat.

Although just 54 when she won the Booker Prize, Penelope Lively is an impressive eighty-years-old when I see her on stage at Daunt Books in Marylebone.

Before introducing her, a Daunt Books representative announces two forthcoming events, each featuring authors of a lesser calibre and appeal than tonight's drawcard. He then warns us to be mindful of filthy thieving bastards [or words thereof]. This follows the theft of a bag from the store's previous event. As the youngest audience member by a generation or two, dressed for a visit to the landfill, and coughing in a manner accustomed to one living under a bridge, I feel the finger of suspicion hover before my hooter, ready to give it a good press. Honk, honk!

Daunt Books' Marylebone store is a particularly delightful venue. Originally an Edwardian bookshop, it has retained its antique oak furniture and classic wooden counters, making it resemble a library from some period drama. If it were a book, it would be a character-filled hardback, its tactile pages well-thumbed, its cover illustration and typography well-crafted and considered. Tonight's event is in the rear of the shop, and Penelope Lively and her interviewer Boyd Tonkin, literary editor for The Independent, sit on a modest stage before a large stained-glass window with an almost biblical arched design. The audience is seated on green fold-out chairs, alongside stacked shelving, which continues above on separate mezzanine levels. Penelope Lively must be in her element here. She tells us about her love of libraries, and how she thinks homes laden with books have a real heart to them. People who read digital books, she once said, are 'bloodless nerds'.

Unfortunately, her bookshop experience is somewhat tarnished by technology. In fact, she's been lumbered with the very same microphone trouble that Hilary Mantel faced. In this case, the microphone of Boyd Tonkin is working perfectly, while hers, quite clearly, is not. This is particularly evident after she reads a long passage from her book, and Boyd Tonkin suddenly speaks. Due to the speakers being set up behind the audience, he sounds like a random man shouting at the back. Fortunately, Penelope Lively is an old pro. Her clear, well-projected voice makes her easily heard, even above my god-awful hacking.

Despite the elderly audience, who are more susceptible to the seasonal ills, I'm the only one with a diseased throat. My constant coughing really is most unpleasant. I sound like I've been smoking a mosquito deterrent coil. An older woman sitting in the row in front appears to be cowering at my rasps. She is wearing a coat, but her arms are not in the sleeves, so when she reaches for her complimentary wine her arms don't actually move. After the theft announcement, she and a woman alongside both pulled their coats forward, to deter me from fingering their wallets and phones. But they can't escape my germ-riddled barks.

Penelope Lively isn't wearing her trademark glasses, perhaps because she doesn't want to see her audience. It's a really clever idea, fellow authors. And to build on this I would just add that, should your vision be satisfactory, you could always close your eyes throughout your event, or wear a blindfold.

Her new book is a non-fiction work about the 'old', and her being part of that category herself.

Penelope Lively: I've been making things up for 40 years, so I wanted to write something that was true.

Penelope Lively was born in Cairo and now lives in North London. Her ideal age, she says, was fifty-five. As an eighty-year-old, she thinks she understands more because she's 'been there'. Unlike her grandmother, who always remained very rigid in her views, she has managed to 'adapt and mutate', perhaps, as she says, because she grew up in the middle of the twentieth century, a time of great change. I wonder if this has helped her 'mutate' from a normal author into a public author. It all seems effortless to her tonight, making me feel like *I'm* the old-fashioned one. Instead of being a cool young author, ready to hit the scene, I'm more like a fusty old grandma. A great, *great* grandma.

Penelope Lively: I swore this afternoon. I was quite obscene, actually.

At the signing afterwards, I quietly apologise for my coughing.

FP: You can swear at me too, if you like.
Penelope Lively: No, I wouldn't do that.
FP: *I'd* be swearing. With your microphone problems and all.
I'd be effing and blinding.
Penelope Lively: I didn't even notice, to be honest. [*Pause.*]
Francis Plug. Is that you?
FP: Yes.
Penelope Lively: I suppose these must be yours, then…

She reaches into her pocket and produces my wallet, my phone and my bus pass.

FP: Oh yes, I expect I'll be needing those. Thanks.
Penelope Lively: Not at all. Good day to you, *Francis Plug.*

The Penelope Lively book belongs to Mr Stapleton, my banker client. To be honest, so do all the other Booker books I've had signed. His collection of first editions are deliberately unread, by him, for investment purposes. He'd probably thank me, for getting them signed, but so far he's none the wiser.

JAMES KELMAN

How Late it Was,
How Late

*to Francis Phe
from James Kelman*

SECKER & WARBURG
London

all the best

On the pretext of having a wee, I sneak *Moon Tiger* inside to its place on the bookshelf, smuggling *How Late It Was, How Late* back out in my sackcloth. It's Saturday, and Mr Stapleton and his girlfriend are sitting on the patio reading the weekend papers, while I make a show of working the land.

With the James Kelman novel safely inside my kit bag, I announce my intention to head off for a lunch break. Mr Stapleton grunts, and I walk slowly backwards, fanning my arms up and down.

A round black tray leans on the leg of my pub table, resembling a wonky wheel that has become dislodged from a pub table car. On the table itself are many different glasses, resembling an architect's model of a future city. When I raise a glass skyscraper to my head, I notice a couple sitting down at a distant table. At first I only half clock them, but my drifting gaze suddenly darts back to their faces, as if I've been scanning the bar through a pair of binoculars. The woman is Mr Stapleton's girlfriend, and the man is Mr Stapleton, my client.

Despite the drinks I've consumed, and the swimming calm they provide, I instantly straighten to attention, like a sleepy fox that hears a far-off bugle. In my agitation, I knock a glass over, like a Godzilla giant. Mr Stapleton looks over at the tinkle.

Mr Stapleton: [*Mouthed, unheard.*] What the fuck?

As he begins walking over, I try to mask the multitude of empty glasses by lessening their broad expanse, piling them up into a few key towers representing a designated business district.

Mr Stapleton: Half-day, is it?
FP: Look at this messy table, from the previous occupants.
Mr Stapleton: Right.
FP: The staff should clear all this up, shouldn't they?
Mr Stapleton: Are you planning on going back to work anytime soon?
FP: Yes, it's just way too messy here.

Like Pat Barker in Wanstead, fellow Booker Prize-winner James Kelman is foregoing the bells and whistles of the major auditoriums for a modest event in a small independent bookshop.

Finsbury Park Station is full of warren-like burrows, and as I helplessly seek an exit to Stroud Green Road, I feel like a Pac Man figure being chased by big-eyed ghosts with fluttering, raggedy ends.

The red frontage of New Beacon Books has faded in the sunlight, as have a number of the book jackets in the window. Normally I would suggest some deciduous beech or hornbeam, both of which are proven shade providers, even during the winter months. But to plant these would require digging up the concrete-blocked pavement, and may restrict the pedestrian traffic. Failing this, perhaps the folk at New Beacon Books could hang a thick black-out curtain in their window embroidered with the word ADULT in sparkly silver letters.

A familiar-looking man is standing outside the shop, smoking. He is a black fellow with a pronounced pointy beard, spectacles, and a sandy hat wrapped with a black band. I stop for a smoke also, racking my brain.

Mystery Man: Alright?
FP: Yes, yes. Sorry, you're…
Mystery Man: Linton.
FP: Ah, Linton Kwesi Johnson!

Like Nick Cave, Linton Kwesi Johnson is a hugely respected musician, although it's his poetry, often recited as verse over his music, for which he's most widely known. It's rare to spot an author at another author's event, apart from myself of course, so I slap my head, convinced I've got my dates wrong.

FP: I was supposed to come for the James Kelman talk.
Linton Kwesi Johnson: It's alright. Jim's inside.
FP: Jim?

A decent-sized crowd are milling around eating crisps and drinking wine out of clear plastic cups. Unlike most author events I've attended, everyone seems to know everyone else. New arrivals, such as myself, are still greeted warmly and welcomed, as if we've been expected. The shop itself specialises in black culture. It's small and there's little space to hide.

Older Woman: Do you know Jim?
FP: Jim?
Older Woman: Yes, Jim. It's his book launch tonight…
FP: I thought it was James Kelman's…
Older Woman: Yes.
FP: Oh, James *is* Jim. Right. Yes, yes I do know him.
Older Woman: How do you know him?

FP: Oh, well I don't actually *know* him. I mean… he scares me, if I'm honest.

Older Woman: He scares you?

FP: Yes. Does he scare you?

Older Woman: He scares you! [*Laughs and laughs and laughs.*]

James Kelman, it turns out, has a close affinity with New Beacon Books. I spy him wandering around the little enclosed aisles, having something personable to say to everyone, and as he moves forward, I keep a step ahead, scampering out of his way with my plastic cup of wine. He talks in a thick Scottish accent, a bit like Billy Connolly, only much rougher, as if he were a gravel road and Billy Connolly was a tarmacked driveway. I'd like to see him arm-wrestle with John Berger. That'd be worth putting money on, especially if it was other people's money.

James Kelman is speaking in the George Padmore Institute, situated two flights above New Beacon Books. There's a real homely feel to the room, with framed photos on the walls, and a mantelpiece above the fireplace that supports a bust of a black man, and some plastic cups recently stained by red wine.

James Kelman and his interviewer, Roxy Harris, are both introduced by Linton Kwesi Johnson. They sit with their backs to the street, facing us in our plastic bucket chairs. James Kelman talks about growing up in the 1950's, and how some of the dads in the 'heavy' area of Govan in Glasgow used to steal grass by digging it up in rolls of turf.

Roxy Harris talks about the night of the Booker Prize ceremony and how, after winning, James Kelman chose to ditch the awards crowd, journeying instead to meet his New Beacon mates at a pub near here, on Liverpool Road. A few tuxedoed publishing types managed to tag along with him, and it wasn't mentioned whether they talked much louder than everyone else in the pub, but I can't help thinking that they probably did.

One of the big criticisms of *How Late It Was, How Late* was the explicit swearing. James Kelman, in real life, swears too. Even when he's talking about his interest in linguistics.

James Kelman: 'Do you dig' means 'do you understand' in Gaelic. It became a cool thing to say in the 60's, but it's fucking Gaelic!

Is it OK for authors to use the 'F' word in public? No one seems particularly bothered. Maybe that's because most of the crowd here are good mates of the author. Which is a great concept in itself. Rather than fronting up to a bunch of doll-faced strangers, just arrange a meet-up with your mates and call it an 'author event'. It's not a ruse I could hope to benefit from myself, you understand, but for those of you with the means it makes all the sense in the world.

James Kelman has removed his brown felt suit jacket, revealing a very dark blue polo shirt. It's certainly hot upstairs, and feeling a bit flushed, I move my chair directly beneath an overhead fan.

My lank hair is whipping about like crazy when, I swear, my chair begins lifting off the ground. For a moment or two I hover above the lined grey carpet, but then the fan dislodges from the ceiling and veers off across the room. My chair and I follow directly beneath. I'm travelling at very high speed inside the George Padmore Institute, my limp, dead legs sending spare chairs tumbling as I tip and turn my way among the crowded room. If I had some kind of lever, I could attempt to direct the flight path of my bucket chair, but instead I'm at the mercy of the overhead blades. And when they decide to fly out of the window and directly towards the lowering sun, I'm forced to follow along blindly.

YANN MARTEL

To Francis Plug,

May you reach the

coast of Mexico,

Yann

life of pi

A NOVEL

CANONGATE

Wordsworth Books in Chalk Farm is closing up shop. It's the busiest bookshop I've ever seen. The locals have all come out of the woodwork, and the barren shelves resemble the rationed remains of an apocalyptic disaster. The staff look flustered. I feel terrible for them, so I look studiously amongst the dregs for something to buy. But I can't escape the fact that I'm picking over their bones.

It's interesting to see which books are left, and therefore the very lowest on the pecking order. Interesting in a mean way, like staring at the last kids to be picked for amateur sports teams. The 'nerd' books include travel guides to countries no one wants to visit, an American football compendium, a handful of chick-lit titles, and a book about high combustion that should have been £14.99, but has been reduced to just £2. They're practically being given away, even though someone's slogged their guts out writing them. An author probably pulled their hair out finishing *Fun With Indoor Ferns*, and that's £2 too. A marriage may have ended over the writing of the Paris mystery novel, now just a quid.

A couple near me are having a whispered argument:

Man: Look, there's nothing here. It's just the shit stuff, let's go.
Woman: We have to support them. It's our local bookshop. It's independent.

Man: A bit late for that, isn't it? It's closing down.
Woman: We have to get *something*.
Man: Alright, let's get this. Come on…
Woman: *101 Balloon Tricks*? Nick…!

I have to wait to be served. The expression of the man behind the counter blends feelings of embarrassment and barely concealed anger.

Bookseller Man: That'll be £2 please!

Darkness is descending upon the Thames. As I cross Hungerford Bridge, random flashes of light emit from the compartments of the London Eye, like gunshot bursts. Perhaps they're being fired by members of a religious cult in fancy trainers who are shooting themselves in the face in order to jettison to some miracle planet behind Mars.

Squeaky train brakes screech from the rail bridge in front of Charing Cross station. They sound a bit like a German electronic music track, and for an instant I picture myself in a green open field, dancing in a robot style to this sound. Looking eastwards, I see the fading light catching the tip of the Gherkin, a building controversially modelled on a battery-powered penis replacement, and therefore a fitting statement from the City to the English taxpayer.

With Yann Martel's book under my arm, I stand outside the Queen Elizabeth Hall brandishing a smoke. Below is the riverside path, the Queen's Walk, and leading off this is Festival Pier where river taxis arrive and depart. An orange lifeboat passes on the Thames, its simple rudder being steered by a large tiger, also orange. An orange flint glows from the pipe in its mouth.

Beside the stone-chip wall at which I stand are some well-trimmed boxwood plants in a rectangular tin box. Rather than disposing of my butt in their foliage, I attempt a flick that, if successful, will spin my cigarette end above the Queen's Walk path, over the high jump bar as it were, onto the soft foam mattress of the dirty cold Thames. Blood starts to build in my forefinger as my thumb exerts upwards pressure, creating adequate tension for the spring. This is for the Olympic gold, and the World Record.

The launch is silent and the butt takes flight, spinning in slow motion, powering through the chilled air, the inevitable breeze, however slight, that follows the river's path. The successful firing of the forefinger perfectly propels the cigarette, its smouldering end shooting like a warning flare towards the boats on the river.

Well, we'll never know if it cleared the riverside wall or not, because I really don't care for sporting pursuits. Sport was something I did as a kid, but I've grown up now and there are more important things for us adults to worry about. Leaving sport for the children, I turn towards the side double doors of the Southbank Centre, rubbing my hands, shivering.

I'm interested to know if Yann sounds like *bran* or *barn*. I hope he doesn't give the ending of *Life of Pi* away, because I'm only halfway through it. At this point, I'm convinced the tiger character is actually a man, possibly a fugitive from the law, dressed in disguise, inside a tiger suit.

My hands are perspiring heavily, as is my brow. It's the alcohol, trying to escape from my ravaged body. Yann Martel, I suspect, isn't particularly sympathetic to drinkers. Early on in his book he refers to the animals being 'as unhygienic as alcoholics'. And later he writes: 'To be drunk on alcohol is disgraceful, but to be drunk on water is noble and ecstatic'. He also blames the 'drunken insanity' of the ship's crew for releasing the animals. Just as well I brought along some of that minty gum.

LADIES AND GENTLEMEN. PLEASE TAKE YOUR SEATS IN THE PURCELL ROOM. THE PERFORMANCE BEGINS IN FIVE MINUTES.

It's a 'performance'. I better drink up...

LADIES AND GENTLEMEN. PLEASE TAKE YOUR SEATS IN THE PURCELL ROOM. THE PERFORMANCE BEGINS IN TWO MINUTES.

Quick, quick, down the hatch. These empty plastic glasses will probably kill some seagulls one day.

LADIES AND GENTLEMEN. PLEASE TAKE YOUR SEATS IN THE PURCELL ROOM. THE PERFORMANCE IS ABOUT TO BEGIN.

The passage just inside the entrance door is congested with latecomers. As I shuffle forward, I notice a microphone sitting on one of the attendants' chairs, unattended. That'll be for question time a bit later. Feeling light-headed from the fast-drinking frenzy, I tuck the microphone beneath my coat and proceed to my seat.

The top of the microphone resembles a scoop of ice cream, and my light tapping fingers create a series of depth charge thuds throughout the auditorium.

BOOM. BOOM. BOOM.

It's nearly ten past seven, and Yann Martel still hasn't appeared. I literally poured my drinks over my eyes to take my seat on time. For the *performance*. I slowly raise the microphone towards my whiskery face.

FP: [*Tap, tap.*] Hello? Hello? Yann? Yann? Where are you, Yann? Or is it Yarn? Yarn? Yarn? It's ten past seven, Yarn. Yann? Yarn? Yann? Yarn? Yann?

Have you used a microphone before? For the uninitiated, it's worth getting some practice in. You don't have to actually touch it with your mouth, like rock stars do. (This must be confusing for Nick Cave, at his poetry readings.) Also, if you're provided with a hands-free mic, clipped to your lapel, don't forget to turn it off when you visit the toilet, or if you need to vomit before your event.

After Yann signs my book, expressing sympathy for my needless rush earlier, I return to Chalk Farm, to have a drink for those independent bookshop folk.

Before entering the Enterprise pub, I spy the bookshop staff themselves, sitting inside. I remain outside, peering in at them through the window, unobserved. The man who served me earlier still looks angry. Another man looks despondent. With them are two women, and another man. Beneath me are two metal flip-up doors, used for the delivery of large heavy kegs to the pub's basement. Uncertain whether they're strong enough to stand on, I jump up and down on them, just to be sure.

A short time later, clutching my *Fun With Ferns* book, I cautiously approach the bookshop crowd.

FP: Hello. Sorry about your shop.

All: Ta, thanks.

FP: Um, I bought this book there.

Woman On Bench Seat: Good on you.

Man On Bench Seat: Cheers.

FP: Can I get anyone a drink?

Woman On Stool: Oh, gin please.

Woman On Bench Seat: Something strong would be great, thanks.

Man On Stool: I think *bitter* would be a suitable drop, thank you. What's your name?

FP: Francis. Francis Plug.

Man On Bench Seat: Francis *Plug*?

The bar counter is traditionally wooden and curved. Glass droplet lampshades are suspended overhead, illuminating the patrons, ensuring they don't pay for their drinks with plastic toy money by mistake.

I buy a bottle of wine for myself, filling my wine glass up to the top, with wine.

Woman On Stool: Is Francis Plug your real name?

FP: Yes. [*Pause.*] It's not Francis Adirubasamy.

Woman On Stool: No, that's quite different...

Woman On Bench Seat: *Francis Plug.* It's very memorable. [*Laughs.*]

Man On Stool: Why were you jumping up and down on those metal doors outside?

FP: Um... [*To Woman On Stool.*] Have you read this fern book? From your shop...?

The woman on the bench seat wants to move on to Little Venice, so we proceed on foot, along the narrow banks of Regent's Canal. We're all a bit drunk, walking like Pi, *pitching and rolling in the wild sea that was the steady ground.*

When it emerges that I'm an author, the others begin feeding me advice.

Man: If small bookshops are stuffed, then so are the writers. Especially emerging writers like you. The money ends up going towards a small pool of boring, populist shite chosen by marketing departments. You'll be writing for yourself.

Woman: Nah, it's all going digital, isn't it? You'll find an audience, Francis Plug. You just won't get paid.

Third Man: It's the bloody banks' fault. They bankrupt themselves, and then they come running to us, the public. But when they're making their huge profits, suddenly they're privatised and we don't see a bean.

Second Man: Hey, it's May Day this Saturday. Let's smash some banks!

Houseboats are moored along the canal, and I expect at this time of night the occupants are trying to get a bit of shut-eye, in their houses. We're probably being a bit noisy, especially when we hold each other's hips in a chain, like an inchworm, kicking our many legs out, singing *Who Stole the Cookie From the Cookie Jar?*

Soon the cages and foliage of London Zoo come into view, and it's my suggestion that we should leap the fence and hang out with the animals. I'm the first one over, leading the way, but the others have second thoughts.

Other Man: Nah, forget the zoo. I'm starving. Is there McDonalds in Little Venice?

Woman: Oh yeah, McDonalds.

Other Woman: Hungry, Francis Plug?

I peer through the wire net fence with a despairing face, like a puffin.

FP: No. It's the animal kingdom. Come over.

The others begin to wander off, and the other woman shrugs.

Other Woman: Well, nice to meet you, Francis Plug.
Thanks for the drinks. And good luck with your book.

She tries to kiss me goodbye through the fence, but I have a pursed puffin beak.

The zoo is surprisingly dark. I was expecting the grounds to be lit throughout with tall lamps, like a park, but the place is eerily black. I can't find the two mighty Indian rhinoceroses, like in the *Life of Pi* zoo, nor is there any trace of a hungry elephant, or hippopotamuses floating in a pond. And there's no train, no one-wattled cassowary. Where are the turtles, the yummy turtles? Mmm, I want some of those delicious turtles...

I find the tigers, but they're the wrong ones. I'm after the species from Bengal, but Raika and Lumpa are Sumatran. Both of them are pacing like crazy inside their enclosure. One of them trots over and eyes me like a tough pub drunk. Before I can tame them I have to show them who's boss. Unzipping, I let forth a cascading fountain of wee through the bars of their cage, staking my territory. I am the ringmaster.

FP: [*Shouting.*] This will be the greatest show on earth!

I don't have a whistle, which is a major setback. My own on-board whistle is nothing short of weak and flubbery. Picturing myself in there with Raika and Lumpa, I see the quieter of the pair sitting on the roof of their small shelter, gnawing on my leg that's been removed at the thigh. The more dominant beast is crouched by the protruding tree stump, tucking into my sausage-like intestines. My severed head dangles to one side, still attached to my torso by a single neck tendon. My face is locked in an expression of half amusement, as if I've just been told a joke that makes fun of a disadvantaged minority group.

Elks, where are the elks? Elks are great.

Rubbing my hands together, I eagerly set off in search of the elks.

Amsterdam

Ian McEwan

To Francis Plug
with very best wishes

[signature]

Jonathan Cape
LONDON

I've got a few days' work, which I'm grateful for, especially after shelling out on those Chalk Farm drinks. It's a chance to regain a financial footing, pay back some of my owed rent, and placate other riled bodies, such as my energy suppliers, my local council, the Inland Revenue, and various gardening equipment hire firms. I'm also hoping to go to the Hay Festival. And I need a bucketful of eggs.

A blue bucket full of eggs sits between my legs on the tube train. It looks like I've just laid one big blue egg. No one in the train mentions the eggs, or asks me if I've laid them. If I'm their father.

Warren Street is the closest Underground station to Ian McEwan's house, but I get off at Goodge Street because I really like the name 'Goodge'. It sounds like a good name for a pet chicken. I sometimes help people with suitcases and prams in the Underground, but no one helps me carry the bucket of eggs up the steps at Goodge Street, even though I'm clearly struggling.

In my satchel is a copy of the Booker-winning novel, *Amsterdam*. I've bought it along on May Day because Ian McEwan lives in Fitzroy Square, and I thought I'd try and visit him, and then throw a few eggs at the BT Tower.

I'm not sure which house is Ian McEwan's. All the houses look pretty much the same in Fitzroy Square. The BT Tower is right there, just one street across, so the residents must be getting their brains fried by the billions of signals from those massive satellite dishes. I worry for Ian McEwan in this exclusive neighbourhood. I hope his neurons aren't melting with all those text message bleeps. He must be banging the sides of his head with two closed fists, like an alarm clock, making his glasses shudder about his face.

I choose a huge Georgian mansion at random.

Rap, rap, rap.

A man opens the door. At first I think it's Ian McEwan because he looks very familiar and about the right age. But he doesn't really look anything like Ian McEwan.

Man: Yes?

FP: I'm looking for Ian McEwan.

Man: Ian McEwan doesn't live here, I'm afraid.

FP: Can you tell me where he lives? It's somewhere on Fitzroy Square.

Man: Is he expecting you?

FP: No. I've got a book for him to sign. And I need his help, for this book I'm writing.

Man: I see. I can't help you there, I'm afraid.

FP: Griff Rhys-Jones! That's who you are... Griff Rhys-Jones!

Griff Rhys-Jones: Yes... [*Pause.*] That's a lot of eggs you've got there...

FP: I'm going to throw them at the BT Tower because it's May Day. And also the banks, a bit later.

Griff Rhys-Jones: Aha. Do you have a strong throwing arm?

FP: Well, I do a lot of digging and hoeing and pruning. But I suspect it's a different muscle needed for throwing. The *flexor carpi radialis*, perhaps?

Griff Rhys-Jones: Yes, I was going to suggest the *bracioradialis*, but you may be right. Anyway, good luck with the

eggs.

FP: Thank you, Griff Rhys-Jones. Very nice to meet you.

Griff Rhys-Jones: And you. What was your name?

FP: Francis Plug.

Griff Rhys-Jones: Francis *Plug*. That's a very fine name indeed. Well, mind how you go, *Francis Plug.*

FP: [*Waving.*] Goodbye, Griff Rhys-Jones. Your name's funny too.

This bucket is blimmin' heavy. I spread the eggs out on my carpet earlier, all forty-eight of them. And then I ran back and forth very fast, from one wall to the next, trying not to stand on any of the eggs, or kick them. Maybe I'll head to the BT Tower first, then come back and find Ian…

PAAAARRRRRPPPP!!!!

Lordy. That car almost ran me down.

Motorist: What do you think you're doing?

FP: I'm carrying a bucket of eggs.

Motorist: You're in the middle of the road!

FP: You shouldn't be driving your car today. It's May Day.

Motorist: What the hell's that got to do with anything?

FP: Ha, ha… You're Ian McEwan!

Ian McEwan: Oh, Christ.

FP: I've been looking for you. Griff Rhys-Jones wouldn't tell me where you lived. Look… [*Fumbling in satchel.*]… I've got your book. The Booker Prize one.

Ian McEwan's head slumps forward onto the steering wheel. PAAAARRRRRPPPP!!!!

167

FP: Mind your glasses...

The BT Tower looks like a battery-powered toilet brush. I'm not sure whether to throw my first egg at the doors or at the higher windows. I decide to aim for the doors because I have a lot of eggs.

No! I threw it too high. It hit one of those first floor windows. We'll call that a practice throw. The shell is still stuck there, on the window, due to the sticky egg yolk. It was a good splatter, that. Splat!

The next egg is slightly browner. How on earth does the shell get made inside the hen? It's completely illogical. Hens eat seeds, pecking the little fragments. But this egg is smooth and completely sealed. There are no joins, no seedy bits. It's a work of genius. BT might have the technology to let you talk to someone in Samoa, but they can't make a perfectly smooth egg, no matter how hard they really try.

That was a good throw. Straight into the left entrance door. The BT Tower is starting to look a bit messy now, but not the actual Tower part, to be fair. Some of the staff are looking out at me through the windows. They're working in there, on May Day. My arm is starting to get sore. I forgot to stretch my *flexor carpi radialis*.

I head towards the City with my eggs, looking for riots. The crowds on Oxford Street aren't angry. They're swinging shopping bags and buying things they don't need on May Day. I'm swinging the blue bucket, looking for smashed windows.

A small mob has congregated outside Holborn station. There's no shouting, and the police haven't turned up, but the crowd seems on edge. Some of them appear well into their seventies, and there's a polite-looking Japanese couple, and some tidy Americans with their shirts tucked into their pulled-up trousers. One guy seems to be wearing a Nike cap, but that can't be right. The 'swoosh', I think, must be a turd. Yes, that'll be it. A man holding a sign approaches me.

Man: Are you here for the walk?
FP: The walk? Oh, the *march*, yeah. Right on.
Man: The Literary London Pub Walk?
FP: Damn right.
Man: That's the spirit. Five pounds, thanks.
FP: Five pounds?

We're off. The pedestrian light is green, but as we all cross the road it turns red and a horn honks. I gesture to the offending car with my hand.

FP: Come on then, you want to take us all on?

As we walk along Bloomsbury Way, I approach the guy with the sign. His name's Robin and he's our leader.

FP: So, what's the plan of attack?
Robin: Well, we're going to head towards the British Museum now, then up to Russell Square, stop into a pub in Queen Square, then around towards Tavistock Square, Gordon Square, the University of London and then back down to Bloomsbury Square to finish.
FP: Did you bring a megaphone?
Robin: [*Laughs.*] No, I'm used to projecting my voice. I'm theatre-trained.
FP: Hmm. Well, let us know if you need some back up. We'll scream at the bastards if we have to.
Robin: Pardon?

FP: Listen chief, I've brought loads of eggs along, see? So if you could let everyone know that the eggs are in the blue bucket and that they can help themselves.

Robin: Sorry, what? What do you…

FP: Look, no joins at all. Unbelievable.

Our mob forms a stationary blockade right outside the British Museum. According to Robin, Karl Marx had his most productive years there, researching and writing in the Reading Room. And Lenin had a pseudonym on his Museum library ticket while he was putting together the newspaper of the Russian Socialist Democratic Labour Party. This spiel is all calculated, designed to fire up the mob. I'm not sure if Robin is a Socialist or if he holds more Marxist views, but all this preamble is working, because the group are holding off every word. We'd better not run into any bankers, because I tell you what, they'll probably get lynched on the spot.

There aren't many banks in Bloomsbury. Or supermarkets, department stores, fast-food chains. Most of the streets are comprised of huge stone-block Georgian buildings, which appear to be used for small business operations and rented accommodation. Our leader's route seems a bit misguided therefore, and unsurprisingly, my brothers and sisters appear rather passive when they should be really angry. Robin tells a mild joke, and the others laugh lightly. I decide to turn my own laughter into a chant, banging the blue bucket in time.

FP: HA HA HA!
HA HA HA!
HA HA HA!
HA HA HA…!

I have to stop on Montague Street for a wee, because I've been chugging on a hip flask. While weeing, I sing a relevant track, I think, to May Day.

FP: All I need is the air that I breathe…

One of the American men comes back to find me, shouting as he points:

American Man: There he is. He's in there. He's urinating against a wall.

When I rejoin the group, Robin announces, somewhat impatiently, that there are toilets at the pub, our next stop. We're standing outside a Georgian house, and I ask a middle-aged northern woman if I've missed anything.

Northern Woman: Well, this house is where Oscar Wilde spent his very last evening in England.
FP: Hmm. Did you bring any weapons?
Northern Woman: Sorry?
FP: Did you bring any weapons?
Northern Woman: [*Looking worried.*] Any weapons?
FP: Like… a bicycle chain? Or… a switchblade, a cut-throat?
Northern Woman: No… why? Is it dangerous around here?
FP: It could get nasty, madam. Look, you can help yourself to eggs, they're in here.
Northern Woman: What do I do with them?
FP: Here, let me show you.

I shovel my hand into the bucket, plucking out a smooth oval egg, like a lucky dip prize. I throw it towards Oscar Wilde's former residence and it splats against a window, near the Georgian door.

FP: Ow! My sore arm!

We take over the tiny Queen's Larder pub. Behind the serving

171

area is a photo of a cute miniature dog with the message: WELL-BEHAVED DOGS ARE ALWAYS WELCOME.

Robin has all the money, but he's only bought a drink for himself. Indignant, and a bit drunk to boot, I half-heartedly toss an egg at him. Unfortunately, it hits another customer in the face. Splat! An incident develops involving the wronged patron and his angry mates. Our group is larger however, and up for a tussle.

FP: May Day, May Day, May Day...

The man behind the bar shouts at our lot to get out, so Robin herds us towards the door.

We regroup at the picnic benches outside. Robin is finally looking angry, so hopefully things will start to kick off. But he simply tells us to put our drinks down because we're leaving. That's a shame I tell him, 'cos we just got there. He points at me.

Robin: You! You can go and get lost! Go on! Leave us alone!
FP: Hang on, I paid five quid. *And* I brought all the eggs...
Robin: You're out of your mind!

He's shaking his head and his red face. The others look at me over their shoulders as they walk away.

FP: Well, thanks for nothing. You bunch of frauds.

I toss an egg after them, towards Queen Square, but my arm is weak and it hits a parked car, setting off the alarm. Robin beckons the cowardly group out onto the road and they begin trotting away, even the oldies. The sound of the car alarm is drowned out by sirens. The police have arrived in their armored trucks, blocking off the mob. They leap out, seizing arms, squeezing necks. The Japanese woman falls and is dragged away. The others protest, especially Robin with his high and mighty voice, but they're all rounded up and packed off quick smart.

They've left quite a few unfinished drinks. I think I might drink those drinks...

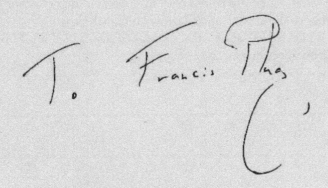

To Francis Plug,

The Inheritance
of Loss

❤❤❤❤

Kiran Desai

My warmest wishes,

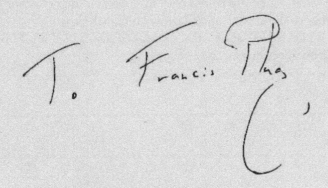

A
Atlantic Monthly Press
New York

I need a wee. But it's the same old story. If I leave my table, I'll lose it. And if I put my case on the seat, to save it, the police will be called and my books and pants will be destroyed in a controlled explosion.

My table's outside the Mad Bishop & Bear pub in Paddington station. I decide to leave a note beside my prominently displayed full pint, and cart my case to the loo. The note reads: PLEASE LOOK AFTER THIS BEER. THANK YOU.

When I return, the beer has gone, the note has gone, and my table has been claimed by a family of foreign visitors, who become alarmed by my fist shaking, and curses in the English tongue.

I thought about driving to Hay-On-Wye, but the chance of my van making it to Wales is next to nil. There's also the pressing matter of cost. I've already shelled out on accommodation, miles from anywhere, and the additional fuel costs would bury me. So I'm hoping to go by train instead, for free.

My suitcase is filled with full-strength alcohol, shrouded in underwear, and carefully placed around this are a selection of books, awaiting signatures. I'm hoping to read Kiran Desai's novel on the train, before I drink too much and am forced to hold the book to my face, slowly moving it from right to left, as if eating a cob of corn with my eyes.

I'm wandering tableless around Paddington Station when I recognise Ruth Rendell. She is sitting on a row of grey metal seats, turning a large newspaper page, vigorously shaking it, as if to rid a bath mat of unsightly hairs. Are there spy holes cut in the pages? No, her vast imagination is not in any way engaged. She isn't pointing at the train at Platform 4, exclaiming: *earthworm*. She does not gaze at the huge, ribbed beams encasing the station roof, scribbling: *Blue whale, Jonah, blowhole*. No, the news of the day is more than enough to keep her mind occupied. Her mind will be mushed later, as a featured author at the Hay Festival. The interviews, the questions, the scrutiny; all that horror comes later. In the meantime she's right to kick back, blob out and spare herself the glare of prying eyes, like mine.

A man seated in the row behind Ruth Rendell prepares to leave, so I run hard, sending grounded pigeons skywards, their little hearts bursting like popcorn.

As an author, it's important to be presentable in front of your public, and Ruth Rendell is particularly dapper and a credit to her profession. My best clothes, in comparison, are better described as 'lucky' clothes. Lucky pants, lucky socks, lucky shirt. In the public's eye, I suppose I resemble a dog dressed up for a school fair. Of course, if Ruth Rendell didn't have to 'flash up', she could use that money for other things, like rope, or bin liners.

I can smell her perfume. Choosing the right brand, as a celebrity figure, must be a trial. I find it hard enough not breaking wind. If Ruth Rendell were to break wind in a public place, it would be big news. A scandal. Which is a sad truth about this whole author business, reader. You can't even fart.

Not buying a train ticket is foolhardy, but I have to risk it. It's an expense I simply cannot shoulder, especially when the fare is broken down into single and double malt whisky measurements.

Most of the seats have reserved cards protruding from the top like bookmarks, so I sit in an unclaimed spot by the aisle, my case in sight on the overhead rack. The driver announces that Reading will be the first stop, causing me to share the joke with the passenger in the window seat beside me.

FP: That's appropriate, isn't it?
Reserved Passenger: What?
FP: Reading. *Reading.* Given we're going to a book festival.
Reserved Passenger: Are we?
FP: Oh. Sorry, I just assumed…
Reserved Passenger: Look, this is a *quiet carriage*, see?
  [*Pointing to sign.*] So if you don't mind…

I can't resist buying extra drinks from the trolley that's being pulled through the carriage by an Eastern European woman with powerful arms. The travel-sized bottles are mere splashes of alcohol, but they can provide one with the bare fuel to line the bottom of the tank, enough to start the engine as it were, and travel a small distance.

Ruth Rendell is sitting at a table seat in front of me and I'm watching her. I lack the courage to sit at the spare seat alongside because, like many of the authors I'm attempting to join, she terrifies me. They all seem to share a confidence, arriving fully formed, ready to tackle any public speaking roles, or in-depth analysis of their work. Hopefully everything will fall in place for us too, right? [*Fingers in ears, cross-eyed.*]

Murders are quite common on trains. In my opinion, the Eastern European woman poses the biggest potential threat. The story unravels like this: An Eastern European woman serves drinks on a Great Western service. She slips polonium-210 into the tea. The victim dies. There, I've solved it already. But who's the victim?

I have to find the victim. And then I have to tell Ruth Rendell.

I wander through the carriages, looking for the victim. My search is hindered by all the readers. The festival-goers. Their expressionless eyes are cast down on their books and reading devices, making the identification task more challenging. I should be immersed in *The Inheritance of Loss*, but a life is at stake.

The countryside passes at a rapid rate, as if thumbed. We pass a series of wind turbines, their blades swiftly spinning like the hands of clocks, counting down to the murder. I must act now.

FP: Do you mind if I sit here?

Ruth Rendell: [*Waving the back of her hand vigorously.*] Shoo! Shoo!

FP: But... you have to solve the murder...

Ruth Rendell: Shoo! Shoo!

FP: I'm a criminal. I don't have a ticket. You could use me in one of your...

Ruth Rendell: SHOO! SHOO!

I manage to avoid Ruth Rendell when we arrive in Hereford. As I board the bus, she is whisked off by a driver in a private car.

Shortly before reaching Hay, I see a giant squid laid out end to end in a grassy field. It's mottled pink in colour, and its tentacles thrash about because it's alive on the dry land, under the late sun. It also has a very, very large eye. Our bus doesn't stop on its account, and no one mentions the squid when we're removing our cases outside the festival site.

I join the queue for a shuttle bus into Hay township. The distance between the festival tents and Hay itself is so ridiculously close, I laugh when we arrive.

FP: [*To a fellow passenger.*] I didn't realise it was so close. Blimmin' heck. It's like getting a bus to put the rubbish out. Seriously, you'd have to be a proper lazy old shite to take the bus when you know how close it is, right?

The Wheatsheaf is a blue corner pub. It's a large, multi-level establishment, brimming with festival diners and frantic waiting staff.

FP: A Scotch, thanks.
Bartender: A rowboat of Scotch?
FP: Pardon?
Bartender: One rowboat of Scotch coming up. That'll be twenty-six thousand pounds.
FP: Twenty-six thousand pounds?

It's started to rain outside, which doesn't bode well for my lodgings search. I'm staying somewhere in the surrounding countryside, in an isolated rural location. I'll have to walk there later, in the dark, out of my bleeding mind.

Bartender: Are you going to order some food? Today's special is Entire Mouse Baked Inside a Sunflower Loaf.
FP: No, I'm fine...
Bartender: Here's your bill. Seventy-eight thousand, four hundred pounds, plus nine thousand for the loaf.

When I finally reach the cottage, it's well into the early hours and the lights are out in the larger farmstead alongside. The farmstead houses a family who work the land, and I think I see someone at the curtains after I fall over a wheelbarrow. As arranged, the key to the cottage is under the flowerpot on the window ledge. Soon after I've entered there is a knock on the door, but I don't answer because I'm having a poo.

179

During the night I awake, confused, to the sound of a loud, blubbery noise. Finding nothing inside the cottage, I wander across the large driveway to a darkened field in my pants and bare feet. There, spread out on the rough pasture is a giant, rubbery squid. It's crying. Water is sliding down its huge eye like a glass shower door. I pat its tentacle soothingly, but its slimy skin is repulsive to the touch, and I stick out my tongue.

FP: Urgh!

It keeps blubbing, so I sing it a lullaby.

FP: … Feels like you're frying, you're frying.
YOU! Your sex is on a fryer!

The next morning, a woman stands at the door to the cottage, peering in at all the plates and bowls and saucepans and mugs and cutlery that I have meticulously laid out across the carpet of the living area. She looks up nervously at me.

Woman: Hello. Francis, is it?
FP: Yes.
Woman: I'm Meg. The owner.
FP: Hi, nice to meet you.
Meg: Everything alright?
FP: Yes, it's really great.
Meg: Um… there was a bit of noise last night.
FP: Yes, sorry. I fell over the wheelbarrow. It was right in front of me.
Meg: No, not that. It was some sort of clanging inside the cottage.
FP: Oh, yes.

Meg: [*Pause.*] Um, what was that?

FP: I was just doing a bit of a dance with the saucepan. And the dessert spoon.

Meg: Right. It was very noisy actually, so if you could... not do that again please.

FP: Of course. Sorry about that. Sorry.

Meg: And you were singing in the field...

FP: Yes, the poor thing. Got him to sleep eventually.

Meg: Who... ?

FP: The giant squid.

Meg: The giant squid?

FP: Yes, the giant squid in the field. He was singing too. So noisy.

Meg: [*Awkward silence. Meg looks at the plates etc on the floor.*] Everything all right with the plates and things?

FP: Yes, thank you.

Meg: Good. [*Pause.*] Oh, I brought you these. Just some fresh fruit and veg which... we grew them here on the farm.

FP: A turnip? Ha, ha. A turnip...

Meg: [*Pause.*] Well, anyway... enjoy your stay.

FP: [*Laughing.*] A turnip!

I try to wave, but my arms have gone all floppy, and Meg has already retreated down the weathered stone steps.

I've got my own garden for a change. A place I can actually wake up to, rather than arriving at, for work. Meg and her family manage the area around the lawn, but the untended grass beyond seems to stretch on forever. Most of the flowers are growing wild too, sown by the birds and Mother Nature. Creeping buttercups, birds-foot clovers and little tufted forget-me-nots. There's even brugmansias, the flower that features in Agatha Christie novels, due to its almost untraceable poison.

It's mid-morning when I start the long walk back into Hay, juggling the turnip.

The pointed white tent roofs give the festival the appearance of a travelling circus. Most circuses provide entertainment and fun with clowns and performing animals, but here the performers are, for the most part, authors. We authors, of course, are actually quiet, solitary figures. In this sense, the stage is set for some kind of freak show.

The makeshift nature of the festival is unavoidable. The tents, walkways, shops, and even the on-site pub have been hastily erected, like pages in a pop-up book, each scene briefly revealed before being closed and flattened. Once the crowds have gone, the only remnants of the festival, I imagine, will be holes in a muddy field. A blank, muddy field. The Hay Festival is a blank field filled with words.

The Hay Festival is a blank field filled with words.

– Francis Plug

I might try and sell that line to the Hay Festival's marketing team.

The queue for Kiran Desai has been bombarded with people for A.C. Grayling. Even the 'Friends of Hay' in the fast-track queue are confused. Apparently Kiran Desai's event has been moved. I can't schedule my day if things are going to keep changing like this.

The new venue is a tent sponsored by a major financial institution, a contributor to the recent banking crisis. I find this a bit off, understandably, but it's not like I have a choice. I can't see Kiran Desai in a tent sponsored by something I like, such as cheese. Nor, I imagine, will she herself have any say in the matter. It's a big nasty bank tent or nothing.

The huge bank tent has sixty-eight different stage lights. A formal black curtain frames the stage area, while behind the tiered audience seating is a hi-tech control desk, like you'd find at a stadium gig. Above this, on the back wall, a huge round clock faces the authors on stage, letting them know how much longer they need to sit there, exposed like ducks.

An older couple sit in front of me on green plastic chairs. The old woman scampers off, perhaps to the toilet. Then the old man departs, to answer his phone. I put Meg's turnip on his seat before the old woman returns.

FP: Excuse me.
Old Woman: Yes?
FP: The man that was sitting there…
Old Woman: Yes?
FP: He turned into a turnip.
Old Woman: [*Laughs.*] Really?
FP: Yes. There was a huge thunderous flash and a burst of purple light and smoke and he was gone and he'd turned into a turnip.
Old Woman: Wow!
FP: You don't understand… the man turned into a turnip!
Old Woman: It's alright, here he comes now, see? There he is…
FP: Ah, yes.

The stage is grey and carpeted, without sand or flaming hoops. Kiran Desai is being interviewed by the literary editor of the Guardian, who was talking during the Roddy Doyle event in London.

Live footage of the event is being projected onto a large screen behind the stage from four different camera angles, plus a zoom. It pays to be prepared for this, authors. Although signing up for a modest gig in a field, you may find yourself suddenly appearing in extreme close up, on the big screen.

There's a slight time delay between hearing the voices and seeing the two women speak behind. It's a bit like watching a subtitled kung-fu film. I find it rather funny. The audience however, is laughing at things I don't find funny. Things Kiran Desai is saying that aren't even supposed to be funny. Serious things. They're desperate to be entertained, the audience. They're laughing their heads off.

Kiran Desai gets annoyed, she says, by trivial questions.

Kiran Desai: Once an interviewer asked me: What needs to be thrown out of your refrigerator?

I want to ask her what it feels like to be a writer on stage, on TV, in a tent sponsored by a greedy bank, but my hand is only very slightly raised, just off my thigh.

The ushers are old ladies, just like in London, except here they wear fluorescent vest jackets. One of them is walking near me, but she doesn't notice my hand.

Anyway, it's too late because the literary editor has announced that Kiran Desai will be signing books in the on-site bookshop.

FP: Oo, oo.

The change of venue has confused me, and with no idea where the bookshop is, I panic.

FP: [*Aloud.*] Don't clap, run to the signing queue! Clap! Run and clap, run and clap...

The flimsy bookshop only sells books by the festival authors. There are three separate signing desks, each with its own queue. While Kiran Desai was on stage, other events were taking place too, and now everyone's converging on the little bookshop for their respective signing sessions. It's like a sausage factory of book signings.

The three queues are a good gauge on who the popular authors are and who aren't very popular at all. For instance, one of the queues is very long, whereas another has only two people. The author with the very short queue arrives first, possibly because no one stopped him for a chat after his event, or to say thanks. The two people in his queue must be happy that they don't have to wait long, although they might also feel ashamed for wanting a signed book from an author who isn't popular. When the author first eyes the other queues, he winces. It's quite noticeable. Not wishing to have a queue of no one, especially with the other two queues looking on, the author takes his coat off in a very slow, drawn-out way, as if taking a coat off was a new thing that he's still learning to do. Next, he makes a big performance of fishing in his coat for a pen. The person at the front of his queue has a pen, and they're waving it at the author, but it clearly isn't the right pen. It isn't the special signing pen. Perhaps it's in his other pocket...

Kiran Desai arrives soon after, and is directed to a table in front of a long queue where she quickly ushers the first person forward. The unpopular author, meanwhile, is giving his wine a taste to make sure it's drinkable. To make sure it's the right wine.

Kiran Desai is a young Indian woman, and she has long tangly hair, like a mermaid.

Kiran Desai: 'To Francis Plug...'
FP: I've seen an adult giant squid, a live one.
Kiran Desai: Really? I thought no one had ever seen one. Because they're so solitary...
FP: I know, I read that in your book. But I've actually seen two of them.
Kiran Desai: Two of them? Where?
FP: Right here. In Hay.
Kiran Desai: In Hay? Now that *is* a surprise.

FP: One of them was crying, so I sang him to sleep and he started snoring.

Kiran Desai: [*Laughing.*] Well!

That wasn't supposed to be funny, what I was saying.

FP: I really liked that kung-fu stuff.

Kiran Desai: Kung-fu stuff?

FP: Yeah. *That* was funny.

Kiran Desai: [*Handing my book back, not laughing.*] OK. Well... watch out for those giant squid.

The unpopular author is in deep conversation with the first person in his queue, and the second person is starting to look a bit annoyed. When you're an author, with a signing queue of your own, you may wish it to be short too because that means you'll finish quickly, job done.

In my satchel is a large stack of fliers, each one handwritten by me on scrap paper. I'm trying to drum up some gardening work, to pay for the cottage.

GARDENING WORK
HAVE YOUR GARDEN TENDED BY AN AUTHOR.
[*Crude illustration of me writing
in a notebook while holding a spade.*]
LIVE IN NORTH LONDON?
HAVE A MASSIVE GARDEN?
LIKE BOOKS?
CONTACT FRANCIS PLUG
THE 'AUTHOR GARDENER'
COMPETITIVE RATES.

Festival Goer: What's this?

FP: I'm an author. But I do gardening work too.

Festival Goer: [*Pointing.*] What's that?

FP: That? That's me. I'm writing a book, but also gardening.

Festival Goer: Oh, right. I wouldn't have got that, to be honest.

Our conversation is interrupted by a member of security.

Security Man: Sorry, you can't hand out fliers at the festival.

FP: Why not?

Security Man: It contravenes our environmental policy.

FP: But I'm an author.

Security Man: This says 'GARDENING WORK'.

FP: I do both. See?

Security Man: What's that?

FP: That? That's me. I'm writing a book, but also gardening.

Security Man: I wouldn't have got that, to be honest.

Festival Goer: I didn't get it either...

FP: Look! Open your friggin' giant squid eyes!

V. S. NAIPAUL

In a Free State

ANDRE DEUTSCH

The weather looks promising, but it's famous for inflicting misery on the festival, so I'm sure to wear my polka-dotted saffron neck scarf. If worst comes to worst, I'll have to cadge one of those hooded festival sweatshirts. The merchandise features quotes from famous festival participants like Bill Clinton and Arthur Miller. Now I've got my own quote, I might try and flog it.

Shopkeeper: 'The Hay Festival is a blank field filled with words.' Umm… right.

FP: How do I get paid?

Shopkeeper: Well, it's not actually me that decides on the designs. I just sell them.

FP: I'm an author, so you can put it into production straight away.

Shopkeeper: Oh, you're an author? 'Francis Plug'. I'll have to look out for your books.

FP: How will I get paid?

Shopkeeper: Well, the Organisation Committee will need to debate its merits first I guess, before deciding whether to use it. Or not.

FP: It's very catchy.

Shopkeeper: Mm. Well, I'll do what I can. What's this?

FP: It's a flyer. I'm all out of business cards.

Shopkeeper: What's that?

FP: That? That's me. I'm writing a book, but also gardening.
Shopkeeper: Oh. I wouldn't have got that, to be honest.
FP: Fine!

I wish they could pay me up front for my quote. It'll be everywhere next year. But they'll probably credit someone else. Someone more marketable and glitzy. Like Desmond Tutu.

The festival gift shop is a bit pricey, so I settle for a postcard. I decide to send it to my sister's daughter Anna, my little niece.

Dear Anna,

I'm at a book festival in Hay, which is a small village in Wales. I realise that handwritten words are quite boring for you young folk, so to spice up this letter I'm attaching a real leaf that I picked this morning, from a deadly poisonous brugmansia plant. Whatever you do, don't grind it up into your mum's biscuit mix or you'll all die horrible deaths with your guts falling out!

Love,
Uncle Francis.

A large man wearing tweed clothing has just slumped onto a deckchair featuring the cover design of *The Garden Party* by Katherine Mansfield. His big bum is contorting her book. It's only Day Two, and already people are completely tuckered out. Their new wellies are covered in filthy, dirty mud. Their brains are exploding. They're flopping down, collapsing like castles of sand before the oncoming tide. Fortunately, to help festival-goers soldier on, a range of amenities are on offer:

Luxury yoghurt variations inspired by the Continent.

Sixteen flavours of locally made sheep's milk ice cream and sorbets.

Head, neck and shoulder massages to refresh and re-energise.

Thai Massage, Reflexology, and beauty treatments (Facial, Manicure, Pedicure).

It's not really my scene, if I'm honest. But at least the air is fresh. My reputation doesn't precede me in the Welsh pubs, and I'm on holiday, kind of. Still, looking around at the many festival attendees, I have to wonder if these are the circles I want to move in, or whether, as an author, I'll have any choice.

While awaiting V.S. Naipaul's event, I sheepishly sit on Virginia Woolf's *A Room of One's Own*. It's very embarrassing. I feel like a wood beetle on my back with my little arms kicking. I can't even reach my drink properly. Ashamed, I hide behind a newspaper produced by the chief festival sponsor. One of its headlines reads: *BANKERS PAID £14 BILLION IN BONUSES.*

Unbelievable. Authors are stuck in the real world of interviews and book signings, while bankers seem to be living in some bloody fantasyland. The world's gone mad.

Seizing one of the pages, I rip it in half, and then in half again. Grabbing at more pages, I set about tearing randomly. Other festival delegates look up nervously at the coarse shredding sound, and the surrounding grass is soon littered with scraps of newsprint. When I'm done, I neatly fold together the remains of the tattered newspaper, and with much effort lever myself up, discarding my empty glass and paper debris.

The festival toilets are in makeshift white containers, like the ones that construction workers have their lunch in. There are huge queues outside the Ladies, on account of their need for larger weeing areas. But I walk without delay into the Gents, almost piling straight into music legend, Billy Bragg. He's having a pee right there. I stand next to him and give him a very big smile.

Billy Bragg: You 'right?

FP: Yes, thank you.

Billy Bragg: These authors think they're flaming rock stars, don't they?

FP: [*Quietly.*] I'm an author.

Billy Bragg: Oh...

FP: Here's a flyer.

Billy Bragg: What's that?

FP: That? That's me. I'm writing a book, but also gardening.

Billy Bragg: I wouldn't have got that, if...

FP: What's your favourite flowing hand soap? Mine's *Milk & Honey*.

Billy Bragg: [*Shaking wet hands.*] I'm not really fussed, to be honest. I'll look out for your books, Francis.

FP: Thank you. Very much. I should be finishing them all up any day now...

V.S. Naipaul's event is in the more palatable Oxfam Pavillion. There are only 35 spotlights above the stage, as opposed to the 60+ in the bank tent, but it's still equipped with camera operators wearing headsets and microphones.

As an author, V.S. Naipaul gives me hope. He says some really crazy things, and yet he's still held up in esteem. Recently he pronounced his belief that no woman writer was his equal, not even Jane Austen. This, he thinks, is because of a woman's 'sentimentality' and 'narrow view of the world'. I sometimes say some mad things myself, in the pub. With any luck, I'll be tolerated and laughed off too.

V.S. Naipaul hobbles across the stage, his arm held by interviewer Alexander Waugh. Sir Vidia Naipaul, as he is officially titled, has a silver goatee beard, and his lightly oiled hair resembles a glistening fish pulled from the sea and caught beneath the dazzling sun. He wears a grey check woollen suit without a tie, accompanied by a purple sweater. A tiny microphone is affixed to his lapel.

Outside the wind has picked up, and the whole structure of the tent is flapping and groaning noisily, as if threatening to lift off. The creaking of the canvas sounds like a person wearing rubber trousers whose bottom is rubbing across a vinyl couch. Overlaying this are assorted bumps and clanks, as if the entire tent is being saddled up and bridled. At the same time, mobile phones ring, a photographer clomps up and down the aisle steps, and a child whinges and fusses in the front side row. It is, without a doubt, the noisiest author event I have ever attended.

V.S. Naipaul has recently published a series of early letters between himself and his father. He is discussing his father's past when he suddenly chokes up, not on the lukewarm water he's been given, but on his sentimental feelings. Wiping away his tears, he agrees with the interviewer that his father remains a raw subject.

Meanwhile, the wind continues to batter the tent. Could it be that the wind is actually A.S. Byatt? Perhaps she's blowing up a storm at V.S. Naipaul's remarks about women writers. Ho, ho! That'll learn him.

V.S. Naipaul begins delivering an address, reading from A4 sheets. It's rather difficult to hear him, due to A.S. Byatt outside. Two o'clock arrives and passes. V.S. Naipaul reads on. Many people begin leaving for their next events. Seemingly oblivious,

V.S. Naipaul continues. Eventually, during a pause for emphasis, the audience jump in and begin clapping. Alexander Waugh quickly winds things up, apologising to the crowd for A.S. Byatt, and I dash off to join the signing queue.

A young woman paces the length of the queue announcing that V.S. Naipaul will be signing two *old* books per person. On a side table are modern paperback editions of V.S. Naipaul's many books, and a quote on one of them reads: 'A man who more than anybody else embodies what it means to be a writer.'

After queuing for twenty minutes, I am two people away from the signing desk when a different, older woman sees my *old* book and announces the new rules.

Older Woman: New books only. No old books will be signed.
FP: But… the other woman said that he was signing *two* old books.
Older Woman: I'm the boss. New books only.

V.S. Naipaul is privy to this outburst, but refuses to be embroiled. He looks delighted as he scribbles away, avoiding eye contact with his readers, protected behind the desk from his old books.

I suppose it's for the best. V.S. Naipaul will receive a percentage of his new book sales, while he doesn't stand to make anything from his old titles. He's made his money on them already. It's disappointing for me, especially since I've been queuing so long. My only hope is to wait outside. To hide and wait.

Eventually, with the help of an assistant, Sir Vidia begins sneaking off. I chase him, my book raised high, like a club. But he is quickly ushered into a discreet tent nearby where a makeshift sign reads: ARTISTS ONLY.

A-ha. The elusive Green Room.

A security guard is posted at the door, acting as a buffer between myself and my fellows.

I return soon after carrying a large potted plant.

Security Man: Hold on, can I see your pass please?
FP: Ah... sure, it's in my pocket here. Can you just hold this for me? [*Offering plant to security man.*]
Security Man: [*Rolling eyes.*] In you go.
FP: [*Laughing.*] You bet!

Like everything else on the festival site, the Artist's enclosure is made from simple, easily assembled materials. The walls and ceilings are comprised of the same floppy canvas as the event tents, and the floor is raised on small platforms and covered in green felt. But some extra touches have been laid on for the comfort of the artists, including upholstered couch seating, writing tables and chairs, racks of magazines to browse, and a generous selection of food and refrigerated drink. Ho, ho!

There's Alan Bennett! He's just there, sitting on a sofa, one leg crossing the other. He's reading a book.

There's Stephen Fry! He's standing, talking to another man that I don't know. They're drinking wine. Delicious free wine, ha-ha! This is hilarious! I'm shaking the large potted plant with excitement, and people are beginning to stare.

I hover near the refrigerated drinks, trying to put names to faces. Some of the authors and celebrities look older than expected. Maybe their publicity shots need updating. Or perhaps their young and appealing features have been intentionally enhanced for PR and marketing purposes.

My phone's ringing. That's weird. My phone never rings.

FP: Hello?
Man: Francis Plug?

FP: Yes?

Man: I'm calling from Wilson Bailiffs. We have a summons to remove items of your possession from a property in Fortess Road.

FP: No, I'm in the Artist area, OK? The Green Room! With Alan Bennett and Stephen Fry? I don't have time for chitter-chatter!

Man: Mr Plug, I'm serving you notice that we will be accessing your property by whatever...

FP: THANK YOU!

There's V.S. Naipaul, over there. Someone's just fetched him a drink. What a life. I better try and get my book signed before he's off his trolley.

FP: Hello V.S. Naipaul.

V.S. Naipaul: [*Silently staring at me.*]

FP: Yes, I was just at your event. It's a shame that A.S. Byatt had to spoil it by blowing the tent so hard.

V.S. Naipaul: Sorry? What did you say about A.S. Byatt?

FP: She was making a point, I think, by blowing the tent about.

V.S. Naipaul: She was *what*?

FP: Your comment about women writers. That's why she was so wild and blustery.

V.S. Naipaul: Who? A.S. Byatt? Or the wind? What are you saying?

FP: No, A.S. Byatt *is* the wind. She *is* the wind.

V.S. Naipaul: What?

FP: A.S. Byatt. *She* is the blowing wind.

V.S. Naipaul: Are you mad?

FP: [*Laughs.*] I think we're both a bit mad, aren't we V.S. Naipaul?

On my slip of paper, in big clear letters, reads: TO FRANCIS PLUG. But V.S. Naipaul chooses to completely disregard this.

Paul Theroux is at the refrigerated drinks. I have to share my trauma with someone.

FP: Look what V.S. Naipaul did to my book.

Paul Theroux: What did he do, I can't see...

FP: See this note? TO FRANCIS PLUG. You can't miss it, right? He brushed it aside. Like this... [*demonstrates*.]

Paul Theroux: Ah.

FP: And his signature is right at the top, so if I go and ask him again, there's no space...

Paul Theroux: It's probably best if you don't do that.

FP: Why?

Paul Theroux: He can be a bit... crotchety.

FP: Do you know him?

Paul Theroux: Yes.

FP: How come you haven't said hello?

Paul Theroux: Well, we're a bit at odds, currently.

FP: Did he stuff up one of your books too?

Paul Theroux: Something like that.

FP: Hmm. I suppose we can't be too hard on him. He nearly cried during his talk.

Paul Theroux: Did he really?

FP: Yep. He was all choked up. Like a soft little lamb. Why don't you go and give him a big kiss.

Paul Theroux: With respect, you're drunk aren't you?

FP: Oh. Is it obvious? I really have to work on that. For the Booker Prize ceremony...

Paul Theroux: The Booker Prize? Are you attending?

FP: Yeah. Why not?

Because I'm not a 'player' yet, many of my peers in the Green Room choose to pass me over, favouring other 'names' with their time and words. But I manage to corner Martin Amis, pointing out his father's Booker success and place in the literary canon, versus his own yet-to-be-realised talents.

Martin Amis: [*Looking around.*] Security? Can someone get rid of this psycho little fuck?

FP: Let's meet in the Pillars of Hercules. For some drinks. Hey, there's Ruth Rendell. She was really rude to me yesterday...

Conversing with your fellows, while seemingly a relaxed and social side to your duties, still demands a certain rigidity and a keen, intense focus. Writers, particularly lauded ones, are liable to expect pandering, especially from nobodies, like us. Aim for a certain reverence at all times. And try not to laugh too much, or for no apparent reason, because authors have enough to be paranoid about, in this day and age.

Francis Plug

NADINE GORDIMER

THE
CONSERVATIONIST

Nadine Gordimer

JONATHAN CAPE
THIRTY BEDFORD SQUARE LONDON

I've been well catered for with breakfast options. Seven different cereals, a choice of fresh refrigerated milk, free-range eggs, fruits of the orchard, and a wholesome loaf of wheat bread to get my day off to a cracking, countryside start. But I opt for a whisky provided by me, served straight in a clean glass.

It's a three-mile walk into Hay, so Meg has kindly provided me with a bike. After locking the cottage and replacing the key, I pedal down the narrow farm lanes, sitting bolt upright on the seat like Worzel Gummidge's friend, Aunt Sally.

The car park is a field, and the young lads waive any fee for the bike, which I lean on a wire fence. Nadine Gordimer's event is sold out, so I wander beyond the festival tents, up yonder paddocks towards the hills that rise a short distance beyond. The undergrowth is damp and squelchy, and I labour to lift each leg, my arms swatting at mosquitoes and green flies. In her novel *The Conservationist*, Nadine Gordimer depicts buzzing flies in a field, in order to signify the position of a human corpse. Today, a similar swarm buzzes silently around a sunken patch of smelly reeds. I edge closer, my hand covering my nose and mouth, fearing the worst.

Ha. It's just a cow's bowels, unloaded in the bog. It's not the limp body of Ruth Rendell, with her hair-do amuck. It's just a big splat of cow poo.

I share my relief with two Welsh policemen, directing them towards the flies.

FP: I thought there was a famous author out there, rotting in the marsh. But it's just a big old cow poo.
Welsh Policeman: Aren't you the guy we pulled out of the Artist tent yesterday?

After being escorted off the festival grounds, I wander over to see the young car park lads.

FP: Have you heard the news?
Car Park Attendant: No...
FP: One of the festival authors has been murdered and dumped in the field, over there.
Car Park Attendant: What? Really? Who?
FP: Ruth Rendell.
Second Car Park Attendant: Ruth Rendell?
FP: The whole festival will probably be cancelled.
Car Park Attendant: Shit!
Second Car Park Attendant: Bloody hell!
FP: You know what? I think you boys should hot-wire some of them cars and drive them around the field and crash them into each other like muddy dodgems. Do it now, while you have the chance.
Both Car Park Attendants: [*Looking at each other.*]

It's a sad irony that it would probably take a festival cancellation, or indeed a major police cordon, to get the book festival folk away from the marquees and fancy yoghurts into a village full of actual books. Hay has over thirty bookshops, making it the most populated bookshop town in the world. But despite the staggering amount of reading to be had, and the expertise and knowledge that abound in these tiny cobbled streets, it's the authors that attract all the crowds, and the only bookshop they appear in is the flat-pack store in the fenced-off field.

The lady behind the counter of the Information Centre is politely answering queries, her glasses trapped down the end of her nose with nowhere to go but leap. I join the queue and find myself chatting with an elderly woman in front.

Elderly Woman: Are you attending the festival?
FP: I *was*. Until the *incident*.
Elderly Woman: The incident?
FP: You know, the dead body in the back field.
Elderly Woman: No? What dead body?
FP: Ruth Rendell. She was murdered.
Elderly Woman: Oh my goodness! Are you sure?
FP: Apparently her water was spiked with a brugmansia flower. Everyone knows.
Elderly Woman: Good grief! Murdered! How awful...
[*Wipes her eyes.*]

I move, as if to put my arm around her shoulder, but my hand hovers over her head and I give her frizzy hair a pat instead.

FP: So what are you going to do now?
Elderly Woman: I don't know. I suppose I should change my ticket home. I really don't know...
FP: What about bungy jumping? They always have brochures for bungy jumping in these information places, don't they?
Eldely Woman: I have no idea.
FP: Or those Zorb ball things that roll down hills... or, what about chasing cheese down a hill? They do that around these parts, don't they? Yes, chase some cheese down a hill, face first.
Elderly Woman: I really don't know...

FP: Mind you don't end up with your spine poking out of your bottom.

I ask the Information Centre woman where the famous authors are staying.

Information Centre Woman: Well, they stay in a variety of places. Some stay at hotels or B&Bs in Hay, others stay out of town, in lodges or manor houses.

FP: What about Nadine Gordimer, specifically?

Information Centre Woman: Why? Why do you want to know?

I fish out my copy of *The Conservationist*.

FP: So she can sign my book. I don't want to murder her. [*Laughing.*]

Leaving none the wiser on Nadine Gordimer's whereabouts, I walk across Hay Castle Hill, finding a steep grass incline upon which to lie. Hay Castle has been knocked about a bit over the years. In 1216 it was destroyed by the English King John. Not long afterwards, the Welsh Prince Llwelyn set fire to the place. And then in 1977, another fire caused even more carnage. Still, you won't get any sympathy from me. At the end of the day, someone owns a castle and I live in a dingy flat with damp and no fire exits.

I begin writing another postcard for Anna.

Dear Anna,

Hello again from Hay.
The authors at the book festival have been performing in circus tents, but there are no lions or ringmasters. Just the authors,

talking about their books.

Boring, right?

But one of the authors has been murdered and dumped in a field, attracting flies.

So it's not quite as dull as you might think.

Love,
Uncle Francis.

Nadine Gordimer will be getting ready for her event. Perhaps I can catch her before she heads out to the festival site, while she still sits amidst the reconstruction of her writer's room that has been shipped in by large trucks. Perhaps the trauma of her impending stage performance has inspired her to create, to write reams and reams while I pick my nose on Hay Castle Hill.

Eventually, after creeping from hotel to hotel, I manage to track her down. But the kindly woman behind the desk says there's no answer from her phone, so I sigh deeply.

Kindly Woman: Are you all right, dear? You're awfully pale. And you're sweating, big drops.

FP: It must be... the pie. I've just eaten a very hot pie. If I could... somehow... get... this... signed...

Kindly Woman: 'Francis Plug'. Is that you?

FP: [*Croaks.*] Yes.

Kindly Woman: Leave it with me, Francis.

The Hay & District Royal British Legion Club & HQ is a real find. Just inside the door is a Megatough XL Extreme Multi-Game Video Machine, and the only food on view is wrapped in crinkly silver packets. Most of the patrons are a bit scruffy, and they're talking loudly and watching the horse racing. It's fair to say that this is a genuine drinking establishment. It's a hidden oasis of shouting and profanities.

The barmaid flicks up the Brains Beer tap, as if throwing the switch on a Frankenstein creature. Catching my eye, she nods towards some of the rowdy fellows.

Barmaid: Apologies for the terrible language.
FP: That's quite all right. D.H. Lawrence was using the 'C' word in the 1920's.
Barmaid: Was he now? You'll be here for the festival, then.
FP: Yes. I'm a writer. [*Pause.*] Not a pig iron dealer.
Barmaid: Fair enough. Five squid, ta.

With no authors to suck up my time with their natter, I attempt to get some writing done. But the telly proves distracting, and I end up spending long spells focused on the racetrack ambulance.

When my phone suddenly vibrates, I leap with a start. It's a text from Mr Stapleton.

LAWN TOO LONG LEAVES EVERYWHERE
WEEDS NEED SPOTLESS BEFORE I'M BACK 16TH
NEW SECURITY CODE 10000000 STAPLETON

His grasp of the English language really is shameful. I try and set an example with my response.

Hello, Mr Stapleton. Thank you for your text message. I will, of course, tend to the lawn, the leaves, the weeds, and any other requirements that need addressing. Many thanks for the new code. Have a safe and enjoyable time away. All the best, Francis.

See? I wrote that at a pub table, next to a Megatough XL Extreme Multi-Game Video Machine, amidst loud horse racing commentary and shouting and cursing. It's really not difficult.

After many great value drinks, I return to Nadine Gordimer's hotel, feeling like a million dollars. My signed book is awaiting collection, so I do a little dance in the foyer area.

In the heart of Hay Township, Richard Booth's, the largest second-hand bookshop in Europe, is open for business. The books are arranged in a very ramshackle way, and the woman at the desk can't draw any light on an author called 'Francis Plug'. Her colleague and his computer seem to draw a blank also. Nodding my head gravely, I say:

FP: He's very niche.

I stand for a time on the bottom step of the escalator, waiting to be carried to the first floor, before realising the 'escalator' is in fact a very rigid staircase.

The upper level is quiet and calm. All the panic and hysteria of the outside world is soaked up by the mass of printed pages, the books themselves cast like rocks amidst the towering, mountainous shelves. Only the expanding creak of unseen floorboards and the buzz of an expiring bulb emit any hint of sound, until a book falls heavily onto the threadbare carpet.

THONK.

Its title reads: *How To Teach Yourself Accountancy.*

I'm pretty sure it's in the wrong section.

A second book drops to the floor, causing me to bite my knuckle. Then dozens of books begin flying out of the shelves, as if pulled by wires. Walking slowly backwards in terror, I watch aghast as the air fills with books, all descending to the floor in a sprawled, spread-eagled mass.

Edging round the aisle's end, preparing to scramble, I encounter a dignified older woman who stands in the adjacent row silently browsing a book. She wears a long flowing purple dress that buttons up around the neck, and if she hears the sound of bound books clonking, she permits no response. Her dress appears to billow, as if caught in a path of air from a vent or fan. On closer inspection however, I realise with shock that her lower legs are missing. She's hovering above the ground. My body freezes. It's the ghost of Ruth Rendell, in Richard Booth's Bookshop.

Ruth Rendell's ghost has her head lowered in studied concentration, but I recognise her profile, her arched nose, her short, cropped hair-do. I creep closer along the opposite shelving. What is she reading? Have I read it? What's it like being dead? Is she scared of herself?

I think I should apologise for the train incident, even though I'd acted most courteously and she had been really rather rude. Wanting to clear the air, I pipe up.

FP: Mrs Rendell? Miss Rendell? Ms Rendell?

No response. She turns a page with a hand that looks like a thinly cut cheese slice. My timid projection may have been hard to detect, so I raise my voice to a little shout.

FP: Mrs Rendell!

At this she turns, eyeing me with a poisonous stare, dismissing me severely for a second time.

Ruth Rendell: Shoo!

I flush with embarrassment, my alcohol-rich bloodstream accumulating around my face and neck. But I can't just walk away. Perhaps she was murdered after all. I need answers.

FP: Read any good books lately?

Again, Ruth Rendell turns from her book, but this time her face contorts into a monstrous gaping hole, and her wispy, ghostly form makes for me with a roar.

FP: Aaagghhh! You slimed me!

The Blind Assassin

MARGARET ATWOOD

For Frances Phy

best wishes

Margaret Atwood

BLOOMSBURY

It's nice to be home again, although not that nice because my bed's gone, along with all my household appliances, my gardening tools, and also my van. They've been seized in order to cover my unpaid bills. With my work stuff gone, that's effectively my livelihood scuppered, which means I have no way of earning money to pay back the bank or the other demanding bodies. There is also an eviction notice, with immediate effect. But they've left the bedding behind, so I stand in the middle of my tiny flat, pillow fighting myself.

St Michael's is next to the big supermarket in Camden, and it's the first church that comes to mind when I decide to seek sanctuary in the house of the Lord. Unfortunately, the large wooden church doors are firmly bolted. No one leaves their front door unlocked any more. Especially when you have lovely silver goblets and candlesticks about the place, and also hand-stitched embroidered gowns, and maybe a massive Dracula organ. I decide to wait, huddled quietly behind the hydrangeas that paint a pretty picture against the exterior brickwork of the quaint church building.

The last time I entered a church, Margaret Atwood was the iconic figure attracting the adorers. Her curly, globe-like hairstyle even lent a certain aura, as if she'd been blessed with her own angelic halo. The church on that occasion was St James's in Piccadilly, slotted between pricey shops and designer boutiques near the Ritz Hotel. The event, like Yann Martel's, was publicised as 'A Literary Performance'. But in Margaret Atwood's case, it really was a 'performance'.

There were no free drinks, but I assumed as much beforehand, it being a church event. So I dipped frequently into my own supply, cautious not to fall onto the choir and band members directly below me. My balcony view was, I thought, superior to that of the more expensive stalls, and while further away from Margaret Atwood, I felt slightly closer to heaven. Sitting on a tall wooden chair, Margaret Atwood wore a floppy pink hat, a black Thai-dye shirt, baggy black trousers and black shoes. A little stick, painted gold, was attached to her shirt, and also to the shirts of certain performers who were bringing her featured novel to life. Much of the action centred round 'God's Gardeners', an eco-religious group and their Astro-Turf garden. Behind them, the vast stained-glass windows of St James' church featured epic religious imagery, resembling the artworks of Gilbert & George. The most prominent of these depicted a stricken Christ on the cross, and I'm in no way exaggerating when I say that the gaze from his cocked head was directed entirely at Margaret Atwood.

The author acted as narrator for the evening, while the other performers read short passages from her book. Original songs had been written specifically, and as the band performed these, Margaret Atwood swayed in her chair, clapping in time, all the while removing her floppy hat and putting it back on again.

After the show, her new book was peddled in the house of God. A signing took place in the church foyer, but the queue snaked all the way back into the main church. On its journey it passed a display table for the Royal Society for the Protection of Birds, a charitable beneficiary of the ticket sales. I was all for protecting birds, but their plight seemed to pale in significance when compared with other ills in the world, such as the widening of the poverty gap, human trafficking and victims of famine. Jesus Christ was nailed to a cross with a sword gash in his side, his face twisted in agony. Save the birds!

RSPB Spokeswoman: Would you like to sign a petition to protect the hunting birds?
FP: The hunting birds? Aren't they the horrible ones?
RSPB Spokeswoman: No, not at all. They sometimes get a bad rap, but...
FP: They'll poke your eyes out, given half the chance.
RSPB Spokeswoman: Oh, no. No they wouldn't...
FP: They'll make you blind, they will. They'll claw your face while they peck your eyeballs out like little oysters.
RSPB Spokeswoman: No, honestly...
FP: My local pub does a collection for blind people. It breaks your heart. Them blimmin' hunting birds! [*Shaking fist.*]

Margaret Atwood had removed her honey-coloured glasses, and also her pink floppy hat. She seemed remarkably composed and almost serene for what appeared to be a very production-driven task, akin to the hand-rolling of cigarettes in a Third World factory shed made from sheets of corrugated iron. The signing process had a string of subservient youths carrying out menial tasks at every step. An abundance of energetic Post-it note carriers offered their services to those in the queue, and at the signing desk a young man was employed purely to open books at the correct page. A young woman was then tasked with passing the books across the table to the author, and a further woman was charged with moving the queue along, or encouraging people to walk on their own feet. When I finally stood before Margaret Atwood therefore, I felt like I'd just had breakfast at Wallace & Gromit's house. Keen to discuss her theory of bananas coming from outer space, which she'd touched on in her Booker-winning book, I instead found myself swatting away a vicious sparrowhawk, and by the time this was dispersed with, I'd been shunted along the production line.

After leaving St James', I walked along Piccadilly towards The Ritz hotel, hoping to see some million dollar troupers. However, when I passed a luggage shop, I noticed that its grilled metal shutters weren't fully lowered to the ground. So I crawled beneath them, turning to squash my face into the bars like a caged lion.

It was hard not to laugh while growling at passers-by. A group of young lads stopped as I banged my paws on the metal grate, and when one of them pushed the shutters right the way down, there was a distinctive *click*. They found that very funny indeed, the lads, and I laughed a bit too, half-heartedly attempting to raise the cage wall again, without success. After a while the lads walked off, still laughing, and I began to violently pull and shake the shutters, not laughing. No souls stirred inside the darkened shop, despite my banging on the window glass, so I turned my frustration back towards the metal bars. I was furiously rattling these when Margaret Atwood approached with her followers.

Margaret Atwood: Are you stuck?
FP: No, no.
Margaret Atwood: Really?
FP: Yes. No. Yes.
Margaret Atwood: You were at the church event just now, weren't you?
FP: Yes. Thank you.

Margaret Atwood: Are you sure you're not trapped in there?

FP: Yes. [*Pause.*] I'm… I'm a cage dancer.

Margaret Atwood: A cage dancer? What time do you start?

FP: Late. I've got the late slot tonight.

Margaret Atwood: Oh, that's a shame. I'd have loved to stay and watch you.

FP: [*Shrugs.*] Darn.

Margaret Atwood: So, you're sure you're OK?

FP: Ha, ha!

As Margaret Atwood walked away, she turned to look back, finding me dancing softly from side to side, clicking my fingers.

It wasn't the most comfortable sleep I've ever had, but the worst part was having to wee behind the grill and watch it trickle across the path of oncoming pedestrian traffic. My despair was deepened by the fact that I was unable to move on and avoid responsibility for that wee. The shame of this made me drink more from the stash of scotch in my satchel, and thus the vicious circle continued.

The large wooden doors to St Michael's in Camden meanwhile, remain firmly locked and bolted. I have emerged at regular intervals from behind the hydrangeas to check, pounding on the entranceway before running back to the cover of my foliage lair. Has God spied me behind here? Maybe He's smiling down on me, but just a half-smile. A wary, all-knowing smile. As if a part of him recognises me as one of his children, while the other part is X-raying my soul, my oozy innards, like they do in those anti-smoking ads. Maybe I should press my hands firmly in a steeple and hold them up to my face, like slices of bread forming a nose sandwich. Lord knows I have a lot to pray for: employment, drink and cigarette money, tax help, debt repayments, publishing contracts…

Feeling a bit desperate, and unsure what I should pray for first, I begin singing a quiet song to Jesus, hoping he might look with pity on my sad life.

FP: I believe in miracles. Like a nice new flat. You sexy thing, sexy thing you.

Charles Dickens used to offer refuge to the desperate and destitute. If he were alive today, I'm quite sure he wouldn't turn me away. Like our modern authors, he was only too familiar with the public glare. And like Kiran Desai and Anne Enright, he also undertook global book tours, crossing the Atlantic by ship to conduct author events, just as Dylan Thomas later would too. Dickens' health is said to have deteriorated considerably as a result of his 'performing', while Dylan Thomas famously drunk himself to death in New York after his US dates.

Maybe I should escape to the woods. Wild berries are plentiful this time of year, and perhaps I can bed under the cover of some dense bush or a fallen log. Of course, since I'm sat right outside a church, I probably should seek my refuge within. But churches aren't like pubs. They don't even have toilets. Maybe I could be a little church mouse, scurrying around beneath the pews, sustained by the crumbs dropped by all the bribed children. Maybe I'll find some wine, in a chalice. And when I'm not scavenging or sleeping on the hard wooden seats, I can remove the church notices from the bulletin board and write on the back of them, to finish my book.

If there's a god in St Michael's he's having a lie-in. The doors to his house, I've discovered, aren't due to open until 1 pm, and in the meantime I'm getting a sore, muddy bottom. Vernon Gregory Little escaped to Acapulco, a far better choice than a

216

Camden churchyard. Perhaps I'll write to DBC Pierre, former Mexican resident and author of *Vernon God Little*, inviting him here to share in my decampment. We could drink tequila shots and imagine the waves lapping. I hope he still remembers me.

Vernon God Little

A 21st Century Comedy in the Presence of Death

DBC PIERRE

FRANCIS
PLUG

THIS
IS
FOR
YOU

[signature]

ff

faber and faber

DBC Pierre and I last caught up at the Betsey Trotwood pub. He'd been doing one of those Guardian events opposite their old offices in Farringdon, and he invited the entire audience, including me, to join him in the pub afterwards for a drink. Authors don't normally invite their audience to the pub, but DBC Pierre has a bit of a 'reputation'. He's a bit rough around the edges, and he's got the sort of face you might see in the public bars and untarted up pubs in the less agreeable areas of London.

DBC Pierre drunk wine during his talk, not water, and he had a topped-up glass at the signing table.

FP: Is your wine delicious?
DBC Pierre: Yeah, not bad, thanks.
FP: Does it help with the nerves?
DBC Pierre: A bit.
FP: I guess if you drink more of it, and faster, it will help a *lot*.
DBC Pierre: I s'pose...
FP: [*Writing in notebook.*] Sau... vig... non...

I ran to the Betsey Trotwood pub, securing a table and making sure there were extra chairs for DBC and his bag. Even though DBC Pierre is Australian by birth, I bought him a large glass of

New Zealand Sauvignon Blanc, because everyone knows that New Zealand wine beats Australian wine hands down. If he got delayed with the book signings, I could always drink it myself, before it lost its chill, and replace it with another. Although I wasn't made of money, what better way to spend what little I had than on a fine wine for a Booker Prize-winning author.

I sat quietly, smelling the pretty little flowers arranged on my table, inhaling them deeply, like decongestants. The spare tables and seats filled up quickly, forcing the late arrivals to stand around awkwardly. They were standers and I was a sitter. Although eyeing the spare chairs at my table, they didn't attempt to sit on these because I'd turned them upside down. To further dissuade such challengers, I banged my palms on the table surface, occasionally lifting them for a series of handclaps. When I needed to hold a drink, I would slap the tabletop with just the one hand.

DBC Pierre had yet to appear, perhaps due to some official business back at the Guardian's Newsroom. Which was fine. However, in my rush to get to the pub and secure a table, I'd waylaid my need for a smoke.

Since British pubs became smoke-free on July 1st 2007, retaining a table has been problematic. To counter this, I tend to frequent empty pubs. But DBC's entire audience was here, so saving my table, once I ventured outside, was going to be a tall order.

Draping items of my clothing over the upended chair legs, I created a kind of makeshift house. The seething crowd would be less inclined to trespass on my property, and I could return and get my home in order for DBC Pierre when he arrived to visit.

Smoking is supposed to relieve stress, but I felt tense and agitated. The emotion was akin to an antelope mother losing her young calf in a frenzied stampede created by a hungry cheetah. When waiting at the bar to be served, I'm often gripped by a similar desperation. Given the option, I'd prefer a fast petrol pump system where I can quickly fill my own glass and payment can be made instantly via a sample of saliva.

Walking back into the Betsey Trotwood, my shoulders dropped like a pile of heavy oranges in a netted bag. All my upside-down chairs were now right side up, and the flat rounded seats were filled with other people's bottoms. My clothes and my satchel were now in a pile under my table, and the people who ousted me were laughing, as if they were so settled and relaxed that they could just laugh straight away. It was as though my comfortable home had been subdivided and converted into flats while I was down the shops. Not only were my things all cast on the floor, but my various drinks had disappeared too.

The pointy end of my shoe twisted on the floor, stubbing out my fading table seat dream. My knuckles rubbed my eyes, indicating via body language cues that I could no more observe the scene before me. Ordering two more drinks, I joined my possessions beneath the table, adding the fresh glasses and myself to the floor.

My cramped enclave was shared with the shamed legs and feet of wrongdoers. I curled around the table's wrought-iron stand like a troll grasping the foundation pillar of his bridge. Through the floorboards below I could feel the rumblings of a passing Underground train on its way to Farringdon station, but I imagined these rumblings were emanating from my stomach, and that they represented my need to consume a whole goat. The wooden floor made my bottom ache, and my neck strained, forced to bend awkwardly beneath the low-lying tabletop. A glass was placed noisily on the table, inches above my head.

FP: [*Bellowing.*] Who's that trip-trapping over my bridge?

There was no response, so I poked my head up and stared angrily at the faces of the people seated around the table.

FP: [*Bellowing.*] Who's that trip-trapping over my bridge?
Young Man: What are you on about?

I continued staring at each face in turn, daring any one of them to cross. After a short time, the staring and the silence began to feel somewhat strained.

Eventually, a woman at the table diverted her eyes and nudged the others.

Young Woman: He's here.

DBC Pierre had arrived with two officials from the Newsroom. He was scanning the room, searching out a seat. I slithered back under the table, knowing he would pass by at any minute, which he did.

FP: DBC Pierre...

He looked across at those seated above the table, before noticing me beneath, urgently patting the wooden floor.

FP: Sit here, please.
DBC Pierre: [*Laughing.*] Ah, thanks... I might stand for a bit, cheers.

One of his companions strolled off to the bar, leaving DBC standing with the other. I couldn't let him stand up. He'd won the Booker Prize.

On the upper reaches of the wall, alongside the bar, was a platform of unused space. Its proximity to the ceiling excluded any opportunities for standing, but there appeared to be plenty of sitting room. The only way to reach it however, was via the bar counter. So I placed my drinks on this, and followed them up with my feet.

Barman: Here, no! No, no, no...

The espresso machine was a useful foothold, but this meant crunching the upside-down cups and saucers stacked on top. A tumbler glass full of teaspoons clattered onto the floor, and a silver jug filled with hot frothy milk upended onto the counter, coating the angry barman's shirt. Securing my wine glasses on the platform above, I continued my ascent up the tea box shelves until reaching the summit.

The ceiling dipped sharply, due to the slant of a stairwell on the other side. Forced to squat, my knees resembling the arms on a stout sofa chair, I stared down at the many raised eyeballs, as if the pub was packed with zombies.

The bar went silent as the manager began talking me down like a suicide. All I'd wanted was a quiet drink, and the chance for a deep and personal conversation with DBC Pierre at a table reserved just for us. But now I was a spectacle, an *event*, just because I was the guy up really high. I picked out DBC's standing form, and retrieving the book he'd signed for me, I began waving it around like a sparkler, breaking my silence.

FP: DBC Pierre. You can sit up here if you like. There's room.

DBC half-raised his drink, like a handful of dirt to drop into a grave. I began reading his book aloud, starting with the cover, and then the publishing page.

FP: 'Vernon God Little. A 21st Century Comedy in the Presence of Death. DBC Pierre. Faber and Faber. First

223

printed in 2003 by Faber and Faber Limited, 3 Queen Square, London WC1N 3AU. Typeset by Faber and Faber Limited. Printed in England by Mackays of Chatham, plc.

I was just getting onto the copyright details when DBC Pierre broke in. He was now standing directly below, at the bar.

DBC Pierre: Hey, mate. Look, why don't you come down here? I think you're pissing a few people off...

The bar was stony silent as I peered over the edge like a sparrow chick, looking for spilt worms.

FP: I think they might hurt me.

The manager had a phone to his ear, but he wasn't talking.

DBC Pierre: Nah, don't worry about that. Cigarette?
FP: [*Pause.*] I'll race you to the door...

My shoes crept backwards, as if positioning themselves in two wedged starter blocks. A polite cough provided a gunshot and I burst forward, springing off the platform, my legs 'running' in mid-air. I collapsed across a table far below, before falling further to the floor, joining broken bottles and glasses, and those in the process of breaking. Both my legs felt crushed, and my right arm throbbed numbly. My head felt like a button, dangling from a wispy buttonhole thread. But I'd taken out my former table, *and* all the drinks of my usurpers, so that was a total result.

Where was DBC Pierre? I had to win the race. Rising, quivering, to my feet, I hobbled for the EXIT. Pulling the door handle like a lawnmower starter cord, I stole away into the night, shuffling past the finishing line and beyond.

St Michael's is still shut. Acapulco seems a long way away. Mr Stapleton probably goes there all the time. In fact, he's probably there right now...

Standing up, I excitedly pluck my collection of client keys like a harp of happy fortune.

ALAN HOLLINGHURST
THE LINE OF BEAUTY

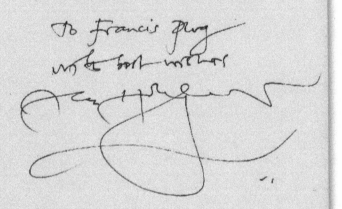

To Francis Plug
with best wishes

PICADOR

Mr Stapleton wears black business socks with gold bands, but right now *I'm* wearing them, stomping around his carpeted bedroom, STOMP, STOMP, STOMP. They're stretched over the top of my thick woollen work socks, and my Bolshevik dancer's legs are leaping up and down, knees pumping like pistons as I chant nonsensical anthems in Mr Stapleton's socks.

FP: YA, YA, YA.

Music blares out of the fancy radio beside his bed, and in between songs, during the commercials and DJ chat, I pause and tip great gulps of whisky into my head. The rim of the cut-glass goblet is streaked with traces of white foam, because my entire face is covered in shaving cream, right up over my eyes. Less than an hour after moving in I've drunk the best part of a whisky bottle, and now my little teeth chatter excitedly, my eyes bright and dancing.

A full-length mirror hangs in the upstairs hallway, and I scream with laughter as I run past it, immediately turning to run past again, waving. In each hand is a bra, belonging to Mr Stapleton's girlfriend, and these are being twirled vigorously, like a floor gymnast's streamers.

FP: [*Screaming.*] BOSOMS!!

Mr Stapleton's alcohol reserves are exceptionally vast, showcasing the finest top-shelf names, presumably so the needs of his high-class guests can be effortlessly met. Cognacs, bourbons, rums, tequilas, ports and gins are all in immense supply, and there's probably enough Scotch whisky to fill an aquarium. These liquor stocks have been partially funded by money from the British public's taxes, so like a character from *The Borrowers*, I'm borrowing it straight back.

I awake on the cool tiled floor of the kitchen. Apart from Mr Stapleton's socks, I'm still wearing the same clothes I returned from Hay in. That was nearly two days ago. I resolve to shower and change just as soon as I have a drink.

The radio's still blaring in the bedroom upstairs. Hopefully it's beyond the neighbours' range. I must be careful about that. They mustn't hear a peep.

A sophisticated security system is installed throughout the house. Individual sensors are strategically placed in key positions, and once breached, a monitoring centre is alerted, who notify the police. Mr Stapleton gave me the run-down on this when I first started working for him. It makes the locks back at my flat seem grossly inadequate, resembling strips of grated cheese dabbed across the door frame with sticky tape. Needless to say, the system in this house is no longer engaged.

The news on the radio is read by a man with a deep and sonorous voice, like Alan Hollinghurst's. When Alan Hollinghurst spoke in the Southbank's Queen Elizabeth Hall, his rich baritone words rolled out like a heavy, seductive fog, unfurling across his audience pasture. While elocution lessons are not essential for the public author, it's probably best if you don't talk like Sweep, the high-pitched squeaky dog puppet.

I imagine Alan Hollinghurst might find this place a bit showy. A bit lacking in taste perhaps, a bit naff. Although a four-storey period home, which Alan Hollinghurst might admire in its original state, Mr Stapleton has chosen to furnish it in a style to match his high-powered corporate life. A painting of a naked lady hangs over a white marble and granite gas-log fireplace. The central sofa is white also, as are the floorboards, but the concert grand piano is black ebony. Every imaginable gadget and appliance has been acquired to ensure that Mr Stapleton is 'with the programme'. His TV, mounted on the wall like a precious artwork, is as big as a sliding door, and if he chooses not to catch up on the news and the melting down of the economy, he can always drive an F1 car, or shoot dozens of Taliban soldiers.

In comparison, Alan Hollinghurst lives in a Hampstead flat, spread over three floors. According to an article I read, it's very tidy, with beige carpet and white walls. When I read 'tidy' I read 'barren'. It took him seven years to write the book that followed *The Line of Beauty*, so he probably had to sell everything he bought with his Booker Prize cheque in order to live.

Still, Hampstead isn't to be sniffed at. It's a very literary place to live, with some massive gardens. And *The Line of Beauty* rights were also bought by a film/television company, so that must have helped. While some authors might live in Hampstead, the majority must live in far more modest surrounds. Newspaper reports suggest UK authors earn 33% less than the national average wage. Most supplement their incomes through other means, such as journalism or teaching. Magnus Mills, an author shortlisted for the Booker Prize, has returned to his original job of driving buses. Others stock shelves or deliver mail. I, of course, garden. I can't stock shelves at the Chalk Farm bookshop because Chalk Farm doesn't have a bookshop any more. And I can't drive a bus because that would endanger lives. Writing is my only hope. Despite the odd exception, the only way to live comfortably as a writer, it seems, is to be rich already.

It feels strange to ascend three flights of stairs and find I'm still in the same house. After turning the radio off, I cautiously engage with Mr Stapleton's bathroom. The shower water projects out of five different wall-mounted vents, hitting me from every side, as if I'm in a boat, riddled with bullets. The shampoo is made from avocado, the conditioner is made from cocoa beans, and downstairs the tea is made from nettles. Nettles? There are no vegetables, no fruit, and no bread or other perishables. I'll have to receive sustenance by eating tinned food, marmalade, and muesli without milk. The massive garden doesn't have a veg patch because veg are only useful to banker-types when they can lather them on their chests.

Although I've not long woken up, it's already starting to get dark. The dimmer switch is useful in maintaining my lovely singing voice. When the light is dimmed, my scales are very low and deep.

FP: LA, LA, LA, LA, LA, LA, LA.

But as I increase the brightness in the room, my scales become higher and higher.

FP: LA, LA, LA, LA, LA, LA, LA.

And then I turn the dimmer down again.

FP: LA, LA, LA, LA, LA, LA, LA.

And up…

FP: LA, LA, LA, LA, LA, LA, LA, LA, LA!!!

According to the kitchen calendar, Mr Stapleton is in the Bahamas, not Acapulco. And he'll be gone for another two weeks. Since I can't garden, I should try and get some writing done. After all, this house makes a rather idyllic writer's retreat. At my disposal I have shelter, warmth, solitude, and an alarming amount of quality drink. I'm surrounded by trees, protected by secure locks, and distanced from the more unsavoury elements of society. I can avoid the bank, the tax people, the garden suppliers, and the general public. This is what it's like to be Mr Stapleton. Nobody can touch him.

Before settling down behind his desk, seeking out the muse, I focus on emptying a bottle of rich liquor. In order to unlock my creative mind, I first must blow up the safe, as it were.

By the time I turn on the computer and attempt to open a word document, I'm simply too drunk to operate the keypad. Despite changing the type size to 72pt, in an effort to aid legibility, I flounder. When I take a new bottle of Podier St-Eustache off to the sofa, all I've managed to write is:

> *How To Be A Public Author*
> by Francis Plug

The English Patient

MICHAEL ONDAATJE

To francis Plus

BLOOMSBURY

My rolled cigarettes dry up quickly, so I take to smoking the contents of a Cuban cigar box. Mr Stapleton has provided crystal ashtrays on his glass-top coffee table, despite the fact he doesn't smoke. His walk-in wardrobe is like a fair-sized room, impressively stocked, as if by Imelda Marcos. I wear his business suits around the house, strutting about like a hotshot banker. But this escapism is limited, and I struggle to progress the role-play. After all, besides looking at numbers all day, what do bankers actually do? Beneath the flashy façade, they're really very boring. I may as well dress like a stone.

One positive outcome of this charade comes from the treasures in the pockets. Mr Stapleton doesn't launder his suits very often, or care too much about money, judging by the wads of scrunched up notes within. Tucked away in his racks of clothes, forgotten, is over £2,000. Two thousand pounds. This is the same man who would question a bill for sunflower seeds.

Since I'm looking after his house for him, I retrieve a small cash payment , in order to purchase a ticket for Michael Ondaatje.

In 1992, *The English Patient* was joint winner of the Booker Prize with *Sacred Hunger*, and like Barry Unsworth, Canadian Michael Ondaatje is rather tall. I sit seven rows back in the

UCLA Bloomsbury Theatre, admiring the plush seating, and the carpet design that resembles bits of brain.

On stage are two leather armchairs with shiny golden feet. Two small bottles of water have been placed on a round wooden table. Behind the chairs is a black-shrouded stand supporting an impressive arrangement of flowers, which gush out of a tall glass vase.

Michael Ondaatje trips slightly as he comes onto stage, due perhaps to some nerve-calming drinks, or maybe just because of his big clumsy feet. Even if you have little feet, like myself, it's worth making a note of this potential hazard should it threaten the stability of an event in which you happen to be partaking. The interviewer, Hermione Lee, introduces Michael Ondaatje, who proceeds to a wooden lectern without incident, where he begins reading from his new book. The house lights have been lowered, and all interest is drawn to the author. It's a minimal stage set-up, and the scene is based around a couple seated on leather armchairs, one of whom stands to read a book aloud behind a lectern. The book is actually filled with the thoughts of the seated woman. The man reads the woman's thoughts aloud as she sits quietly and reflectively in the armchair thinking them.

Michael Ondaatje: [*Reading Hermione Lee's thoughts aloud.*]
This is the good part. I can just sit here in this comfy armchair while he rattles on with his book. My armchair at home is very nice, but the springs in this one are particular springy. Bounce, bounce. I've got my special black shoes on tonight. It should be OK if I gently rotate my dangling left shoe, but not too much. I mustn't distract attention from Michael. My introduction seemed to go bloody well. Not out of the woods yet, of course. I hope he's not one of those self-important bastards.

Michael Ondaatje is very good in his role. He wears a black suit and a black shirt (without a tie), and his hair is grey, and so is his beard. After an accomplished read, he returns to his seat and guzzles all his water. This is understandable, given the demands on his voice, and the fact that the plastic water bottles are very small. The dialogue is not over yet as Hermione Lee has some questions lined up. Despite the assumed comfort of the armchair, Michael Ondaatje sits forward, awkwardly, as if he's preparing to bolt. His hands are clasped between his legs, and his shoulders protrude, pointing towards the EXIT.

Michael Ondaatje: I love taciturn people. I've fallen in love with a character in my book because he doesn't speak. I only write dialogue if I have to. A person in Germany once asked me: 'Is writing like a clockmaker or an escaped horse?' The answer I gave: an escaped horse.

His hand suddenly darts across and seizes Hermione Lee's bottle of water, before guzzling this down too. The empty plastic container makes a 'plick' noise when replaced on the table. Looking over his shoulder, he then stands and makes for the vase of flowers. The protruding foliage settles atop his generous mop of hair as noisy, slurping gulps of water thunder through his clip-on microphone. After draining the vase, he wipes his dripping beard with his suit sleeve. But the flowers in the empty vase, deprived of their saving nutrients, make a lunge for his throat. There is a strange guttural cry and the curtain falls and I begin clapping.

Michael Ondaatje is signing his books on stage right, and we queue at the bottom of the steps. A tall book dealer stands behind me. His long hair is grown in an unfashionable way, and his moustache doesn't fit well on his strange, elongated face. He's loudly showing off, boasting to a younger man about the good old days at the Hay Festival.

Book Dealer: Back then it was just a small tent at the bottom of a field. William Golding, I remember, was only signing one book per person, so all the dealers got one book signed and then went to the back of the queue to get another book signed and so on.

Hmm. He wouldn't think himself quite so clever if he knew that the Hay Festival had turned into a Murder Fest.

An attendant slots the front dust sleeve of my book into the title page, so that Michael Ondaatje can immediately open the book to the right spot without any unnecessary page turning or time wastage. My little feet trip when clambering up the stage steps, due to earlier drinks, for the nerves.

FP: Is *The English Patient* a mental patient?
Michael Ondaatje: Pardon?
FP: Is *The English Patient* a mental patient?
Michael Ondaatje: You haven't read it?
FP: Not yet, but I plan to. This isn't actually my book.
Michael Ondaatje: Oh. So who is Francis Plug?
FP: That's me.
Michael Ondaatje: You're Francis Plug? And you want me to write a dedication in this book, to you, even though it's not your book?
FP: Yes.
Michael Ondaatje: Hmm.
Book Dealer: Oh God, he's getting a dedication in a first of *English Patient*.
Younger Man: That's regrettable.
Book Dealer: What a twit. Waste of a good book, that.
Younger Man: And he's getting it signed to 'Francis Plug'.

Book Dealer: Francis Plug? Dear Lord. That'll be easy to sell on!

They both laugh.

As soon as I'm outside the theatre, I call a number at random.

Random Phone Number: Hello?
FP: Is writing like a clockmaker or an escaped horse?
Random Phone Number: What? Who is this?
FP: Is writing like a clockmaker or an escaped horse?
Random Phone Number: Freak! [*Click.*]

Back in Primrose Hill, I'm inspired by the Michael Ondaatje talk and sit at my writer's desk, typing up my notes. Quite often I point at the computer and laugh because what I've written is really very funny. I hold my tummy with my arms and laugh and laugh.

FP: Mercy!

Feeling jovial, I decide to send an email to Mr Stapleton.

Dear Mr Stapleton,

Hello, it's Francis (Plug). How are you?
I hope you're enjoying the tropics. I bet your feet are glad they're not wearing black business socks with gold bands. In that sunshine!
Your garden is going to look quite something when you return. I just need to get hold of some basic gardening equipment,

and mark my words, you'll have an absolute picture on your hands.

Don't be worrying yourself about your empty house in your absence. I'm quite certain it's impeccable, just how you left it. So no need to rush back. Have yourself another ride on that inflatable banana boat – woo-hoo!

Francis.

Although Mr Stapleton's garden is in darkness, it could definitely use some tending. Without any tools, I'm somewhat restricted, but I manage to find a spade in the garage.

The manicured lawn is coated in a fine dew. Perhaps Mr Stapleton has buried his many riches beneath.

The lawn quickly resembles the surface of the moon. I convince myself that the moon above is actually the earth, and that I'm on the moon, digging it up, looking for space treasure. The fact that I'm digging in the dark, while very drunk, means that my excavation efforts are poor at best, and if riches are unearthed, I certainly can't see them. In the end I forget about the moon and the treasure and instead focus on clearing the entire area of landmines.

The God *of* Small Things

ARUNDHATI ROY

For Francis Phip

[signature]

Flamingo
An Imprint of HarperCollins*Publishers*

The bountiful liquor reserves are near exhausted. The kitchen floor is awash with bottles, their empty necks resembling an army of strange singing fish. The cigars too have all but disappeared, their butts littering the ashtrays like bent thumbs. Mr Stapleton's house can be likened to a balloon filled with helium that's slowly but surely losing its air. When depleted, it will fold and collapse. And when it does, I'll be the next to deflate.

So I do a run to the off-licence, using some of Mr Stapleton's forgotten money to purchase cheap liquor replacements, roll-your -owns, and teabags (for the refilling of the whiskies). When I return, the whole place has been turned *upside down*. Ransacked. Drawers have been removed, contents strewn, furniture upended. I pretend to be shocked, but I'm not.

FP: You're responsible for that, you ninny!

The drink running down the walls like wee in an underpass…

FP: It was you!

Then I notice the lawn.

Clasping my new purchases to my chest, I huddle into the bird hide I've fashioned out of cushions, in the lounge.

An unseasonal heatwave has hit England, and even dressed in Mr Stapleton's Speedos, I swelter. As welcome as the cool house interior is however, I'm grateful for a brief escape, particularly from the sight of the crater-filled rear garden. The opportunity to see Arundhati Roy is very welcome therefore, and subsequently seized.

Arundhati Roy, the Indian writer-turned-activist, has taken a very long break from the literary world, hiding away from her readers. But now the Booker Prize-winner is to appear publicly in the UK again, no doubt quickly filling the immense Queen Elizabeth Hall on the South Bank.

Most male authors, I've noticed, wear suits at their gigs, and I'm beginning to understand the appeal: it's a way of blending in. It also gives them the appearance of being successful, when in reality they're in one of the lowliest, most unsuccessful professions going. It's too hot for suits today, though. People are actually sunbathing on the banks of the Thames, reclining with splayed legs amidst the mucky stones on Ferry Wharf shore. It's people like these who create massive bar queues in summer, emerging from their seasonal burrows of abstinence to take all the pub seats. Arundhati Roy's event is indoors and her talk is likely to be political, grim and unsettling, but at least I'll be spared this ungainly flesh and awful carefree laughter. Weaving my way amongst these bouncy castle figures, I head towards the Hall, keen to relax amongst the quiet reserve of the literary audience, no doubt seated politely, avoiding sideward glances at my hairy legs.

With my ticket secured, I'm left with an hour or so to kill before the performance. Not wanting to linger amidst the crowds on the river-facing promenade, I head to the rear of the building, finding the Artists' Entrance door.

Arundhati Roy, having eclipsed the traditional role of public author with her exhaustive human rights campaigning, is likely to have more pressing concerns than a post-show book signing. It therefore follows that I'll miss the chance to meet her afterwards and get my book signed by her hand. By positioning myself in the shadows, some distance from the Artists' Entrance, I hope to avoid suspicion prior to leaping out at her, waving my book wildly.

She'll probably arrive in a chauffeur-driven car fitted with a Hybrid engine. Anticipating this, I ready myself to run alongside the moving vehicle, patting the passenger window before opening the door myself and ushering her out. But what if she's here already and is now having din-dins? A light meal, possibly sprinkled with raisins, to see her through the interview process and the public scrutiny? She'll certainly need some sustenance for the onslaught to come, and I make a point of noting 'Energy Levels' for our own public appearances, reader. Perhaps, in her case, a slice of sugar-rich cheesecake and some fennel tea will suffice; perhaps in ours four vodka Red Bulls.

Maybe she's been lured out to a riverside café by the marketing people at her publishing house. You can't run away when you're pinned behind a table. If Arundhati Roy has doubts at being thrown onto the South Bank's largest stage, they'll bundle her into a sack and carry her lithe, waif figure over their shoulders, unstringing her only when the audience applause has commenced.

Standing nervously in the alleyway, concerns begin to seed in my wet pink brain like magic beans thumbed into the soil. What if Arundhati Roy has already been carted through the Artists' Entrance door, sandalled feet kicking? There's still 25 minutes before show time. On *The Muppet Show*, curtain call is 15 seconds prior to the stage appearance, but at that point the artist is already well ensconced in their dressing room, made-up and show-briefed.

Ms Roy! Ms Roy! Fifteen seconds till curtain, Ms Roy!

Which Muppet said that? Was it Gonzo? Or Ralph, the piano-playing, floppy-eared dog? When I'm a successful writer on the circuit, one of my peculiar demands will be that I'm called to stage by a dog made out of socks and ping-pong balls. Or I'm not going anywhere.

It's possible that Arundhati Roy's interviewer requested to meet her early to run through the proceedings. This would help them get their facts right, so they don't sound completely stupid. They can also pretend to be her friend.

Interviewer: Arundhati and I were talking earlier and she said blah.

Perhaps Arundhati Roy's backstage dressing room has its own private bar, like those kit-set ones in the small advertisements at the back of magazines. Maybe, at this very moment, she's submerged in a hot tub. Or reclining on a towel-covered lounger with cucumber slices over her eyes.

With less than ten minutes until she's scheduled to take to the stage, I recall those GET TO YOUR SEAT announcements prior to Yann Martel and Alan Hollinghurst. Maybe the amplified voice *was* Alan Hollinghurst. Arundhati Roy might still arrive, by the seat of her pants. But she wouldn't have time to stop and chat. She'd probably be running, maybe in bare feet, like Zola Budd. I shuffle off, dejected, like a great big hairy snuffleupagus.

After a brief introduction, Arundati Roy wanders across the vast stage towards the lectern.

Arundhati Roy: I am going to read a couple of paragraphs from my book because I am a writer and I have always felt more comfortable reading than speaking.

Arundhati Roy's phrase resonates with me, but even so, I'm slightly troubled. If *she*, as an acclaimed Booker Prize-winner, feels uncomfortable talking on stage, what hope is there for strung-out, lowly writers like us, dear reader?

Arundhati Roy is wearing a stunning crimson sari, which sure beats some stuffy old suit. But even from way back in Row DD, she appears very exposed. The stage really is obscenely big. It's shameful. You could put five hundred authors on that stage. It isn't Arundhati Roy's fault. She didn't book the venue. Her talk exposes murders, rape, genocide, corrupt judges, and the bulldozing of Indian villages. But that stage looks like a supermarket car park. She must want to crawl under her chair and die.

The sombre mood eases somewhat when Arundhati Roy explains how, as a youngster, she stole carrots from somebody's garden. Ingeniously, she sliced the tops off and carefully placed these back on the soil, thus leaving no trace of her theft. I'm filled with admiration. I want to rush out and perform the trick myself. If caught, I would place the blame squarely on her, my mentor, Arundhati Roy.

FP: [*Whispering.*] Excuse me… do you know which of the Muppets said: *Fifteen seconds till curtain.*

Person in the Next Seat: [*Whispering.*] Hmm, yes. That was Scooter.

FP: [*Whispering.*] Of course, Scooter!

They really are a clever bunch, this literary crowd.

Arundhati Roy is being thanked by the interviewer, and certain pockets of the crowd rise to offer a standing ovation. The other members of the audience applaud too, but they remain seated. It's a bit confusing. Not sure whether I should get to my feet, or sit and clap, I run like a lunatic towards the door.

The balding book investor from the John Berger and Pat Barker events is asking an official representative if there's a signing queue for Arundhati Roy. He's directed towards a table near the windows and I discreetly follow him, almost clapping my hands in excitement.

A line forms quickly behind us, like a squeezed tube of people toothpaste. When Arundhati Roy arrives soon after, she looks at the line as if to say: *What a lot of toothpaste.*

Photographers join the smartly dressed officials around the table, snapping their shutters as soon as Arundhati Roy is seated, offering her no repose from the harsh public glare. The book investor is quickly beckoned up, a willing sacrifice to the cameras in a moment of author/public interaction. Ten minutes before, Arundhati Roy was a figure far below my tiered seat, like a tractor on a large farm, as seen from an aeroplane. But now she's seated across the table, mere feet away. When I pass across my book, the cameras flash furiously.

What lovely hands. Some of the other Booker-winners have fingers like squishy sausages, but Arundhati Roy has delicate, nimble fingers, as if made for cusping a perfect glass sphere. These hands return my signed book, signalling our transaction is complete. Her right hand clasps a glass of water and begins raising it to her mouth. I shriek.

FP: Mind the mites, the little scaly mites! With no eyes!

My boots slap the tiles like sandals as I quickly patter away. Why did I have to blurt that out? What a friggin' muppet...

To Francis Plug

GRAHAM SWIFT

LAST ORDERS

Graham Swift

PICADOR

Mr Stapleton is due back tomorrow, so it's time to abort. After attempting a clean-up/patch-up operation, I select a suit from his vast stocks, along with a pair of nice shirts, some business socks, and some smart shoes, for my author events. I also borrow a Panama hat, like Graham Greene might wear, and four Booker Prize-winning books that still require signatures; two by J.M. Coetzee and two by Peter Carey.

Having grown somewhat attached to my temporary abode, I tip the Panama hat as I pull the front gate to, before shooting Mr Stapleton's house with fingers from both my hands.

FP: Pe-ow, pe-ow, pe-ow!!

I'm fully kitted out, pockets crammed with unmissed money, as I walk towards Camden tube station, destined for Bermondsey.

Bermondsey Underground appears to be modelled on an orbiting space station. It resembles some kind of city of the future, complete with metallic walls and vast spaceship-like caverns. When I exit the train, it's like alighting on the Death Star, and I half-expect

Lord Vadar to be waiting at the top of the endless and imposing escalator.

It must have changed loads since Graham Swift first wrote about the place. His book, *Last Orders*, won the Booker Prize back in 1996, and it follows the story of four men who travel from Bermondsey to Margate with their dead mate's ashes. The novel begins in the Coach & Horses pub in Bermondsey, a pub I've always wanted to visit myself. That's where I'm going now, to see the lads.

Walking from Bermondsey tube along St James Road, I traverse a lengthy tunnel passing beneath some overhead railway tracks. I can't help comparing the tunnel to my life. It too seems long and narrow, but I can see a light ahead, at the other end. The foot passage is filled with leaves, despite the fact that no trees grow inside the tunnel. What the heck does *that* mean? The leaves are neatly lined up, ordered and precise, and I run through them all, kicking them up slap-dash with my worn and weathered boots. Afterwards, I wonder if that was wise, or whether I might have just messed my whole life up.

In *Last Orders*, the bottles behind the bar remind Ray, the central narrator, of a church organ's pipes because he's just been to his mate Jack's funeral. It looks like they've changed the bottle display since 1996. The bottles are still behind the bar, but they're in a single, continuous row, nothing like an organ. There's no shaft of sunlight coming through the speckled window either, because there isn't a window with specks.

FP: Are you Bernie?
Barman: No.
FP: Is it his day off?
Barman: There's no Bernie working here.
FP: I thought this was his pub...

Barman: Nuh. Moss and Julie own this place. See?

A sign behind the bar reads: *Moss and Julie welcome you to the Queen Vic.*

FP: The Queen Vic? But this isn't the Queen Vic. It's the Coach & Horses.
Barman: No, I think you'll find it's not. This is the Queen Victoria. There's no Coach & Horses pub around here.
FP: Hmm. Is Ray here today?
Barman: Ray who?
FP: I don't know his last name. He's a little fellow. Old, he'd be really old by now. He was in the book *Last Orders* by Graham Swift and he drinks here.
Barman: *Last Orders*? With Michael Caine, you mean? That was all made up.
FP: It was the Coach & Horses, Bermondsey.
Barman: Doesn't exist. It was all made up.
FP: But... this is the Coach & Horses.
Barman: No, you're not listening. There is no Coach & Horses. It's not real. This is the *Queen Vic*. Go outside and look at the sign. Stay out there if you want to...
FP: [*Very quietly.*] This is the Coach & Horses. It *is*.
Barman: What'd you say?

In *Last Orders*, the characters sit up at the bar and chat with the barman. But I decide to sit in a raised area by the door instead. Hopefully I'll spot all the lads when they arrive. My Panama hat sits on another chair, and at the table in front of it is a small glass of milk, untouched. It cost me a quid, that milk. A quid.

FP: Come on hat, drink up.

There's a clock behind the bar, but it isn't a Slattery clock, made in Southwark. They probably keep that out the back now, since it's become a really famous clock. Or maybe it's in the shop, getting its hands cleaned.

A dartboard is mounted on a wall to the side of the U-shaped bar, and a shelf above it features two dozen or so cups and trophies. These are adorned with little gold figures holding darts like tiny spears. It would be a really nice touch if Graham Swift's Booker Prize was nestled in amongst the darts trophies, but I look for it and nothing pings out. To be fair, I've never seen an actual Booker Prize trophy, so I don't know what I'm looking for. But as I say, nothing pings out.

Graham Swift signed my book after a reading he gave at the Savile Club in Mayfair. It was an event put on for the benefit of the Club's members, but the public could attend also, and being a member of the public, I decided to join the Club. The talk took place in an ornate, beautifully decorated room. Gilt-framed oil paintings lined the walls, gold trimmings gleamed across the ceilings, and huge pillars were crowned with rich golden decorations. Graham Swift had memorised great chunks of his novel, and despite having the sections printed out on A4 sheets, he read aloud while barely consulting his notes at all. It was as if he'd prepared a well-rehearsed speech. I stood at the back because there were no remaining chairs following my late arrival.

The Savile Club has their own bar, and my lateness was escalated as I ordered a pint of ale and a triple Scotch. My ale took the longest because the barman filled my glass with overpours from other glasses. He did this right in front of me, without apology or embarrassment. Perhaps he knew I wasn't a paid-up member of the Club. Maybe he noticed my attire, deciding my status and credentials didn't quite measure up to his fine standards. Anyway, it tasted OK, I suppose, and as I stood at the back of the fancy room, I drunk my ale of overpours, without complaint.

An old guy comes into the Coach & Horses, but he's not old enough to be one of the lads. It could be Vic, Jack's son. I wave and nod, but he continues past and out to the back. Maybe I'll have a word with him later, in the Gents.

I start supping loudly around every inch of my glass. It's possible that one of the lads in the book have drunk from this very glass themselves, right here in the Coach & Horses pub. It's a long shot mind, given how pub glasses are always breaking, particularly in rough and tumble Bermondsey.

FP: Is it possible that Vince's moustache whiskers have brushed upon the same lip as that from which I too now suckle?

Barman: What? What in God's name are you on about now?

FP: That is, assuming he *has* a moustache. I've always seen him with one, you understand. In my mind's eye.

Barman: You're out of your blinkin' mind's eye.

FP: Same again, please. In an *old* glass.

Back at my seat, I jingle my change, coins that might have been fingered by the lads. I also keep an eye out for Graham Swift, because they like a drink, writers. It helps them/us write better. Artists like a drink too, but they prefer drugs.

Writers = drink.

Artists = drugs.

William Burroughs liked both. You have to hand it to him. I probably would have gone blackberry wild myself.

There's money to be had in planing up some of the unpolished floorboards around the bar area, mounting the shavings on a board, behind glass, and selling them on the Internet to *Last*

Orders fans. A Stanley 130 Duplex Block Plane would do it. Maybe there's a Cheques Cashed Pawn Shop around here with an unclaimed Block Plane.

The item for sale is:

WOOD SHAVINGS. THESE WOOD SHAVINGS HAVE BEEN WALKED ON BY RAY, VIC, LENNY & VINCE, EACH MADE FAMOUS BY THE BOOKER PRIZE-WINNING NOVEL, *LAST ORDERS*. STARTING BID: £125.

Did Vic chew chewing gum? What about Vince? I begin searching under a wooden ledge for moulds of used gum. It's best done from a standing position, as if searching for the catch to lift a van's bonnet. I come across two bits, both old, hardened and difficult to pry. But I have my keys, so I begin to scrape.

Barman: Lost something?

FP: No. I've found something, actually.

Barman: Yeah? What's that?

FP: Chewing gum.

Barman: Chewing gum? As in *used* chewing gum?

FP: Yes.

Barman: What the heck do you want that for?

FP: To chew on.

Barman: Aww shit! [*Nodding to barmaid.*] This guy's looking for used chewing gum. So he can chew on it!

Barmaid: Urrgghh! Is he a bit... ? [*Circles her finger around the side of her head.*]

Barman: And the rest.

FP: Does Graham Swift drink in here?

Barman: Who the bloody heck is Graham Swift? [*To barmaid.*] He thinks this is the pub from that film, *Last*

Orders. Keeps going on about it. This'll be *his* last bloody orders.
Barmaid: [*Shakes her head.*] Nutter.
Barman: He's a nutjob is what he is. A nutjob pure and simple.

The hand dryer in the Gents is a Dolphin Hot Air Dryer. I must confess, I struggle to find the link. Blowholes, perhaps? Or dolphins rising out of the wet ocean into the dry air? Wet to dry? But what happens when it's raining heavily onto the sea? Hats off to the Dolphin Hot Air Dryer Company, because they really make you think.

Outside it's persisting it down. My hands rub together in anticipation of the next pub, but they rub awkwardly because I'm still inside and one of my hands is holding a drink.

A woman with an umbrella is walking a dog alongside the riverside promenade. The dog smells my trousers, probably thinking I smell like him.

FP: Do you know any good riverside pubs by chance?
Dog:
Woman: The Angel's good. [*Pointing east.*]
FP: The Angel? OK, great. [*Pause.*] I'd give the Coach & Horses a miss, if I were you.
Woman: The Coach & Horses?
FP: Yip. It's changed.
Woman: The Coach & Horses?

The buildings of the City loom across the Thames to the west, comprised mainly of financial institutions. There are no high-rise launderettes or off-licences. No skyscraper florists or kebab joints. To have any sort of presence or clout in this city, you need to be a banker or a queen.

Somewhere amidst those towers to money is the Guildhall, where the Booker Prize-winners are announced. What a strange place for a literary award. In the middle of the banks. The longlist for this year's Prize was recently announced, and though I wasn't named myself, I suppose I should attend. After all, it's the most public author event of all, with TV coverage and everything. It's where the spotlight first starts, where authors turn into celebrities, where they become 'names'. I would encourage all emerging writers to attend the Booker Prize ceremony because, as I hope this book has taught you, it pays to be prepared. Unfortunately, tickets for the Booker ceremony are reputed to be the most expensive, exclusive and sought after tickets going. But as long as you have a smart business suit like myself, or a pretty frock, you should be fine.

Angel Barmaid: Wet out?

I awake in my suit and hat in Southwark Park, Bermondsey. At some point, I must have walked here, scaled a fence, and sought out shelter beneath some Norway spruce trees. Quite clever of me really, given Norway spruce trees are ideally suited for rainy weather, due to their tight-knit, water-resistant needles.

Life & Times of
Michael K

J. M. COETZEE

To Francis Ply
with best wishes
J.M. Coetzee

Secker & Warburg
London

DISGRACE

J. M. COETZEE

To Francis Ply
with best wishes
J.M. Coetzee

Secker & Warburg
London

Ironically, J.M. Coetzee, who has won the Booker Prize twice and been shortlisted also, has never attended the ceremony itself. According to reports I've read, he's not one for small talk. An intensely private and reserved man, he has been known to sit through dinner engagements without saying a word to anyone. But perhaps the other dinner guests were complete dullards. It's bad manners to talk with your mouth full, and besides, I would caution against too much chitter-chatter in a setting where influential people are gathered and the wine is free-flowing.

He certainly seems to have an aversion to London engagements, but he's returning to Norwich for a second visit, so this could be a good opportunity for me to leave town for a bit. Trains to Norwich depart from Liverpool Street station, in the heart of the banking district, but I'll aim for discretion, in my new Panama hat.

SMART DRESS ONLY
NO SITE SOILED CLOTHING TORN JEANS OR
DIRTY BOOTS

Normally I wouldn't be welcome at the Hamilton Hall pub, but even though my suit is large and ill-fitting, it gets me through the door. The pub is part of Liverpool Street station itself, and today it's swarming with bankers. Mr Stapleton will be back at work by now, but there's no sign of him here, thankfully. Perhaps he's waiting outside my flat with a shotgun, ha, ha. Ha.

At first glance, the pub interior is most impressive and grand. But a closer inspection reveals faux-gilt trimmings, and Renaissance-style paintings that are darkened and dirtied. A vast chandelier is actually filled with electric candle bulbs, two thirds of which are ashen grey and dead. Triangular strips of ceiling are peeling back like slices of plaster pizza, and a gold radiator is flecked with green, because, underneath, it's a green radiator.

Still, it hasn't put off the wealthy City drinkers. Perhaps they could feed their £14 billion in bonuses through the pub's gaming machines, so at least the average punter, if their shoes aren't too muddy, can have a crack at balancing the books.

Despite being flush with cash, I don't buy a train ticket, instead presenting myself confidently on the platform, engaging with the railway guard, pointing at his whistle.

FP: I used to have my house key tied around my neck like
    that. But one night I was a bit drunk and I put the key in
    the lock and then tripped, nearly hanging myself and dying.
Railway Guard: Mind the gap, you drunken twat.

White daisies resemble churned up water, jettisoned into our wake. Three others share my carriage table, and I want to query them about the whereabouts of the University of East Anglia, specifically Lecture Theatre 1. But they all alight at Ipswich, at a station painted a sickly pale-blue colour. Line congestion slows the onward journey, due to overhead power supplies, so I kill time seeking out the buffet carriage.

Young Barman: If you buy two cans of bitter you'll save
    50p.

FP: What if I buy ten?

Young Barman: Well, you'll save… £2.50.

FP: And if I return the empties? Is there a monetary incentive?

Young Barman: I'm afraid not.

FP: Why don't you make trains that run on empty cans, rather than all that dirty coal?

Young Barman: ?

FP: Ten, please.

The delays mean I'm cutting it fine for JMC. The station is some distance from Norwich township, and the university is on the other side of the township again. I don't want to splurge on a taxi, so I wait for a bus. This J.M. Coetzee event is turning into the *Cannonball Run*.

We make the journey in silence, the passengers and I, although I have to laugh at one point when we turn right at a roundabout onto Unthank Road.

FP: Unthank Road?

On University Drive, little bunny rabbits are hopping about everywhere. They're hopping between the campus buildings and across the entire university infrastructure. They're everywhere. Little bunny rabbits. Twitching their whiskers.

I run through the rabbits, scattering them, to reach J.M. Coetzee. It's after 7pm already and my temples are pounding like a pair of cross-track warning bells.

Of course, I needn't have worried. As with so many other author events, there's no great desire for promptness. Punctuation, it seems, is left to the editors.

The lecture room is large and elephant-coloured. A rear fire exit door is open with a balcony visible outside, and beyond this some foliage. The blue linoleum stage is the exact same colour and material as my table in the train carriage. There are no chairs, just an exceptionally wide wooden lectern with a steel top frontage, and upon this a single plastic bottle of water.

J.M. Coetzee, a South African, is now Chair of Creative Writing at the University of Adelaide, Australia. The grey-haired man who introduces him pronounces his surname Curt-zay-a. I'd always imagined it was Coat-zee. As well as the two Bookers, J.M. Coetzee has also won the Nobel Prize. But where is he? He's not on stage. Maybe he's crouching behind the massive lectern, ready to spring up and surprise us. No, he arises instead from a front row seat, causing me to clap, not in applause, but at the very good sense of this act. By sitting with his back to the audience, he has saved himself the embarrassment of being showboated in the middle of the stage. It's a stroke of genius. I nod vigorously, looking for agreement from those sitting around me.

J.M. (John) Coetzee has a soft, but very well-spoken voice. Despite retaining its South African roots, it also has an element of the BBC. His hair has silvered, and his nimble figure and closely-trimmed beard remind me of a TV magician, or a cruise ship hypnotist. Wearing a dark grey suit, a white collared shirt unbuttoned at the top (without tie), and reading glasses, he begins delivering, in his own words, a 'very long introduction on censorship'.

My own suit jacket feels decidedly scratchy, and as J.M. Coetzee continues, this scratch perpetuates. Not only that, it's jumping about. Reaching inside my buttons, I grip what feels like the large soft leaves of a silver sage plant. Instead, I pull out a very frisky bunny rabbit. It begins kicking and thrashing about, so I shove that little critter straight back in there, quick smart.

Having delivered his introductory address, J.M. Coetzee turns his attention to his novels. He's not reading from his Booker Prize-winning titles, however. He's not going to 'play the hits'.

Instead, he selects a passage from *In The Heart of the Country*.

I'm not sure if I should look at him as he reads, or direct my eyes elsewhere. It's a dilemma I've often faced at author readings. Where to look. Some people stare at their shoes. Others zone out towards some nondescript point in the distance, slightly cross-eyed. And some of the more 'Zen' people even close their eyes completely. Usually I stare transfixed at the author, getting my money's worth.

A very noisy motorised scooter passes behind the lecture room, powered by a tinny little engine. Because the fire exit doors are open, the noise travels in and repels us. On the pretext of chasing the confounded scooter noise away, I slip outside, to dispense with the rabbit.

Holding the fluffy ears, I complete three circular turns before heaving it skywards, towards the grassy lawn. I'm just finishing a cigarette when the scooter makes a return pass.

FP: Oi! Shut up, you noisy shite! J.M. Curt-Zay-A is reading! He's trying to read!

After winding things up, J.M. Coetzee makes his way back to his front row seat like a distinguished Italian gentleman, rather than a South African living in Australia who happens to be in England. I'm very impressed. There's no discussion, no interviewer, and no questions. From an author's point of view, it's pure poetry-in-motion. And it makes complete sense. If the public have feedback, the author can offer their response in writing. Public interaction, without interacting with the public. Genius.

Afterwards, J.M. Coetzee moves to an on-campus Waterstones store to interact with the public. I run there. Running on university grounds is probably one of the most uncool things you can do, but I've long found that the right quantities of alcohol will waive any illusions to hipness and a trendy style. The queue weaves its way throughout the fiction aisles, filling the shop like a very passive flash mob. However, J.M. Coetzee's immense popularity does not appear to please him. He seems annoyed even, as if he's been forced to write another chapter in a book that he'd already imagined was finished, proofread and printed.

His glasses, nestled in his shirt pocket, could be likened to him, as a South African joey, who now peers out from an Australian kangaroo pouch. When he sees my note, TO FRANCIS PLUG, he pauses and looks at my face quite intently, before slowly lowering his head to write. His goatee, on closer inspection, appears more whiskers than beard. After passing back my books, he reaches for a water bottle, scowling.

FP: Unthank you.

For a student pub, the Union is pretty tame. The noise is muted at best, and none of the windows are broken. Empty pub glasses await collection on the courtyard steps, rather than being stolen by tanked-up opportunists. There aren't even any puddles of soup-like congealed vomit. Prior to my arrival, I was half expecting to find the whole campus on fire, because the University of East Anglia is famed for its creative writing school and you'd expect those young writers to be fuelled with outrage given the state of the world and the injustices perpetuated by the greedy bankers. But instead, the place is just filled with little fluffy rabbits.

Alongside the pub courtyard is the Waterstones shop, its golden 'W' sign dangling enticingly. It seems like an obvious target for theft, given it would make a lovely gift for a woman called Wanda or Wilma or Wendy or Winifred. A few young women are seated outside, but I have no wish to approach them or engage in conversation. I've read *Disgrace*, and I'm not stupid.

J.M. Coetzee remains stuck in the bookshop signing autographs. He must have removed his suit jacket because I can see the back of his white shirt through the window. The snaking queue inside the shop has not abated, and while I can't see J.M. Coetzee's face, I imagine it's turning crimson as the intense grip on his pen causes pages of his books to tear.

J.M. Coetzee and fellow South African, Nadine Gordimer, weren't always on the same page, but when she died very recently at the age of ninety, he joined in the tributes, highlighting her 'exemplary courage and creative energy'. I was sad that I never got to meet her myself, due to her event being sold out, and the fact that I was frogmarched off the Hay Festival grounds by two burly security chaps, my pleas and protests falling on ears made from cloth.

ff
PETER CAREY

Oscar and
Lucinda

*For Frances Plug
from
Peter Carey*

faber and faber
LONDON BOSTON

For Francis Plug from

True History of

the Kelly Gang

Peter Carey

ff
faber and faber

Lately I've been crashing out in pubs, hiding behind their curtains at closing time, and kipping on their sofas. In truth, I've had some very close calls. Because I've been helping myself to drinks and setting off alarms and scaring cleaners out of their bleeding minds. And as a Booker Prize-winner in the making, I'm worried about those CCTV cameras, and that programme *Crimewatch*.

Still, despite having no home and no job, I'm not at a complete loss. Peter Carey's in town, which means I can get my final two books signed. And the Booker Prize ceremony is fast approaching, so in fact I have a very busy schedule. The longlist has just been publicly culled into an all-important shortlist. To capitalize on this, events have been organised featuring all of the shortlisted authors. Multiple-author events are not that unusual, but I imagine the Booker events will be a tad more competitive. Like a pageant of sorts, where the authors are pitted against each other, fighting their corners. Given my restricted means at present, I've decided to forego attending these events in person, but my advice, emerging authors, should you find yourself part of such a folly, is to follow a few basic pointers:

- Stay Awake. It's likely you'll have to read passages from your respective books, and we all know how tiresome that can be. When it's not your turn, keep your mind active by grouping all the audience members by their hairstyles, e.g. frizzy perms over there, blue rinses over there, etc.

- Drink In Advance. If your fellows are sipping water and you're necking wine, judgments about your character will be made. However, given the occasions are likely to be long and drawn out (see readings above), it may be advisable to bring your own water glass onto stage, filled with a clear spirit, such as vodka, gin, or absinthe (for greeny water).

- Nod A Lot. You'll probably be asked questions about your book that you have no clue about whatsoever. Hidden nuances, metaphorical meanings, plotting, character development and other ambiguous stuff. Instead of shaking your head and raising your arms in disbelief, just nod. As long as you demonstrate that you understand the question, the answer can be any old rhubarb you happen to dream up.

Like J.M. Coetzee, Peter Carey's won the Booker Prize twice. He's also made the odd shortlist, but unlike J.M. Coetzee, he actually turns up for his events. This year though, he has some respite. Instead of being lumped on stage with a group of his peers, he'll be up in front of a packed theatre audience all by himself.

I decide to walk to the South Bank from Tufnell Park. Charles Dickens used to walk twenty miles a day, in the middle of the night. If alive today, he might have run into me in the early hours, making a wide berth around my flailing arms.

A security truck is parked on Kentish Town Road. A guard appears carrying a small grey suitcase handcuffed to his wrist. He wears padded clothing, possibly bulletproof, and his head is encased within a reinforced helmet. Reminded of Ned Kelly's protective armour, I imagine myself similarly kitted up, keeping the world at bay. Outside Kentish Town Station, I see just the thing. A solid, waist-length mask with *Camden* written on the side.

After a strong physical grappling with the black cover, I eventually separate it from the bin beneath. The heavy weight drops with a thonk on my head, its rectangular slot finding alignment with my eyes. It's a bit pongy, and because my arms are pinned at the side, the apex of my head is forced to take the entire weight. But now my identity is safe and I'm indestructible. Unless they shoot my legs.

Before long I'm sweating relentlessly, breathing like a plough horse with the strain of carrying the cumbersome shield. The inner dome has rubbed my scalp raw, so I take refuge inside the brightly coloured frontage of Quinn's corner pub.

The pioneering Irish spirit is kept alive at Quinn's, but to sample their wares, I must drop to my knees, before falling heavily, face-forward, onto the carpet. Wriggling backwards out of my armour, I breathe in the fresh pub air.

Barman: Stag do, is it?
FP: No. Just on my way to see Peter Carey.
Barman: Peter Carey? Is he the new Dr Who chap or something?
FP: No, he's a learned author from Bacchus Marsh. He wears glasses…?
Barman: [*Shaking head.*] Can't say I do.
FP: Brandy, please. Some of that illegal brandy grog…

The pub regulars are forced to veer around the black tubular shell that remains lengthwise on the patterned carpet. The barman, towelling a rack of glasses, nods discreetly towards my huddled form seated at a nearby booth, brandy vapour purifying the whiffy air around my head.

The rest of my walk is fairly eventless, apart from clonking into people who can only attack me with their hurtful words.

At the Southbank Centre, my knee cracks into the ticket desk.

Receptionist: Are you alright there?
FP: I can't see where I'm going.
Receptionist: Can I...
FP: Don't look at my eyes!

The Peter Carey event, like Nadine Gordimer's, and John Berger's before, is sold out. The best I can do is return for the signing.

The armour, meanwhile, is proving burdensome and attracting unwanted attention, so I abandon it near the street performers' area by the river, after doing a little dance show, for no money.

To fill time while Peter Carey is on stage, I head towards Downing Street, hoping to have a quick word with the Culture Secretary about the plight of the modern author. I walk rather briskly into the crash barriers outside, turning my gripped hands in the air, as if steering a large truck filled with explosives.

Downing Street is England's third most famous street after Coronation Street and Electric Avenue. Three policemen guard two gates, one of which is a huge monster of a gate, such as one might find at the entrance to a city, or a children's theme park. A separate side entrance allows access to camera crews and other 'in the scene' people, once their passes have been checked and verified. For us nobodies stuck behind the gates, it's all very mysterious and secret. We're kept in the dark while the rich and powerful make deals out of sight, in private rooms. They pretend to be our friends at voting time, but when we pop around for a chat they close the gates with a clang, and the policemen pull their helmets over much of their eyes.

When a delivery van shows up, the gates are opened and a raised metal barrier in the middle of Downing Street is lowered into the ground. Specially clad officers shine torch beams beneath the undercarriage, prodding about the wheels with long sticks affixed with mirrors. The bonnet is lifted, and the boot is opened and checked. Inside the van is the Prime Minister's new kite.

Prime Minister: Yay! My new kite!

After carefully studying these goings-on, I devise a plan whereby security can be breached and No. 10 can be blown sky-high. A Monster Truck waits until the gates are opened and careers through, sailing across the raised metal barrier. The policeman with the machine gun goes for the windscreen, but it's too high, and the Monster Truck ploughs on, releasing the attached rockets and blowing out the front walls of the PM's house. The explosive-laden Monster Truck fires its rockets, taking out the ridiculously lavish furnishings inside, but I, the driver, eject before impact, swinging my legs about as I slowly drift to earth, hoping to dodge the arsenal of bullets that are spraying at me like fast, upward rain.

Another idea I have revolves around a Flying Robot Pigeon Bomb. That's *two* subversive plots in just ten minutes. Hello?

FP: [*Pounding palm with fist.*] Yeah! Yeah! Yeah!
Police Officer: You all right there?
FP: Yes, thank you.

The Red Lion is the closest pub to 10 Downing Street, so it's the Prime Minister's local. But I bet he's never brought his guts up outside. He's the Prime Minister. It must be the worst job in the world, because despite being so very famous, no one in their right mind would want to pin your picture up on their bedroom wall. Except your parents perhaps, and the very saddest people in our community.

Politicians are professionally coached in the art of smiling, which may point to their success as modern authors. But sometimes a smile is not enough. Tony Blair also needed a strong fending arm at his Dublin book signing when eggs and shoes were hurled at his smiling face. Some of his big political decisions were probably made right here in the Red Lion. Perhaps after making a particularly big and far-reaching decision, he noticed that his tie was submerged in his pint, and maybe the others all laughed. And perhaps he tried to whack the others with the end of his tie, pretending it was a wet fish.

A newspaper is folded on my pub table, and the current Prime Minister has made the front page yet again. In households across the country, this newspaper will be used to line kitty trays, and kittens' wee will soak into his face over the coming days and weeks. Could this be why vast quantities of printed material are suddenly being digitised? Is it a government conspiracy, all tied back to the cat piss on the Prime Minister's face?

As I stand in the signing queue, the old nerves reappear. Even plied with drink, I never fail to get butterflies at the thought of meeting a famous author. At least, as a punter, it's over quickly and you can run away. But as an author, on the other side of the desk, you're stuck. And the more famous you are, the longer the queue. It's almost an incentive to write silly books, that no one will read. Of course, you can't win the Booker Prize with a silly book, authors. So you'll simply have to muck in and bare it.

The book investor is just behind me in the queue. He tries to blank me, but I swivel about, like Noddy's friend Mr Wobbly Man. His pile of first editions is larger than mine because Peter Carey has a string of 'hits'. While J.M. Coetzee has moved from South Africa to Australia, Peter Carey has moved from Australia to New York. It seems to be the thing if you win the Booker twice. In Hilary Mantel's case, it appears she has moved to a place in the far reaches of her own imagination.

Peter Carey is another tall author, following in the large footsteps of Barry Unsworth, John Banville, and Michael Ondaatje. I'm sure he'd like to stretch his long legs, but that would impede the standing area in front of the desk, and most readers choose to stand right there, as close as possible. The queue is moving slowly because of all those books Peter Carey has written, which need signatures. He's wearing out his hand by writing his name, when he really should be writing another prize winner.

FP: Hello, Peter Carey.

Peter Carey: Hello.

FP: Um, I really liked that bit in *Oscar & Lucinda* where those glass things get snipped and explode into zillions of pieces.

Peter Carey: Ah yes, Prince Rupert drops.

FP: Right, those. Um, do you think the same premise would apply to much larger glass things?

Peter Carey: I'm not sure. What do you mean?

FP: Well, say skyscrapers, for instance...

Peter Carey: Skyscrapers?

Outside the Southbank Centre, I scan the London skyline for glass churches. But it dawns on me that the glassiest ones are probably to be found in Canary Wharf, the new financial district.

When the book investor emerges, I beckon him over.

Book Investor: Yes?

FP: Are you going to the Booker Prize ceremony?

Book Investor: No. Why?

FP: Well, I'm heading along myself and I was hoping I might see a familiar face.

Book Investor: Why are *you* attending?

FP: I'm actually up for the Prize.

Book Investor: What, you mean you're on the shortlist?

FP: Yes. Not this year's shortlist. Next year's. I'm up for it next year.

Book Investor: ?

FP: Listen, you know what? Why don't you have these Peter Carey books?

Book Investor: Really?

FP: Yes, a gift from me. Here, take these J.M. Curt-zay-a books too. See, they're signed and dedicated also. *To Francis Plug.* They might be worth shedloads one day.

Book Investor: Hmm... right...

Canary Wharf is on the DLR train line, and appropriately, I start my journey at 'Bank' station. The train jolts and bumps along the tracks like an amusement park ride, causing my handwritten notes to resemble a graph on the televised cricket that shows where all the runs have been hit.

Unlike other tube stations, Canary Wharf has a Tiffany's. It's also swarming with police in bulletproof vests, but there's no sign of a major incident. In fact, all the young tanned bankers in their suits are laughing and carefree. Why do they need armed police protection? Is it because the rest of the country, having lost their jobs in the recession, or their basic services due to the bail out, now want the bankers dead? Or is it because the bankers themselves simply think they're as important as their good friends in Downing Street?

There are more armed police outside, very conspicuously

dotted about in open public areas. They have sweeping eyes and twitching trigger fingers. My own fingers twitch around the handle of my blunt-nosed pliers.

A central square is filled with after-work drinkers spilling out of modern bars and cafes. The very latest financial news is being broadcast to them on electronic outdoor signs and cinema-sized screens.

FP: Yawn.

I wander off down some back streets, my eyes craned skywards, looking for bank logos and the glassiest glass towers.

A security man, wearing a security tag, approaches.

Security Man: Can I help you there, sir?
FP: Just looking, thank you.
Security Man: Perhaps you might consider...
FP: Yes, I'm thinking about that one. How much for the really tall building with the flashing light?
Security Man: Might I suggest you stick to the Cabot Square area, back in this direction. You'll appreciate that security around the office buildings is paramount...

Waving his hands, he attempts to coax me towards the square, as if fanning a meat patty on a barbecue. Circling around another street, I approach the glass monoliths from a different angle.

A huge glass tower, belonging to one of the major financial groups, sits beside the Thames, opposite the Millennium Dome. A smattering of world flags above the entrance, together with a doorman, gives it the appearance of an international hotel. But of course, it's no such thing. Squatting beside the glass corner frontage, I retrieve my blunt-nosed pliers and begin squeezing the edge of the glass.

Of course, if it explodes into zillions of pieces, it'll be like in that film *The Mummy*, when the pyramids blow up and sand goes everywhere. Except it'll be glass. Crouching at the base, I ponder being buried in a mountain of fine glass shards, and perishing.

I find a great pub in the Isle of Dogs called The Ship, and after I've had a few, I show the barmaid my pliers and explain how I was *this* close to being buried alive in glass, earlier.

The Luminaries

Φ

ELEANOR CATTON

To Francis Plug with all good wishes,

GRANTA

The Old Doctor Butler's Head is a traditional dark-wood pub situated down a narrow pedestrian street in the heart of the City. It was first founded in 1610, rebuilt after the Great Fire in 1666, and its modernization continues today with lighting fixtures powered by electricity and a centrally positioned widescreen TV. It's 6:11pm. I've been here since half past two, writing my acceptance speech.

The pub is very close to Guildhall, the venue of tonight's big ceremony. I'd hoped to rub shoulders with the Booker Prize crowd, but instead the patrons are boring financial types, given to a bit of shouting. Mind you, the sponsors of the Booker are an investment management business, so maybe it's their lot. The shortlisted authors are probably holding out for the free drinks at the awards do. I suppose I ought to head off soon, to join them.

The channels on the pub TV keep changing. One minute it's cricket, then rugby, boxing, golf, snooker. None of it bears any relation to the cultural domain. At present, a row of footballers are singing their national anthem. Some of them are smiling and winking at camera. It's as if they know that tonight's £50,000 Booker Prize cheque can be earned by them in a day.

A circle of men stand near my table talking shop and eating crisps. They're all naturally balding, or their hair is cropped so tight they appear to be. All of them. They're discussing a colleague's £2.3m house. One of them was out in his boat over the weekend. Their suit jackets are draped over chairs and they're licking their fingers to avoid any greasy, salty suit shoulders.

I pull out my acceptance speech, softly reading it aloud. A man holding a champagne flute looks over.

Man: Wow! Check out his tiny handwriting!
Man II: What are you writing?
FP: It's an acceptance speech. Tempting fate, I suppose.
Man III: You're not up for the Booker Prize, around the corner?
FP: Yes. I'm attending the ceremony tonight.
Man II: Wow! What's your name?
FP: Francis Plug.
Man: [*Laughs.*] Francis Plug! That's just your pen name, right?

They insist on buying me a drink, so I ask for a triple Scotch.

Man: Calm your nerves, right?
FP: Yes. A little.

Gesturing towards the champagne flutes, I ask:

FP: What are you guys celebrating?
Man III: IT'S TUESDAY!

After thanking the men for my drink, I pocket my speech, explaining that I have to meet my agent.

Walking down Mason's Ave, I cross Basinghall Street, striding purposefully through a little side passage. The passage, like the nozzle of a balloon, inflates out into a square. Two suited men approach, and I hear them likening my walk to that of an arm-swinging *Super Mario* character. They both laugh. I didn't even know I did that. But so what? I've written a book. Almost. You bloody idiots!

Sitting on a bench in the square, in front of the Guildhall, I watch men in black suits and bow ties, and women in pressed blouses and skirts, arriving for the ceremony. It is a clear, still evening, and a very prominent moon in three-quarter phase is visible in the south-east. The only alcohol I now have is swimming in my bloodstream, and once it wears off I'll be tired and weak and sad. Inside that building the free drinks are flowing. The big names of British publishing are in there, along with a handful of notable writers. Booze and books. My short little legs swing furiously beneath the bench.

The red carpet outside is actually more of a salmon colour, and on either side are two raised cauldrons of fire. Tucked away discreetly behind one of these is a medium-sized fire extinguisher. Suddenly a motorbike policeman with flashing lights bustles into the square, escorting a black sedan with its own flashing light system. This is flanked further by a large black 4WD car. The front passenger leaps from the sedan and opens the rear door. Out steps an elder, silver-haired lady who I recognize as Camilla, Duchess of Cornwall. A waiting female official curtseys, and the immediate scene thereafter contains flash photography. Opposite my bench is a huge mobile broadcasting unit, which is capturing all this action for TV sets throughout the land. A satellite dish is installed at the rear of the vehicle, but it's not facing the Guildhall – it's facing the opposite way, towards the moon.

It really is a lovely night out, but I don't want to be out. I want to be in there [*pointing*].

Things grow quieter after that. Attendees continue to arrive on foot, their heels scraping and clattering over the tiled square.

281

A younger woman in a white dress emerges from inside, followed by three fittingly attired gents. Having assured their attendance and seats, they're catching a quick cig before the official proceedings commence. Raising myself from the bench, I brush down my suit trouser thighs and walk briskly across towards them. Nodding amicably to the group upon arrival, I produce a cigarette and politely ask for the service of a light. A tall gentleman, his eyes smarting from his own smoke, raises the flap of his thick suit pocket like a mail slot and posts his hand inside. The hearty conversation has been paused in the wake of my interruption, and they wait for me to step back out of the circle, so as to resume, but I don't.

FP: Too early for cigars, right?

Heads are lowered, looking at polished shoes. Mr Stapleton's shoes have become proper mucky. I forgot to buff them.

FP: Are they putting on a DJ tonight? After the Booker bit?

The four look amongst themselves, suppressing grins. The woman answers.

Woman: That's a good question, actually. I daresay I'd rather fancy a *boogie* later. What do you boys think?

The gents don't seem so keen on the idea. A handsome fellow with a blonde parting is the only one to pipe up.

Handsome Blonde Man: I don't think the Guildhall does *discos*. They're not really my thing...
FP: Sure, sure. [*Pause.*] Unless they played that track HEY MAM-BO! YA, YA, YA, YA, YA, YA, HEY MAM-BO!

Furtive eye movements are exchanged, barely-smoked cigs are flicked and stubbed, and the group make a general movement towards the lighted doorway. Discarding my own tab like a scalding hot chip, I slip between their shielding frames, laughing at some imaginary joke as we enter the concourse, past the doorman, veering left. My laughter becomes a kind of splutter, like an aeroplane that's lost its second engine. The others are silent as we continue down a lengthy carpeted corridor before approaching a Man Booker table manned by women. Our group is recognised, and we putter through a doorway where a tunnel of groomed waiting staff smile and welcome us with trays and flutes of champagne.

It's like Harry Potter's house inside. Like some huge medieval castle. It's full of suits, of course, and it actually belongs to a corporation. Still, I can't wait to see what the loos are like.

Like the Old Doctor Butler's Head pub, there are modern additions, such as light projections and voice amplification technology. The upper balconies have been commandeered by headphone-wearing camera crews, and the stage has been backlit with illuminated electronic screens. But the rest of the Great Hall retains its original, centuries-old fittings, its beautifully preserved wall mosaics, and its exquisite polished stone statues. If books are phased out tomorrow, these fine surroundings won't alter a bean.

My smoking friends have mysteriously dissipated, dispersed amidst the buzz. With no contacts or 'touch points' to converse with, I stand somewhat awkwardly by myself. There are many empty chairs at the arranged circular tables, but most of the attendees are up mingling, so it's difficult to know which seats are spare.

Clutching my champagne flutes, I ask after absentees.

FP: Is this seat taken?
Man At Table: Yes.
FP: What about this one?

Man At Table: Yes, that's taken too.
FP: And this one?
Man At Table: It's taken.
FP: And this seat here?
Man At Table: That's taken also.
FP: What about this seat?
Man At Table: That seat is also taken.
FP: And this one?
Man At Table: Yes, it's taken.
FP: And this one?
Man At Table: It's taken.
FP: And this one?
Man At Table: It's taken.

It's anyone's guess which table tonight's winner is sitting at, but I'm keen to know because maybe it's a lucky table. And if it's too far from the podium I may have to practice my gait. Does the winner seek out the losers on their way up for their prize? Do they offer a sympathetic shrug, or a mild shoulder punch? Do they laugh aloud as they walk? Do they skip? I need to be prepared, and so do you, dear reader.

Unable to join a core group, I strike up conversations with anyone who'll listen.

FP: ... And then, after consuming a small capsule containing the novel of your choice, the text will be projected out of your eyes onto whatever surface you see fit to read it, such as a bathroom door, your wrinkly old palm...
Old Gent: That's your theory on the future of publishing, is it?
FP: Yes, sir. I just made it up, just then.
Old Gent: Have you been taking *pharmaceuticals*, by chance?
FP: No, no. *Artists* take drugs. *Writers* drink alcohol. There are some exceptions, mind...

The Corporation of London is housed in this building, which may explain why the mood is so formal and staid. That and the royal presence, of course. Despite the free-flowing booze, no one appears to be letting their hair down. I suppose there's a lot at stake. The publishers will all have *ker-ching* eyes, hoping for a winner to rocket sales. The judges will be chewing their fingers, knowing they'll be publicly flayed for the 'wrong' decision. The sponsors will be stressing about their speeches, as well as their large investment and reputation. And one of the authors is set to pocket the life-changing sum of £50,000. All the more reason to lighten up. The Bank of China has held events here too, and I bet they were a real hoot.

The waiting staff are very busy responding to waving hands and clicking fingers. It seems like a rather thankless job. They've started serving the hot bread, and already that table is asking, 'Where's *our* bread?' And that table needs their glasses topped up, and that man's dropped his knife. They're really up against it, these waiting staff. Perhaps I can help.

FP: You didn't finish your bread.
Man: It would appear not.
FP: Was it not to your liking?
Man: No, it was fine. I'm saving myself for my main.
FP: What about the hungry little orphan children?
Man: I beg your pardon?
FP: A small child could run to school on all that fibre.
Man: Are you *drunk*?
FP: That'll be me up there next year, collecting my prize.
Man: [*To a fellow at the table.*] This waiter is completely drunk!
FP: It's in here [*taps pocket*]. My acceptance speech. All set.
Man: Your acceptance speech? For what?
FP: My book, silly!
Man: Your book?
FP: Yep. My Booker Prize-winner.

Man: [*To fellow.*] Says he's written a book!

FP: Yes, it follows the author events of real authors, offering tips to aspiring writers on how to face their public.

Fellow: Well, I'm afraid I see a rather pointed flaw with your award hopes. You see the Booker Prize only rewards literary *fiction*.

FP: Yes, but there's a singing squid in it... and a man turns into a turnip.

Man: A singing squid? What was your name?

FP: Francis Plug.

Fellow: Francis *Plug*? Well, a name like that certainly belongs on a dust jacket!

FP: Like Dick Francis, you mean?

Fellow: [*Laughing.*] Yes, except your horses sing!

Man: [*Laughing.*]

FP: [*Not laughing.*] I think you'll find it's a squid.

The shortlisted books are displayed on plinths. One of them is going to win the Booker Prize. If I knew which one, I could borrow it for a bit and get it signed by the winner, hot off the press. They might even draw a picture for me as a special personalised addition to the standard signature. Perhaps a sun at the top of the page, grass at the bottom, some trees growing up through their name and the title, and maybe a love heart around my name with an arrow through it.

On a separate plinth is the actual Booker Prize trophy. It looks like a toast-shaped gravestone, with a hook to keep your tea towel on. If I'm honest, it doesn't sail my boat. I'd prefer something more zany, like a stuffed badger's head draped in a Christmas lights halo. It's not up to me, of course. I'll get what I'm given. Catching the eye of a passing, well-coiffured woman, I point towards the trophy with raised eyebrows, grimacing.

If you don't enjoy talking, you'll probably find this evening terribly, terribly boring. There are no category prizes, no runner-ups, and nothing to keep us amused and stimulated as we await the sole announcement of the evening. It's little wonder that, despite a snippet on the late news, the event is not televised. Other than talking and eating, nothing actually happens. When I come back next year, I must remember to bring a good book.

The main dishes are being served. It's all happening very fast and very efficiently. Dithering around Table 6, desperate to be useful, I make a sudden lunge for the salt.

FP: SALT! SALT! WHO WANTS SOME? WHO WANTS SOME SALT? YES, MADAME! SALT? YOU WANT SOME SALT? ON YOUR POTATOES? JUST YOUR POTATOES? JUST YOUR POTATOES? THERE IT GOES! SALT! SALT! LOVELY SALT!

Senior Waiter: Excuse me sir. We can't have you doing our job for us [*half laughs*]. You're a guest…

FP: I'm an author! I really am…

Senior Waiter: Well, indeed. Here, let me take that…

FP: I'll tell you what, you do the salt, and I'll go and check on the fire extinguishers.

Senior Waiter: But… there's no need…

The fire extinguishers are mounted on wall brackets, discreetly positioned on the perimeter walls. The instructions are clear:

HOLD UPRIGHT
PULL OUT PIN
AIM AT BASE OF FIRE FROM
A MINIMUM DISTANCE OF 1 METRE
SQUEEZE LEV…

There's Eleanor Catton, one of the shortlisted authors.

FP: Hello, Eleanor Catton.

Eleanor Catton: Hello.

FP: It's so nice to see an actual author at this thing. I was beginning to think you'd all done a no-show. Of course, the free drinks...

Eleanor Catton: Right.

FP: I'm an author too, as it happens.

Eleanor Catton: Oh. What was your name?

FP: Francis Plug. I'm not on this year's shortlist, but I'm all set for next year's.

Eleanor Catton: Good for you. It should be really interesting next year. I'm glad it's opening up to a wider audience.

FP: Oh, I forgot all about that. It's all changing isn't it? It's going to be full of Americans.

Eleanor Catton: Yes, but...

FP: Thanks for reminding me. I better change my acceptance speech.

Eleanor Catton: You've already written your acceptance speech?

FP: Yes. Have you written yours?

Eleanor Catton: Well, yes... but not for next year...

FP: Did you see the moon outside? It's just like on the cover of your book. If that's not a sign, what is?

Eleanor Catton: I...

FP: Actually, let me just go and grab your book. Where are you sitting?

A compere is up on stage and he's saying things that really aren't very funny. The sponsor from the investment place is up next, so I can't see the bar being raised. Authors might not be the life of the party, but a banker on stage doesn't exactly lend itself to 'good times'. If the literary world wants to shed its stuffy image, it has to ditch these banker types. They're giving us a bad name. It's no wonder today's kids think books are really boring.

We're being championed by people who like maths.

Here he comes now, the banker chap. He's got a suit just like... oh my god. It's...

Mr Stapleton: Your Majesty, ladies and gentlemen...

Oh no. Oh no, no, no. What's *he* doing here? This is *my* gig. This is *my* lot. Why did *he* have to go and stick his beak in?

Mr Stapleton: ... proudly continuing our close association with the finest literature...

This is just awful. It's just about the friggin' limit.

Still, as tired and dreary as his speech may be, I have to take my hat off to him. He looks at home up there. Sure, people are talking over him, and he's blathering on a load of old nonsense, but fair dues, he's up in front of the biggest names in publishing, not to mention Her Royal Highness. I'd like to see myself do that.

When he finishes, it's to mild applause, akin to the sound of a metronome tick. I'm in two minds about whether to stay. The free drinks are terrific, granted, but it's a bit noisy, and I don't know anyone except Eleanor Catton. And she didn't draw a picture in my book, not even a little kiwi, or a tuatara, or the central clock tower in Hokitika. Added to that is the fact that, given half a chance, a certain banking representative of high standing will gladly rip my skin off.

I suppose I should be taking notes, jotting down tips. But the longer I stay here, the more I feel like I'm done with all that. At least in theory.

The stage isn't tall and imposing, it's just a piddly little stage. I'll be quick. I don't want to keep everyone from their chitter-chatter.

FP: [*Tap, tap of microphone*] Hello? Hello? Hello? Hello? Hello? Hello?

Someone: WE CAN HEAR YOU!

FP: Thank you, sir. That man there, thank you. Um, I won't be long, Your Majesty, ladies and gentlemen. But I'd just like, first off, to applaud the previous speaker, Mr Stapleton.

The crowd resume talking loudly.

FP: Mr Stapleton... EXCUSE ME!

To get the attention of the naughty crowd, I discharge a burst of dry powder from the fire extinguisher I'm holding. *HOAARRR!*

FP: THANK YOU. As I was saying, Mr Stapleton is a banker. Bankers, of course, despite their immense wealth, are a bit fusty. More than a bit, even.

There is some mild laughter from the crowd. That wasn't supposed to be funny, what I was saying.

A security man approaches the podium, beckoning me down. I ignore him so he mounts the stage.

FP: Still, I thought Mr Stapleton did pretty well up here, considering. Excuse me...

Compressing the handle release, I blast the security man with a deafening burst of white foam.

HOAARRR!!

HOAARRR!!

He staggers back to the side of the stage. Gasps swell up from the audience. Even with the microphone, I have to project my voice to be heard.

FP: I'm wearing Mr Stapleton's trousers, as it happens. This suit, shirt, shoes and socks, they're all his. Really. Did you know, he has first edition copies of all the Booker Prize-winners? It's true. Of course, he hasn't actually read any of them...

This produces more laughter, confusing the security guards that have gathered, preparing to mount the stage.

FP: But more importantly, Your Majesty, I'd like to discuss *next* year's Booker Prize ceremony. I'm hoping to bag the Prize myself then, so if you don't mind, I'm just going to practice my acceptance speech.

I retrieve the speech from my pocket and unfold it.

FP: Thank you. Ahem. [*Reading.*] Thank you for this Booker Prize award. In particular, thank you for the £50,000. It mightn't seem much to some of you, particularly when spread over the many years it took to write my book, but to me it's a lot. Tonight's free drinks are great, but tomorrow I'll have to buy my own.

I look for some water on the podium, but there's none. I can see why you might need it.

FP: Apologies, Your Majesty, ladies and gentlemen, if my presentation skills are not yet up to scratch. Although writers are now expected to be showmen and showwomen, some of us aren't very good at that. Perhaps you Americans out there can start teaching us a thing or two, right? [*Two thumbs raised.*]

As if on cue, my speech slips off the lectern, down to the floor. What a dickhead! I'm floundering about for it when a pair

291

of security guards rush the stage. I manage to keep them at bay with some further blasts of foam.

HOAARRR!

HOAARRR!

But I've lost my stride, and now the room is erupting. Ditching the speech, I leap into the crowd firing randomly. The guards are in hot pursuit, so I make towards a side wall and a fresh extinguisher. Crouching to unfix the pin, I run to meet the first guard, coating him like a scarecrow in a blizzard.

HOAARRR!

The second guard wisely holds back, but in the distance I spy a new threat. The police have arrived. Mr Stapleton is escorting them along the perimeter of the hall, and now they break cover and run.

The security guards rejoin the pursuit like little lion cubs bucked up by their big, scary parents. Attempting to make for a side door, I discover more police approaching from the other side of the hall. With all exits blocked, I discharge a final fog of foam, and turn to the wall, preparing to scale.

Near ground level is a bronze monument to Sir Winston Churchill. Traversing his person, squeezing a sculptured arm (all muscle, sir!), I use his smooth head as a springboard to clamber further up the fifteenth century walls. A clustered column and its accompanying mouldings provide useful footholds, assisting my ascent, and I have to admire the craftsmanship of the rich decorations, which are splendidly cast. Like a wonderfully aged and weathered tree, the walls of the Great Hall have many textured surfaces to clasp and pry, aiding me as I clamber beyond the enforcers below. My fingers work nimbly on the edges of the mosaics and gilt frameworks, while my feet, encased in black banker footwear, progress beneath at a clumsy, plodding pace. Another hindrance is the dust. A wet finger is seldom applied to these grooves and rounded edges, clearly. They certainly don't tell you that about the Booker Prize ceremony. About how dusty it is.

Continuing my climb, I feel like Hughes in *Sacred Hunger*, scaling the solitary heights of the Liverpool Merchant towards his crow's nest. Barry Unsworth was once lauded here, sharing the evening's prize with Michael Ondaatje. John Berger declared his support for the Black Panthers down on that stage, and James Kelman shot off early to join his mates in the pubs of Finsbury Park. When Hilary Mantel first collected the Prize, she said she felt like she was flying. Perhaps she had a similar view to this one. Same as that pigeon inside Earls Court, way up in the rafters. Like me, it somehow found a way in. Hopefully it found its way out again too. Getting into these places isn't the problem. It's the getting out, that's the thing.

I'm starting to sound like Confucius. Or Pat Morita in *The Karate Kid*.

They're serving dessert. The sea of craning faces has been replaced with scalps, many balding, as the guests tuck in. A smell of pastry wafts up. Crumble, perhaps. It must be a hundred feet from floor to ceiling, which would pitch my present height at around seventy feet. The demanding calls from the police spokesperson have ceased. I expect the fire brigade will arrive soon, with a very tall ladder. I hope I can hold out. Because despite resembling a stealth Spiderman figure, wedded to the wall, I'm actually attired for a cushy day at the office. The shoes have got to go, so like an Iraqi journalist, I send them hurtling towards the heads of those below. It doesn't help that I have the full weight of Eleanor Catton's massive tome in my satchel either. I'm in a bit of strife, truth be told. I think I might be losing my grip.

Further up are some small stained-glass windows. If I can get to those and open one, perhaps I'll gain access to the roof. Just what I propose to do once I get there is anyone's guess. Maybe I could shimmy down the satellite mast on the mobile broadcasting unit. It's parked quite close, I think. I wonder if they televised my speech. It was a poor show, shameful even, but if I watched it back I could study my mistakes and apply the corrections next year. Anyway, I've broken the ice, dear reader, cleared the first big hurdle. It wasn't as terrifying as you might think. No one died. Of course, it wasn't exactly natural either, not a bit of it. And it probably helped that I was brimming with booze. And it's possible that I may still die yet…

Down below, they're pressing on with the ceremony. I've managed to edge up towards the roof, but these old window latches are as stiff as you like.

NOTE TO THE READER

As you may have realised, *How To Be A Public Author* is a work of fiction. Francis Plug does not see or reflect the real world – he occupies a very different realm. Thanks for reading.

ACKNOWLEDGEMENTS

A book of this magnitude and importance cannot be achieved without the help of many people. Acknowledgements are therefore due to Dan Rhodes, Craig Taylor, Peter Hobbs, Cathryn Summerhayes, Fergus Barrowman, Jane Howe and Ilona Leighton-Goodall at the Broadway Bookshop, Dave Le Fleming, Steve MacDonald, Ryan Shellard, Dave Askwith, Andrew Gallix, Andrew Stevens, and Laurence (Lol) Weir and Gordon Keddie (for gardening tips).

Huge thanks to Elly and Sam at Galley Beggar, and also to my London family, Linda, Violet and Vincent, and my family back in New Zealand, and in Hawaii.